MW01700410

The Baffled Beatlemaniac Caper

First book in the Sandy Fairfax Teen Idol mystery series

By Sally Carpenter

Oak Tree Press Taylorville, IL

Oak Tree Press

Oak Tree Press books may be purchased for educational, business or sales promotional purposes. Contact Publisher for quantity discounts.

First Edition, September 2011

Cover Art by Reese-Winslow Designs

Book Design by Linda W. Rigsbee

ISBN 978-1-61009-031-5

LCCN 2011933061

Dedication

Janis Johnson
theatrical producer and friend

Acknowledgments

MANY THANKS TO the following people. Without them this book would not be possible.

To Steve Carlson for invaluable advice and unflagging enthusiasm.

To Brynne Chandler, Leslie Haukoos and Idie Emery for friendship and encouragment.

To Sunny Frazier and Billie Johnson of Oak Tree Press for their willingness to take a chance on a new author.

To the sisters and misters of Sisters in Crime, especially the Los Angeles chapter, for inspiration, advice and support. You're a writer's best friend.

To the wonderful teen idol fans I've met over the years.

To the Beatles fan conventions that inspired this book, Beatlefest (now called the Fest for Beatles Fans) in Chicago and Liverpool Days in Pasadena.

The character of Sandy Fairfax is fictious, based on a compilation of the lives of real teen idols and a heavy dose of imagination. All of the Beatles-themed records mentioned in this book exist and, with the expection of the "butcher cover," are in the author's personal collection.

Foreword

Forward - Into the Past!
By Steve Carlson

MYSTERY—A GREAT place for any writer to hang their hat.

Sally Carpenter's premier shot across the bow with this Sandy Fairfax Teen Idol mystery series is a hit out of the park.

Boomers who yearn for the spark of Nancy Drew or the Hardy Boys can amp up the volume and go nose-to-nose with the gritty style of a modern film noir-style hero. Fairfax's only problem is—he suspects he may be past his rock n' roll prime. And that ain't doing anything for his ruptured ego, as he wades armpit deep into the dark world of crime busting.

Reading this first project was more than an eye-opener for me. Carpenter hit on the insecurities of a middle-aged man with a warriors' heart and forty pounds of extra weight muffining around his waist. Out of shape, out of step and maybe running out of time—with one more chance to create a new life for himself--using his vast knowledge of the music world to help him through a myriad of crazy confluences. The best part is Carpenter pulls it all off with flash and humor. The results are hilarious, stunning and insightful. (And where did she go to school to learn how guys think?)

"Too Old to Rock n' Roll—Too Young to Die" is a title from a classic album by Jethro Tull, but this phrase puts our main character right into focus.

If you are a young reader, this book might help you better understand your crazy, mixed-up dad. If you appreciate the history of pop culture and are into the retro "thang," you are in the right place.

And if you are in the mood for fun, turn the page . . .

Sandy Fairfax Discography

All records and singles except *Sessions* and *Black Wave* originally released on the SuperTonic label

Sincerely Yours, Sandy. "Girl of My Dreams"/"Spark of Love" 1975

Soda Shoppe. "Cuddle Close"/"Sweet As Can Be" 1976
Walk In The Park. "Weeping Willow"/"Every Jack Has His Jill" 1976

Stars In My Eyes. "Little Bunny Bright Eyes"/"Morning Glow" 1977
Dancin' Sandy. "Meet Me At The Disco"/"Swing To The Beat" 1977
Sandy Sings Live For You (concert album) 1977

Knight In Shining Armor. "Tell Me True (I Love You)"/ "Tomboy In Pink Ribbons" 1978
Sandy Rings In The Holidays. "Mistletoe Kiss"/ "Sugar Plums and You" 1978

Castles In The Air. "Moonbeam Melinda"/ "The Picture In The Locket" 1979

Sandy's Tastiest Treats (greatest hits) 1980

Peanut Butter And Jam Sessions (independent label) 1985

Black Wave (with the band Shipwreck) 1988

Movies And Television

Buddy Brave, Boy Sleuth (live action TV series)	1975-1979
Buddy Brave And The Suspicious Spy (movie)	1976
Buddy Brave And the Dangerous Demon (movie)	1977
The Secret Files Of Buddy Brave (animated TV series)	1979-1980
Charlie's Angels (guest appearance)	1980
Fantasy Island (guest appearance)	1983
The Love Boat (guest appearance)	1985

❖ CHAPTER ONE

(Just Like) Starting Over

"SO WHAT YOU'RE telling me is that my career is dead."

"I wouldn't say your job prospects are that hopeless, Ernest. More like they're in intensive care on life support." Marshall yanked open the door of my side-by-side refrigerator, a monstrosity large enough to hold a frozen moose, and rummaged around. "Why don't you ever buy what I like? A guy could starve around here."

"You're an agent. You're only entitled to ten percent of my food."

I pushed him aside long enough to nab some sandwich fixings from the fridge. Marshall resumed his foraging while I took a package of hoagie rolls from an overhead cabinet and built a monster of a sub using leftover tri-tip and plenty of hot mustard and horseradish. When finished I placed the sandwich on a paper plate. So much for the culinary skills of bachelor living.

In the background, classical music played low over the speaker system hidden throughout my Hollywood Hills house that I'd bought in 1975 with royalties from my first album, *Sincerely Yours, Sandy*. I love all types of music, but classical relaxes me the most.

"You're out of beer," he said.

"I dumped it down the sink."

Marshall removed his curly-topped head from the inner depths of the fridge and cocked a black eyebrow at me.

"I quit," I continued.

He'd heard this many times before. "Oh?"

"I mean it, Marshall. This time's for keeps."

He opened the cabinet where I used to store my wine and hard liquor. Empty. "Looks like you're right. Congratulations! I'm happy to hear it. When did this happen?"

I checked my wristwatch. "I took my last drink twenty-two hours and fifteen minutes ago, but if I don't get out of the house and do something I'll go crazy."

I reached into the fridge for a cold bottle of O'Douls, popped off the cap with a metal opener fastened to the end of the island and took a big swig. It didn't have the same kick as beer, but going through the motions made me feel better.

Marshall took a fountain pen from the inside pocket of his burgundy pinstripe jacket, made a note on a page in his leather-bound memo book, tore off the paper and handed it to me. "That's the day and time and phone number of one of the Alcoholics Anonymous groups that meets at my temple. The groups are open to the public. This one's mostly power players in the industry. You might meet some people you've worked with."

"Thanks, I'll check it out." I stuck the note under a magnet on the front of the refrigerator so I wouldn't lose it. "Now, about that job. . . "

Marshall held out his hands and shrugged. "What am I, a magician? Times have changed since the '70s, Ernest. The music industry of the '90s wants techno and hip-hop, not cute boy acts. The old producers are gone and the new kids in charge don't know Sandy Fairfax."

My agent let my stage name hang in the air as he returned to ransacking the refrigerator and took out a paper plate with a leftover piece of Marie Callender's chocolate pie covered in plastic wrap and a can of PowerPunch energy drink. The rat—I was saving that pie for later. I don't know how that young guy can pack away food the way he does and stay skinny. Must be all that golf he plays with the studio heads. Marshall opened a drawer under the center island and picked out a dessert fork.

I scratched my scraggly beard. "Yesterday I talked to my ex. She won't let me see my kids again until I'm sober and working. All right, so I'm working hard on the drying out part, but Marshall, I need your help in finding work."

"Are you sure you feel like working? You haven't made a public appearance in five years."

"Yes, I'm sure. C'mon, Marshall, what do you say? I'm open to any gigs you got. At this point I'll even sing at a high school prom. I'll do *anything* to get my children back."

"Believe me, Ernest, if I have a job for you, I'd—" He snapped his fingers. "Wait a minute, now that I think about it, something did cross my desk late last week."

"You didn't tell me?

"I assumed you wouldn't be interested."

"So let's go outside and we'll talk about it."

I opened the sliding glass door that led to my backyard. I carried my sandwich and the bottle of O'Doul's outside, my flip-flops slapping the tile as I crossed the poolside patio. I eased my lanky six-foot-two frame into a wrought iron chair. Marshall followed me with the pilfered pie and the PowerPunch in hand, and sat across the wrought iron table from me. He unbuttoned his jacket, the closest he gets to casual. As for me, I was comfy in an old ragged T-shirt and shorts. We ate as we talked.

The mid-morning California sun glinted off the pool ripples. The birds chirped merrily in the trees and the honeysuckle growing in the bushes smelled good. In my sobriety I could notice little details like that. But I had no time to stop and smell the roses. I need this job that Marshall dangled in front of me.

"I took a call from a woman who wants you to speak at a Swingin' Sixties Weekend event," said Marshall. "It's more or less a gathering for Beatles fans."

"They want me for a Beatles convention?" I tossed my head back to get my long blonde hair out of my face. "Why?"

"Because Ringo guest starred on your TV show. The woman wants you to come and talk about working with him."

"Oh, that. Now that you mentioned it, I remember Ringo." I chuckled at the fond but distant memory. "Haven't thought about him in years. We had some good times together, but I don't know what I can say about him. We hung out a few times after he did the episode, but we're not close."

"Doesn't matter. Beatle fanatics adore anyone who so much as caught a glimpse of the guys walking down the road."

"When is it? This convention?"

"Labor Day weekend."

"That's at the end of this week. Not much lead time."

"I got the impression that this wing ding is being slapped together at the last minute. The organizer whom I talked to sounded rather disorganized herself."

"Keep talking. Where is this gig?"

"Evansville, Indiana. Midsize city on the Ohio River."

"Never heard of it."

"Sure you have. You sang there back in '72 at Roberts Stadium."

"Did I?"

"The woman I talked to said she saw your show." He opened the can of PowerPunch, took a sip, held the can at arm's length and scrunched up his face. "How can you drink this stuff? What's in it? Gasoline?"

"I gave up booze, not caffeine. Cut me some slack." I'd finished with the O'Doul's, so I grabbed the can from him and gulped some down. "This gig sounds easy enough. How much trouble can I get into at a fan convention?" If I had known the answer to that question, I'd have run inside, locked the doors and never left the house again.

"Now about your fee." Marshall rested his elbows on the table and leaned forward. Nothing made him happier than talking about money. "They're not offering much, just expenses and an insult of an honorarium. Frankly, Ernest, it's a small shindig and the organizer said they can't afford your usual fee."

"I don't care. I have to start working somewhere. In a couple of years I'll turn forty and I don't want to end up on a TV show like *Whatever Happened to Your Favorite Washed-up Seventies Has-been?*"

"Anyway, the money doesn't matter. I turned down the offer."

I snatched Marshall's plate away from him.

He tried to grab it back. "Wait! I'm still eating!"

"Lunch break's over. Get on the phone, call that girl back and tell her I'm coming."

"You're kidding. Do you really want to do this convention?"

I stood up, kicked back my chair and carried the plates into the kitchen where I dumped the remains of lunch into the garbage bin. I'd dreamed of making a huge splash of a comeback like Elvis and his riveting '68 TV special, but you can't always get what you want. At least if I start at the bottom, there's nowhere to go but up. "Yes, I really want to do it."

He stood at the sliding glass door. "You won't make any money on it."

I eyed his expensive clothes. "Then you'll just have to buy your suits at a thrift store."

As always, Marshall got in the last word. "In that case, the first thing you're going to do is to call my stylist in Beverly Hills for a shave and a haircut. The fans are paying to see Sandy Fairfax, not Grizzly Adams."

❖ CHAPTER TWO

Come Together

I SPENT FRIDAY morning of the Labor Day weekend on a six-hour flight (with one layover) from Los Angeles International to Evansville Regional Airport. On the plane I worried about how I'd face the public again. What if the fans mobbed me? What if they *didn't*? In show biz, five years off stage may as well be five hundred. Did anyone still remember me?

When the plane landed, I grabbed my carry-on bag and stumbled onto the tarmac where a summer heat wave of ninety-five degrees and fifty percent humidity smacked me in the face. I hadn't toured in so long I'd forgotten about the harsh Midwestern weather. I slipped on a pair of aviator-style sunglasses and walked to the terminal as the sweat rolled off my ponytail and down the back of my blue Hawaiian shirt with the white flowers on it.

I assumed somebody would meet me, but Marshall hadn't given me the name of a contact person. I never thought to ask. In the past my handlers made all the arrangements and dealt with the people in charge, so all I had to do was to show up and sparkle. I stood inside the gate, set my bag at my feet, and glanced around. Where were the hundreds of screaming girls who used to line up to greet me? At least one fan still remembered me.

"Hi, Sandy! Hi! Over here!"

A short woman waved her arms and ran towards me. Her hazel eyes, magnified by rimless glasses, danced with delight. A large round metal button with a photo of yours truly and the words "Sandy's girl" was pinned to her Beatles T-shirt. A Beatles baseball cap sat atop her fuzzy brown hair. The woman wore a denim skirt as well as a Sandy Fairfax watch and charm bracelet. She carried a tote bag depicting the Yellow Submarine sailing through the Sea of Monsters. Around her neck on an elastic cord hung a purple nametag that said "Convention Host." Didn't take a detective to figure out where she planned to spend the holiday weekend.

I instantly shifted internal gears from tired Ernest Farmington to delightful Sandy Fairfax. I pushed the sunglasses up on my head, slapped on that toothy smiled, that once graced a million lunch boxes and held out my hand. "Hello, and you are—?"

She gripped my hand with both of hers and wouldn't let go. "Bunny McAllister. My real name is Beatrice, but ever since I heard your song 'Little Bunny Bright Eyes," I go by Bunny. I adore that song! It's my favorite! Welcome to Evansville! We're so glad you could make it! I'm so thrilled to meet you!"

Yes, she spoke with exclamation points. She gazed up at me so longingly that I expected her to kneel down and kiss my feet; thankfully, she didn't. "Did you have a good flight?"

"Yes, fine, thanks." I extracted my hand from her clutches and glanced around, hoping to find someone else I could talk to. "Who's in the charge of the convention? Where's the director?"

"That's me. I'm one of the organizers. Red Hardiman and I are the co-chairs. Red's back at the hotel setting things up. I'm in charge of you. I mean, I'll be looking after you. If you need anything at all, I can help." She reached for my bag. "I'll take that for you."

I grabbed my suitcase with my left hand (I'm a southpaw). "No, thanks, I'll carry it." The last thing I needed was some excited fan running off with my belongings.

"The airport has a restaurant. We can have lunch here."

"I'd like to go straight to the hotel, if you don't mind."

True be told, I was starved and lunch sounded wonderful. My meals so far today consisted of coffee at LAX and chips and soda on the plane. But first I wanted to clean up and rest in a quiet room. Besides, passers-by were staring and I was afraid they might start bothering me. I wanted Marshall here to run interference.

"Sure, no problem. Follow me."

Outside in the parking lot, I stopped by the curb and put on my sunglasses.

"Where's the limo?"

"Sorry. The convention's on a tight budget and we didn't have money for a limousine. But that's all right. I'll get you where you need to go."

Bunny wove her way between the parked cars to the far end of the lot with me trailing behind. She stopped beside an old, two-door blue hatchback in need of a wash. A novelty license plate on the front bumper featured The Beatles logo. Bunny opened the rear door and I loaded in my bag. The back license plate was a personalized Indiana state plate that read BUDI BRV—my TV show, *Buddy Brave, Boy Sleuth*. I shot her a look and she giggled. What a goofy girl. I considered hailing a cab to take me to the hotel, except I had no idea where I was going.

Bunny opened the passenger side door, picked some trash off the floor and dumped the mess onto the back seat. "I didn't have time to clean the car, what with getting ready for the convention."

I checked to see if the door had an inside handle so I could escape in case this enthusiast wanted to take me home and keep me in her basement. I eased into the front seat and my knees wedged up against the glove compartment. Bunny reached under my car seat and yanked on a lever. My seat slid back with a jolt. I stretched out my long legs and fastened the frayed safety belt.

Bunny climbed in the driver's seat. "You might want to roll down the window. The car doesn't have air conditioning."

The clunker had manual crank windows, not automatic. I rolled the window all the way down and rested my elbow on the ledge, entirely at Bunny's mercy of wherever she planned to take me. She turned left out of the airport parking lot to travel south on a four-lane highway that ran through rural scenery. I thought she was headed for the hotel just south of the airport, but she passed it by.

"Where are you going?" I asked.

"Downtown. That's all we could get. Red and I called every place in town, but all of the hotels were booked or too expensive."

Moving at 55 mph generated a breeze of hot air through the car, which did little to cool me off. A handful of vehicles passed us, mostly SUVs, pickup trucks and old Cadillacs driven by senior citizens. Bunny turned on the car's tape deck and George Harrison's "33 and 1/3" album blasted at full volume.

She said something, but with the wind noise and the stereo booming, I couldn't hear. Giving concerts in stadiums full of screaming fans had left me a little hard of hearing in one ear.

"Could you please turn down the music?"

"Sorry." She twisted a knob and lowered the music to a low roar. "Is that better?"

"A little, yes. What were you saying?"

"I said, you cut off your beard. I think you look better without it. How did you get that scar on your face? Does it hurt?"

I touched the faint line that ran down my left cheek. "I cut myself shaving."

Now that was a bald-faced lie. The scar was a souvenir of my barroom fight last year when I was drunk and tried to beat up a guy. After the bum cut open my face with a broken bottle the police arrested me for causing a disturbance. With my whiskers gone, the scar stood out like a California wildfire against my fair skin. How embarrassing.

"Anyway, Sandy, I'm happy you could come on such short notice. I was afraid you were too busy with all your other bookings."

What other bookings? I thought. "No trouble at all."

"So how are your kids?"

The strength of the teen idol industry is its ability to create a bond between fan and star. Rock bands attract their followers for the music, but teen idols draw in fans through their personality, or rather, the persona created by the studio's publicity machine. The '70s teen magazines like *16* and *Tiger Beat* printed endless articles on me, all with the goal of making the reader feel like she knew me intimately. As a result, strangers come up to me and ask the most personal questions as if we were lifelong friends.

Even though I hadn't seen my kids in months, I answered Bunny with "They're fine." I changed the subject to stop any more intrusive queries. "What's the agenda for the convention? What do you need me to do and when?"

She stopped for a traffic light. Cars with Kentucky and Illinois license plates joined us on the highway. "The convention officially starts at ten o'clock tomorrow morning, but we've got a mixer tonight at eight for the early birds here already. I hope you can come. The guys in the Beatles tribute band are here and they're dying to meet you. They're playing tomorrow night."

"What's the band?" Every garage in L.A. has a Beatles tribute band, ranging in quality from pathetic to pretty good.

"The Mersey Marvels. They're from Indy."

"Indy?"

"Indianapolis." The light changed and Bunny accelerated. "You're on tomorrow at two. You'll talk for about an hour and sign autographs. Mr. Ellis sent some photos you can sign for the fans that don't bring anything. He was so helpful in getting you here."

Now it all clicked. "Are you the one who contacted my manager?"

She beamed. "Yes, I am."

"See Yourself," the last song on side one of the tape, finished playing. Bunny ejected the cassette, flipped it over and reinserted it to start "It's What You Value" on side two. According to the road signs, the car had turned onto the Lloyd Expressway.

"We got some last minute registrations when people heard you were coming," she said. "You have lots of fans around here, especially with the kids. One of the local stations runs *Buddy Brave* every weekday from four to five."

"Is that so? I didn't know the show was still in syndication."

The car left the expressway for a surface street and we entered downtown Evansville. The streets looked woefully deserted for the Friday of a holiday weekend. Not much to see except for a library, small civic center, mom-and-pop shops and modest apartments. We drew near a large, nice looking hotel, the Executive Inn, upscale and modern. No doubt the facility offered many amenities such as an indoor pool, fine dining, comfortable rooms. . .

But Bunny drove by.

"Isn't this the place?" I asked.

"Oh, no, we're not at the Executive." She turned a corner. "Our hotel's right up ahead."

Ahead to the right loomed a faux-medieval castle, an eyesore covered in gray siding molded to resemble rough-hewed stone. Faded banners hung from the round turrets. A shield-shaped sign identified the deformity as the King Arthur's Arms. The black letters on the marquee announced "Welcome First Annual Swingin' Sixties Weekend, Sat.-Sun. Special Guest Andy Fairfax." My anticipated comeback had failed before it began—the people in charge couldn't even spell my name right.

Bunny pulled up in the circular drive in front of the lobby entrance, a gate with a drawbridge lowered over a shallow concrete-lined "moat." Through the open car window I could smell the stagnant algae-green moat water.

"I'll drop you off here so you won't have to walk. I'll go park the car." She gestured at the parking structure across the street.

The thought of entering unfamiliar territory alone frightened me. "Go ahead and park. I don't mind the walk."

An SUV pulled up behind us and the driver honked the horn. Bunny glanced over her shoulder at the impatient driver.

"You better get out, Sandy."

"Where do I go?"

"You'll see the registration table. Can't miss it."

The rude driver honked again. Bunny reached across my lap, yanked the door lever, and pushed the passenger side door open. She said something, but I couldn't hear with the idiot behind us honking. I unbuckled my seat belt, stepped out and shut the car door. Bunny drove off and narrowly missed a car coming from the other direction. As I watched her leave I realized she still had my suitcase in the car. How much would my old socks fetch on eBay?

As the sun baked my head, I decided I could wait more comfortably inside the hotel. The drawbridge swayed as I trod across. The lobby's glass doors automatically slid open with the sound of grinding gears. Inside, the sixty-five degree air conditioning froze the sweat on my face. Between the outside heat and the inside chill, I'd probably catch a cold. The other guests walked by and smirked, probably because I was the only guy in the hotel—possibly the entire city—dressed in a Hawaiian shirt. I looked more like a tourist than the real sightseers.

The lobby tried dismally to carry out the Camelot theme with dark wood paneling on the walls, hung with metal swords, shields and a painted, not woven, tapestry of a unicorn. Rusty suits of armor stood guard beside the entryway. A candelabra made of a metal wheel with electric bulbs hung from the wooden ceiling beams. In the center of the lobby stood a discolored metal fountain of a peasant boy pouring a dribble of real water from a pitcher. For a moment I toyed with the notion of leaving and checking into classier Motel 6.

A sign hung on the far wall read: "Swingin' Sixties Weekend 1993. Beatlemaniacs sign in here. We hope you will enjoy the show." Around the sign were brightly colored banners with sayings such as "Far Out!" "Groovy Man!" and "Are You Hip?" Sparkly plastic strips dropped from the ceiling.

In this corner stood a long table holding with cardboard cartons filled with manila envelopes. In a chair behind the table sat a fortyish African-American man sporting a neatly trimmed beard and a touch of gray in his red hair. He wore black pants, dark rimmed glasses and a red T-shirt with a white Beatles logo on the left chest. Around his neck hung a purple nametag that said "convention host." One thing about fans is that they're easy to spot.

A short man standing in front of the table was talking to the convention host. "Dana and Scott can't stay in the same room."

"Why not?" The African-American man had a deep, rich voice.

"They're not getting along."

The man consulted a clipboard. "I don't know what we can do about it. We only reserved two rooms for the band. Dana and Scott are in one room, and Grant and his wife in the other. We can't afford another room. You're staying with folks in town. Can one of the guys bunk with you?"

"No can do. My friends have a small apartment and I'm taking up the sofa bed in the living room."

"Excuse me." I wanted my room, not a discussion of someone else's housing problem.

The African-American man stared at me. "Are you here to register for the convention? What's your name?"

He didn't *recognize* me? Had I changed that much in eighteen years? My face had filled in a little and a few wrinkles had set in around my big baby blue eyes, framed in long blonde lashes, but I still couldn't shake my boyish features.

"I'm Sandy Fairfax." I tried not to sound as indignant as I felt.

The man broke into a wide smile. He stood up and reached across the table to pump my hand. "Sandy Fairfax! It's a pleasure to meet you! I'm Red Hardiman."

As we shook hands I removed my sunglasses, folded them and slipped an earpiece onto the front of my shirt so I won't lose the eyewear like I usually did. From his hair color, I can see where he came by his name. Red had an air of authority and seemed like a person who could handle things without fawning over me.

"Where's Bunny?" he asked. "Didn't she pick you up at the airport?"

"Yes, she did. She's out parking her car."

Red peered over the table and at my feet. "Didn't you bring any luggage?"

"I've heard of traveling light, but this takes the cake." The short man guffawed and offered his hand. "Good afternoon, I'm Arthur Becker." He slipped into a bad Liverpudlian accent. "But you can call me Ringo. I play a mean set of skins, if I do say so meself."

Red added, "Art's one of the Mersey Marvels, our tribute band for the weekend."

I can tolerate most tribute bands when they play, but I can't stand musicians who live out their fantasies off stage. I shook Art's hand anyway. "Nice to meet you."

"Hey Sandy, maybe later we can get together and jam."

Good lord, no! "Thanks, but I doubt that I'll have the time. I'm on a tight schedule." I turned to Red and hoped Art would disappear. "I'd like to go to my room."

"You'll need to check in over there for your room." He pointed to the reception desk across the lobby. "But I can give you the convention packet. Everything you need's in it. Map of the hotel, program schedule, list of restaurants and places of interest in town."

"I'm afraid I won't have time for sightseeing," I said. "I have a flight booked for tomorrow evening."

"I understand."

"What about the extra room for Dana and Scott?" Art asked.

Red signed. "Can you give me a minute, Art? I need to find Sandy's packet. I'm the only one working registration until Billy Shears gets here."

"Who's that? That can't be his real name." I couldn't imagine any baby boomer crazy enough to name their kid after a character in a Beatles song.

"Billy Shears, eh?" Art chimed in. "Does he get by with a little help from his friends?"

If this clown didn't stop with the Beatles jokes, I'd whack him senseless with Maxwell's silver hammer.

Red explained, "That's the name he uses on the Beatles discussion groups on the World Wide Web and that's how everyone knows him. Billy's helping out with the convention. He can't come until tomorrow because he works second shift at the Toyota plant in Princeton."

"Princeton?"

"Little town about thirty miles north of here. Ah, here's your packet." Red pulled an envelope from one of the crates and handed it to me. Then he pointed to several stacks of booklets on the table. "Some of the local kids are giving out free samples of the Beatles fanzines they produce. Help yourself, Sandy. One of those is about you."

Most of the amateur fan publications were of photocopy-and-staple quality, with the pages covered with tiny type to use the fewest number of pages. Although lacking in writing or print quality, the 'zines were full of heart. Four newsletters were devoted to one fab apiece: *Flying With Wings* focused on Paul; *Life With The Lions* for John; *Spiritual Sky* for George devotees and *Really Gear Ringo,* which Art picked up and slipped it into his travel bag as he continued arguing with Red about another room.

I thumbed through a quarterly periodical called *Dreamy Detective,* put out by the Sandy's Buddies fan club. Unlike the other 'zines, this beautiful booklet rocked. The glossy cover had spots of glitter glued on and calligraphy lettering. The color photos inside were high quality. The text looked professionally printed. A thin gold ribbon, threaded through holes punched in the paper, held the pages together. Someone had spent time and money handcrafting each copy.

"That's Bunny's newsletter," Red said. "She runs your biggest fan club. She has members from all over the United States and in Canada, England, even Japan."

The lobby doors creaked opened and a group of adults charged in, all carrying backpacks or suitcases and heading for the registration table. I needed to clean up and collect my wits before meeting the public, so I thanked Red for his help and, with the manila envelope and fanzine in hand, stepped away from the table. The group besieged Red, all clamoring for their registration packets at once. Red tried to keep his cool as he tried to serve them. Art struck up a conversation with anyone who would listen.

"When can we meet Louise Harrison?" one fan shouted, referring to George's sister who lived in America.

"She won't be here," Red said.

"I heard she'd be here this weekend."

"I'm sorry. We tried to contact her, but couldn't reach her."

"That stinks! I drove all the way from Dayton just to see her!"

"We have another special guest. Sandy Fairfax."

"Who's he?"

Ouch! Some people really know how to hurt a guy. I slipped away before I was further insulted and stood in a short line at the hotel's front desk. Over the counter hung a mangy stuffed elk head with cracked glass eyes that peered down mournfully at the guests. While I waited my turn and as the wobbly elk head threatened to fall on me, I studied a freestanding map of the state for lack of anything else interesting to look at. Marshall made my reservation under my real name, Ernest Farmington, so I got my keycard from the desk clerk with little fuss. I hurried to one of the empty elevators before the fans got on, and rode up to the fifth floor.

After hiking a few miles through a maze of identical hallways, I found my room, unlocked the door, stepped inside and nearly passed out from the fumes left by the previous occupant. Several years ago I used to enjoy cigarettes but I quit when the smoke began to affect my voice and now I can't stand the smell of tobacco. I couldn't open a window to clear the air because the heat would shrivel me. I tossed the registration packet, fanzine and my sunglasses onto one of the double beds (didn't I rate a king-sized bed?), called the front desk on the phone and complained about the smoke in the room.

The clerk replied, "Does it bother you?"

"Of course it bothers me or I wouldn't have called."

From across the line I heard the tapping of computer keys. "I'm sorry, but you didn't request a non-smoking room."

"Yes, I did. The person who took the reservation made a mistake." Marshall's meticulous about details and he wouldn't make an error like that. "I need another room, please."

More keyboard clicking. "I'm sorry, but we don't have any non-smoking rooms available. We're filled up for the weekend."

"You're kidding. How could a hotel in this little town be filled up?"

"We're holding five rooms for late arrivals but that's all."

From my experience of touring, at least one, if not all, of these "late arrivals" would never show. "You can give me one of *those* rooms and the late arrivals can take *this* room."

"But you're in a smoking room and we can't give a smoking room to someone who asked for a non-smoking room."

"Yes, you can, you gave a smoking room to *me*!"

"We're holding those rooms."

"Can I speak with the manager?"

"He's not in the office. Can I take a message?"

Before I could give a heated reply, someone knocked at the hall door. "Sandy, are you in there? It's me, Bunny. Are you busy?"

Since arguing with this clerk was fruitless, I hung up and opened the door. Bunny stood there, her face flushed, with her tote bag hanging from one shoulder and my heavy overnight bag in her hands.

"I brought your luggage," she panted.

"You didn't need to do that, Bunny. You should have asked one of the clerks to haul that for you."

"I don't mind." She set down my bag with a sigh of relief, took a step into my room and glanced around my humble surroundings. "How's the room? Is everything okay?"

"Actually, no. The hotel gave me the wrong room. I asked for non-smoking."

Bunny sniffed the air. "Yeah, I can smell it out here. I'll ask the front desk—"

"I already checked. The clerk said nothing's available."

"I'm sorry, Sandy, I—" She smiled. "Tell you what. I'll trade rooms with you. My room's non-smoking and it doesn't smell at all."

I raised an eyebrow in surprise. "Bunny, you don't need to do that."

"No, I don't mind. Hoosier hospitality, you know. I want you to feel comfortable while you're here. Come on, I'll take you there."

Before I could object she grabbed my bag and raced down the hall to the elevator. I didn't want to lose my luggage again, so I dutifully followed. We rode the elevator down one floor to Bunny's room on the fourth floor. The space had a lived-in look. Beatles memorabilia cluttered the desk and table and Beatles posters were stuck on the walls with dabs of sticky putty. A wind-up Beatles alarm clock sat on the nightstand. A boom box played "I'll Follow The Sun" from a *Beatles '65* cassette.

One corner was devoted to that loveable Sandy Fairfax guy—teen magazines and *Buddy Brave* Gold Key comic books from the '70s, a *Buddy Brave* Secret Underground Laboratory play set and the authorized *Buddy Brave* board game urging youngsters to "solve a mystery along with the world's greatest boy sleuth" (I played that game once with my kids and lost). How did she manage to pack all of this stuff into her tiny car?

A woman about Bunny's age sat cross-legged on one of the twin beds, sewing a Beatles patch onto a denim jacket. She wore a peasant blouse and long crinkle skirt. Bunny introduced her as Trish, a member of her fan club. They were sharing the room for the weekend to save on expenses. Bunny explained my predicament to Trish and the roommate, bless her heart, agreed to swap rooms. Trish began packing up the collectibles (I couldn't image how she planned to move all that loot without a forklift) and Bunny suggested I wait in the hospitality suite until they cleared the room.

"Hospitality suite?" I asked.

"Yeah, it's for the people taking part in the convention, where the guest speakers and the band, they can go and relax. And there's complimentary snacks and soft drinks."

Free food sounded great, especially since I still hadn't eaten lunch. Bunny set my overnight bag in a corner of the room, shouldered her tote bag and darted down the corridor, with me trying to keep up. Down the hall we stopped in front of an open doorway. A heavy-set man wearing a purple nametag, a white T-shirt and denim overalls sat in a folding chair beside the door. His girth spilled over the chair seat and his arms resembled telephone poles. A smoldering cigarette dangled from his fingers and ashes dropped into a cheap metal ashtray on the floor.

The man stuck out his fat arm to block my path. "You can't go in there." I heard him speak, but I couldn't see his lips move under his thick black beard.

"Excuse me?" I was annoyed. Bouncers have thrown me out of the best clubs in L.A., but this backwoods bumbler wasn't about to push me around.

"You don't got a nametag."

"I don't *need* a nametag."

"It's all right, Elmer," Bunny said. "This is Sandy Fairfax. He's our special guest speaker. He can come in the hospitality suite."

"Red told me don't let nobody in without a purple nametag," he grumbled. "Don't know why we bother with nametags if people ain't gonna wear them." The mountain lowered his arm and glared at me as I stepped into the room.

The hospitality suite consisted of two adjoining rooms with the connecting door opened and the beds moved out. The inner room contained a desk, file cabinet and reams of paperwork regarding convention business scattered about. The outer room, where we stood, had armchairs, a loveseat, long tables, a TV set on a metal cart with wheels and folding chairs stacked against one wall.

"I'm sorry about Elmer," Bunny said. "I should have told you. Everyone has a nametag inside their registration packets. The yellow nametags are for the fans. The purple tags are all access. It's to keep out the gatecrashers. I hope you don't mind."

"I assumed everybody knew me."

"Why don't you put your nametag on now?"

I patted my pants pockets in search of the elusive nametag and pulled out a broken bit of pottery instead.

"What's that?" she asked.

"Just a memento." I stuffed the object back in my pocket. "I don't seem to have a nametag."

"Maybe it's still in your packet."

"Most likely." Keeping track of one piece of luggage was hard enough without remembering to put on a badge as well.

"Tell you what, Sandy, why don't you relax and I'll go fetch your packet so you'll have your nametag."

"You don't need to—"

"Do you want something to drink?" She opened a plastic cooler on the floor. She stuck her arm up to her elbow into the half-melted ice, felt around, pulled out a can of soda and handed it to me. "Mr. Ellis told me you like Mountain Dew."

"Yes, thank you." I took the can, popped the tab and took a long, grateful gulp to quench my thirst. "That tastes great. Where are the snacks?"

The paper-covered tables were bare except for a bag of potato chips, a plastic box of store-bought cookies and a bowl full of green Granny Smith apples.

"Oh, no. Billy's in charge of stocking the suite, but since he's not here, I guess it didn't get done. I brought the apples. That was my idea."

I got the joke immediately. After the Beatles' manager, Brian Epstein, died in 1967, the fabs formed Apple Corps Ltd. to handle their business affairs and the Apple label for recording. The company symbol was a green apple.

"Can I get you something from the snack bar downstairs?" Bunny offered.

Before I could reply, two young men with purple nametags stormed into the suite. One man yelled at the other, "If you ever pull a stunt like that again, I'll *kill* you!"

❖ CHAPTER THREE

Act Naturally

"LEAVE ME ALONE!" The second man's nametag identified him as Dana Mumford. "You don't own me!"

The first man, whose nametag read "Scott Rockwell," waved a newspaper in Dana's face. "Don't go around making announcements like this without telling us first!"

"I can leave the band with three weeks notice and that," Dana punched his finger at the paper, "is my notice."

"Like hell it is!"

"Screw you!"

"Drop dead!"

A third man ran into the suite. "Stop it! I can hear you two all the way down the hall!" The purple nametag on the third man read "Grant Burlington." "What's the problem?"

Dana said. "Scott's acting like a jerk, as usual."

"Go ahead and leave the band," Scott shot back. "I'm sick of dealing with you. I wish you were out of my face."

"I said stop it!" Grant turned to the convention hostess. "Sorry, Bunny. The guys didn't mean to bother you and your friend."

"Don't apologize for me!" As Dana stormed out of the room, he bumped into Art, who was on his way in.

"Watch it!" Art yelled at the retreating man. He shook his head. "Looks like Dana's got his knickers in a twist again. Hello, Sandy. We meet again. Small world, isn't it?"

"Where are my manners?" Bunny said. "I haven't introduced anyone. Everyone, this is Sandy Fairfax. Sandy, meet Art, Grant, Scott. They're in the tribute band, and so is Dana. He just left."

I shook hands all around. Grant greeted me politely but Scott squeezed my hand a little too hard as if he was still miffed from his argument with Dana.

"Hey, Sandy, didn't know that was you," Grant said. "Great to have you here. Always liked your music. I'm 'George' of the Mersey Marvels."

Scott raised his hand. "'Paul' here."

I could have identified the guys on my own. Each one bore an uncanny resemblance to his Beatle counterpart, especially Scott, who had a lady killer face like myself. Poor guy.

"The guy who left must be 'John,'" I said.

"Not for much longer." Scott flopped into an armchair. "He says he's quitting so he can start his own John Lennon tribute band."

"You're kidding!" Art said.

Scott held up the newspaper. "I picked up the paper this morning before I left Indy. Says his new band's scheduled for a gig in three weeks. Guess he was too busy sneaking behind our backs to tell us."

"Let me see that." Grant snatched the paper and scanned the article as Art peered over his shoulder.

"Is something wrong?" Red said this to Bunny as he entered the suite. "I saw Dana in the hall and he looked upset. Blasted right past me without saying a word."

"Scott said Dana's leaving the band," Bunny said.

"You mean now?" Red sounded worried. "What about the concert tomorrow night?"

"We're still playing," Grant said. "I'll see to it. Dana'll be over his snit by then."

"Hello, Sandy." Red finally noticed me. "Just the man I wanted to see. We need another room for one of the band members. Since your room has two beds and you're leaving tomorrow, I was wondering if Scott or Dana could stay with you."

"Absolutely not." I'm willing to work with event organizers up to a point, but this isn't a college dorm and I'm not giving up my privacy for a stranger.

"Sandy, we don't have a choice. Bunny and I have run out of money for the convention and we can't afford an extra room."

"That's unfortunate, but you'll have to make other arrangements."

"Come on, Sandy," Bunny begged. "Sharing a room won't be so bad and it'll help us out of a jam."

I used my never-fail weapon—legalities. "According to my contract, you have to supply me with a private room. If you want to make any changes, you'll have to speak with my manager." I knew Marshall would back me up on this issue.

Scott snipped, "Boy, you must think you're some big hot shot to rate special treatment."

I resisted the urge to tell him that I'd earned the right to act like a prima donna. But as Jarvis Lycowitz, my manager in the '70s, used to tell me, don't piss off the people paying my salary. The best way to defuse the situation was to walk away. I headed for the doorway—but I didn't get far.

"Look at the time, it's four o'clock!" Bunny turned on the TV set and the next sound I heard stopped me cold in my tracks—a downbeat followed by brassy horns playing an all-too-familiar TV theme song.

"Look at that!" Art laughed. "It's *Buddy Brave, Boy Sleuth*! I haven't seen that show in years."

"Sandy, why don't you stay and watch it with us?" Bunny asked.

"No, I have to go—"

"Come on, Sandy, please. You can tell us all about it as we watch."

She pulled the TV cart to the center of the room. The guys moved the armchairs in front of the set. As much as I wanted to leave, something about the show pulled me in, like a whirlpool sucking in the next victim.

Bunny sat on one end of the love seat and patted the empty cushion beside her, the only available seating. "Sit down and relax, Sandy. You must be tired."

Yes, too tired to hike down the hallway to my new room. The hectic day had finally caught up with me. Until I caught my second wind, I wanted to ooze into a puddle and do something stupid and brainless—like watching my show. I grabbed some chocolate chip cookies from the snack table and sat on the loveseat, nearly sinking to the floor through the flimsy upholstery.

Mike Connors had the rugged *Mannix*; Jack Lord, the classy *Hawaii Five-O;*

and Peter Falk the cerebral *Columbo*. But for all eternity I was stuck on celluloid clad in paisley shirts and polyester bell-bottoms with that scarf knotted around my neck. From 1975 to 1979 I ran around damp medieval dungeons ("The Killdary Castle Caper"), hung from flying saucers ("The Make-Believe Martian Caper") and rode the backs of sea monsters ("The Slimy Sea Serpent Caper").

Buddy Brave was an average teenage boy with an after-school job as an undercover spy for a secret government agency. Between household chores and school assignments, he fought dastardly criminals, traveled across the globe and faced deadly peril each week with not so much as an outbreak of acne. Now I realized watching television takes a certain amount of suspension of disbelief. But my show required the viewer to saw open his skull and scoop out most of his brain cells.

The show finished the opening credits and a title card introduced the episode as "The Sunburned Surfer Caper." A happy-go-lucky Buddy, with a head full of tight blonde curls, zipped across the screen on water skis.

"Is that you or a stunt double?" Red asked.

"That's the real deal," I said. "I did most of my own stunts, except for the car cashes. I insisted on it. Stunt doubles never look right. That shot with the water skis took all morning. During the lunch break the line producer gave me a big lecture on why my stunts were running the show over budget."

I munched on the cookies and watched myself as a skinny, twenty-one-year-old kid wearing that ridiculous neck scarf, my trademark. Buddy felt like a separate person from myself, and filming the show seemed like another lifetime ago. I don't remember most of the episodes—I didn't watch them again after the first run. But as the show unfolded, bits and pieces of memories came back to me. Bunny sat on the edge of the loveseat, back straight, eyes glued to the TV screen. She silently mouthed each word of dialogue along with the actors.

Art pointed to the screen and chuckled. "Nice 'fro, man."

Nothing like hitting a sore spot. "Trust me, that hairdo wasn't my idea."

"It's a third season episode from 1977 to '78," Bunny said. "That's the year Sandy had an afro."

"That's the year *The Hardy Boys Mysteries* came on the air and the suits felt like they had to freshen up my show. They demanded I change my hairstyle so I'd look hip or something. I can still smell that junk the hairdresser used to perm my hair." I wrinkled my nose at the memory. "It's a wonder my hair didn't fall out."

The program zoomed along at breakneck speed, something about a surfer champion who disappeared the day before a big contest. Everyone said the champ got cold feet, but Buddy, who was smarter than the adults on the show, discovered the champ's rival had kidnapped the surfer. A mad scientist used a device to transfer the champ's surfing ability into the rival's brain. Unbelievable, I know, but typical of the show's outlandish plots.

The first commercial break came on. Art got up to get some chips and cookies. Red and Scott were still discussing the housing situation. Scott said he could tolerate rooming with the musician for another day, since "tomorrow he's planning on checking out for good."

From the hallway, Elmer, still at his post, shouted. "Go away! You can't look in there."

I glanced over my shoulder. Some people with yellow convention nametags stood in the corridor and tried to peek inside the suite. I gave them a wave and they got excited.

"Let them come in and watch the show, Elmer," I said. "They got good taste."

The yellow-taggers cheered as they spilled into the room. Some grabbed the few remaining folding chairs and set them up around the TV while the others either sat on the floor or remained standing. Elmer growled, slouched in his chair and took another drag on his cigarette.

The commercials ended and after Buddy's obligatory weekly fight scene with the bad guys, the story jumped to the boy detective sneaking into a beach bungalow to look for the missing champ.

"Wait a minute," I said. "There's a scene missing." I leaned forward and rested my elbows on my knees to watch more closely. "I remember shooting a scene about Buddy romancing the girl guest star at a hamburger stand, but I haven't seen it." The show ran along to the second commercial break. "It happened again! That last scene goes on longer, I know. The station's chopping up my show!"

"That's common," Grant said. "They need more room for the commercials."

The fans in the room appreciated my work and I hated to disappoint them. Time for some mischief.

"Nobody mutilates my show." I stood up. "Is here a phone in the room?"

"A phone?" Bunny jumped to her feet. "Yeah, in here."

She picked up the hotel phone from the inner room and brought it to me, stretching the phone cord as far as it would go. I took the phone in one hand and lifted the receiver.

"Who are you calling?" she asked.

I pointed the receiver at the TV set. "That station."

"I know the number. I call them all the time for the *Buddy Brave* trivia contest."

I didn't bother to ask how many times she had won. I punched the digits into the phone keypad as Bunny recited the number. I held the phone to my good ear. The phone rang twice and a receptionist answered.

"WFIE-TV, channel fourteen, how may I help you?"

"I'd like to speak with the general manager, please."

"What is this regarding?"

"I have a complaint about one of the show."

Several people in the room snickered. Art gave me a thumbs up. Bunny gasped and tried to grab the phone away. While I waited for my call to transfer, I asked for someone to please turn down the TV audio so I could hear.

A new voice came on the phone. "I'm Clyde Danvers, the programming director." Sounded like a typical middle-aged, middle management type. "I believe you have a question about one of our shows?"

"Are you the person responsible for making mincemeat out of the programs?" I said.

"Which show are you referring to?"

"*Buddy Brave, Boy Sleuth*. The program on right now. I've seen at least two cuts in today's episode. Why are you whacking my show to death?"

"What makes you think we made any cuts?"

"Because I was there when the show was filmed, that's how!"

Danvers cleared his throat. "Whom am I speaking to?"

"Sandy Fairfax, star of the show."

"No, seriously, who are you?"

"I told you. I'm the kid who's running around on your monitor."

The man spoke softly to someone else in the room before getting back to me. "Where are you calling from, sir?"

"I'm in town this weekend for a convention. I'm at the—" I covered the mouthpiece with one hand and asked the fans, "Where are we?" When I was touring I could never remember the names of the hotels where I stayed.

"King Arthur's Arms!" several people replied. I repeated the information to Danvers.

"Thank you for your concern," the manager said. "We always appreciate feedback from our viewers." He clearly didn't believe me.

"If I see any more cuts in the show, you'll hear from my lawyer." I slammed down the receiver and my audience clapped. I grinned, bowed my head, and handed the phone back to Bunny.

"Are you really going to sue him?" she asked in awe.

"Of course not. I have no control over the show. The studio owns the broadcasting rights, not me."

By now the commercial break had ended, so someone turned up the volume on the TV set and we all settled in for act three of "Sunburned Surfer." Buddy got himself deeper into trouble until he and the pretty girl guest star of the week (who wore a white ruffled blouse with orange hot pants and knee-high boots to match) found themselves dangling from a rope over a pit filled with hungry crocodiles snapping at their heels. The show's real mystery is how the story meandered from surfing to exotic reptiles.

The girl fluttered her foot-long fake eyelashes. "Oh, Buddy, what are we going to do?"

Every classic TV star was known by his catch phrase. I had mine that was used on every episode at the end of act three when Buddy and the girl guest star were tied up or facing certain death at the hands of the villains. The fans in the room recited right along with the kid on the TV, "Don't worry! I'll think of something!" The overblown background music swelled and the show cut to commercial.

"Wasn't that scary, those crocodiles biting at you?" Bunny asked.

"If you look carefully," I said, "you'll notice the crocs and I are never in the same shot. Close-up of me, then close-up of the crocs. It's all in the editing. The insurance people would have thrown a fit if I was that close to a real animal."

"But you acted so scared."

"The director on that episode was scarier than the crocodiles. He hated me. Can't blame him, though. By third season I was a pain to work with."

The commercial ended. Back in the pit, Buddy was literally at the end of his rope. "I've heard that music can soothe the savage beast."

"That's just an old wives' tale," the girl said.

The precocious twerp wrapped his arm around the rope to hang on and played the guitar that hung oh-so-conveniently across his shoulder. He sang one of my hits, a shameless promotion for my records. Sure enough, the crocs swam away.

Buddy mugged at the camera. "Next time I see an old wife, I'll tell her it's true." Small wonder I drank heavily back then. Dialogue that bad would drive anyone to the bottle.

Our hero and the girl swung over to a rock ledge. Buddy climbed up the pit wall—the rocks made handy foot-and-handholds. Once out of the pit, he used the rope to pull the girl up. A crook with a gun jumped them. Buddy seized his guitar by the neck and swung it, slapping the weapon from the villain's hand. Then he used the musical club to whack the criminal on the head and knock him down.

The girl squealed. "Gee, Buddy, that's the first time I've ever seen a guitar used like a real ax!" With puns like that, the writing staff never won an Emmy.

Buddy found the kidnapped surfer, but the athlete was still woozy from the villain's drugs. Buddy used the mad scientist's machine to transfer the champ's surfing skill into his own brain. At the contest, the brash young brat stood in for the surfer—and won, of course. The show ended with Buddy kissing the girl guest star (my favorite part of shooting), receiving accolades from the adults, and getting scolded by his guardian for not cleaning up his room that morning. As the closing credits played out, my audience applauded. I signed some autographs as the fans gushed over my performance. As corny as the show was, I enjoyed their attention. People hadn't treated me this nicely in a long time.

Bunny switched off the TV and the crowd dispersed. Grant left to find his wife. Red headed for the registration table. Scott and Art departed to check on the band equipment. My stomach growled.

"What do you want to do now, Sandy?" Bunny asked eagerly. "I can show you where the meeting rooms are, or—"

"Thanks, but I'd like to get something to eat."

"There's a nice dining room downstairs. Come on, I'll take you there."

I wasn't keen on sharing a meal with Bunny, but my only options were to hop in a taxi and ride around town in hopes of finding a decent restaurant or wait until Trish moved out and I could order room service. We rode the elevator to the ground floor and passed through the lobby to the dining room, Ye Olde Country Inn. The restaurant carried out the medieval theme with round wooden tables and ladder chairs made of rough-hewn wood. The young female wait staff wore colorful but silly jester outfits of tights, pointed caps and doublets.

The waitress guided us toward a table close to four smokers puffing away. I cringed until I spotted a "No Smoking Section" sign and asked if we could sit there instead. The waitress shot me a sour look, but obliged. I suppose L.A. had spoiled me. Some time ago the state outlawed smoking in all public eating establishments. Perhaps eventually the rest of the world would catch up. The waitress sat us at a two-person table up against the four-foot high wall that separated the smoking and clean-air sections. The low partition didn't stop whiffs of smoke from wafting toward me.

I leaned across the table towards Bunny. "I can't handle this smoke. Let's move to another table."

"But the waitress wants us here."

"She's not the one breathing the fumes. Come on."

The room was nearly empty, so we easily found a booth at the far end of the no-smoking area. Our departure flustered the waitress, who returned to our original table, looked around and started back to the kitchen until I hailed her.

"There you are," she said, clearly annoyed. "I thought you'd left."

"We prefer this table." I gave her a big smile. "The lighting's better."

I ordered coffee and the steak dinner, while Bunny asked for a Diet Coke and the baked fish. Miss Congeniality brought a basket of warmed store-bought dinner rolls and a plate of hard butter patties to tide us over. Clogged arteries seemed a better option than starvation, so I grabbed a roll, split it open and smeared it with butter.

Bunny tucked her tote bag underneath the table. "Making a TV show must be terribly exciting. I've lived in Evansville my whole life. Nothing ever happens to me."

"Filmmaking is hard work. Early morning calls, learning lines, retakes, waiting for set ups, getting dirty in the stunt work."

"But you look like you're having so much fun on the show."

A teen idol career isn't as glamorous as people think—stress, rehearsals, fatigue, demands, criticisms, the constant public attention, fights with the studio suits. Fortunately, the good parts were grand enough to balance out the negatives. I shared a few amusing anecdotes from my heyday until Bunny asked if I could do a favor for her.

"What is it?" I better find out what she wanted before I committed to something I'd regret. Fans can dream up some strange propositions, such as the woman who wrote me years ago that she wanted me by her side when she gave birth to her children.

"When the band plays tomorrow night, can you sing a few of your songs for us?"

I put down my roll. "That wasn't part of my agreement for coming here."

"I know, but everyone would like it so much."

"I'll honor my contract, but nothing more. I hope you understand."

Years ago Jarvis had told me to never give away anything for free. Over the years people tried to take advantage of me, probably because of my good nature and clean-cut image. Whenever someone asked for "just one more thing," the request always cost me plenty with little in return.

She gazed at me with hurt puppy dog eyes. "Please, Sandy."

I help up a hand. "I can't, Bunny. I haven't sung in a long time and I haven't rehearsed with this band. You wouldn't want me to put on a bad show, would you?"

She looked down at her bread plate. "No, I suppose not."

Our meals arrived and Bunny attacked her whitefish with gusto. I bit into my steak and the raw meat almost mooed. I asked the waitress to take the meat back to the kitchen and have it cooked. She rolled her eyes at me and clomped away as well as one can stomp in velveteen slippers. As I ate the dinner salad, people with yellow nametags wandered into the dining room and gave me looks of recognition. They smiled and waved, but otherwise left me alone, which I appreciated.

Except for one guy.

"Hey! Hey! You're that dude on TV!"

A guy in blue jeans stood close to my chair and yelled in my ear. His black T-shirt, imprinted with "Mercy Marvels, Indy's Most Authentic Beatles Tribute," was a size too small and stretched tightly across his beer gut. The sight of his hairy belly button nearly made me lose my appetite. He was bald on top, with a fringe of long greasy black hair.

"You're that kid detective!" He jabbed a chubby finger in my face. Patrons at the nearby tables stared. "I watch you every day on TV. Caught any bad guys lately, huh? 'Don't worry, I'll think of something.' That's what you always say, right? Right?"

I put down my utensils and clenched my teeth in a semblance of a smile. I rested my elbows on the table and clasped my hands so I wouldn't punch his big mouth. "What's your name?"

"I'm Hank. Hank Belcher." He grabbed my hand and shook it so hard he nearly separated my arm from the shoulder. "Hey, it's great to meet a big TV star."

"Nice to meet you, too." I yanked my hand away from his grip. "Enjoy your meal."

"Hey, do you know this song?" He grunted like a monkey, scratched beneath his armpits and jumped up and down. The action seemed natural on him. "Huh? Bet you can't guess. Huh? It's 'Gorilla My Dreams.' Like your song, 'Girl of My Dreams.' Gorilla? Girl? Get it?"

I got it, but I sure as heck didn't want it. Hank reared back his head and blasted out a horselaugh. The waitress reappeared with my steak redux. Hank wouldn't move out of her way, so she reached around him to serve my meal. I rose partway from my chair to take the plate from her before Hank intercepted it. I sat down, picked up my knife and fork and prepared to eat. But not yet.

"Hey, that looks good. What is it?" Hank bent over the table and the ends of his nasty hair dangled dangerously low over my steak. If he didn't move in two seconds I'd shove my fork up his nose.

"The steak dinner. Why don't you take a seat and the waitress will bring you one."

"Yeah, good idea. 'Bye now. Hey, I'll be seeing a lot of you this weekend. See?" He showed me the yellow nametag around his neck. I silently groaned as the blob waddled away to a booth.

"I'm sorry about that, Sandy," Bunny said. "Do you want me to keep the fans away?"

"That's all right. I can handle people like him." Bunny and I resumed eating. "How many of these conventions have you set up?"

"This is the first one. Trouble is, we booked it too close to Beatlefest. That's the big annual festival in Chicago in early August. A lot of the fans already attended that convention and ran out of money, so they couldn't come here."

"Are you planning another one for next year?"

"Red and I, we don't know yet. Depends if we can pay the bills. We both maxed out our credit cards to pay for the weekend. We didn't get as many registrations as we expected and we might lose a bunch of money."

Before I could respond, a female voice bellowed from a nearby table. "Tomorrow morning I'm hitting the dealers' room first thing. This time I'm getting me 'butcher cover' if I have to *kill* somebody for it."

❖ CHAPTER FOUR

Apple Scruffs

THE FAT WOMAN had close-cropped black hair and a bad-tempered face that would stop the atomic clock. Two women and a man shared the table with her, all picking at their French fries and avoiding eye contact with Brunhilda. I tried to ignore her, but her voice carried so much that I couldn't help but listen.

"I found a 'butcher cover' at Beatlefest, but some slut, she talked the vendor into selling it to her. This time nothing's gonna stop me from gettin' one." Her audience merely nodded, since the speaker never gave them a chance to talk. I asked Bunny if she knew the woman.

"That's Valleri. Most of the fans steer clear of her. She spreads mean gossip on the fan boards. She hates anyone who knows more about The Beatles than she does or has gone to more concerts or has a better record collection."

Apparently Valleri's memorabilia didn't include the "butcher cover," one of the most rare and prized Beatles collectibles. When Capital released *"Yesterday"...and Today* in America in 1966, the original album cover showed the musicians dressed in bloody butcher smocks and gleefully holding slabs of raw meat and dismembered baby dolls. The photo shocked the suits, who immediately pulled the stock out of the stores and re-issued the record with a more conventional but boring photo of the Beatles dressed in regular clothes and looking subdued. A number of the banned covers managed to slip through and are worth plenty, I'm told.

"If one of the vendors has a 'butcher cover' this weekend, she'll find it." Bunny jabbed a fork into her salad. "Valleri usually gets what she wants."

"That sounded personal."

"Red and me refused to let her help out with the convention because we knew she'd run things to suit herself and treat the other fans badly. Since she couldn't have her own way, Valleri told people *not* to come. We lost some registrations because of her. I bet she'll try to sabotage the weekend to make us look bad."

Valleri spotted us. At first she registered surprise at seeing me and then her face melted into a scowl. She chatted to her table companions. She sounded angry, but with the din of the other patrons I couldn't catch her words and I asked Bunny what Valleri was saying.

"She's jealous because you're sitting with me. She says there's something going on between us."

"Do you think she'll come over here and cause trouble?" I'd rather dangle over a pit of hungry crocodiles than face the wrath of a furious fan.

"Naw. She blusters a lot, but she's a big 'fraidy cat at heart."

We finished our meals around six o'clock. Bunny suggested we skip dessert because the eight o'clock mixer would provide plenty of goodies. I didn't tell her that I planned on skipping the party. I wasn't obligated to meet the fans until tomorrow, so for tonight I anticipated a relaxing evening in my room with a hot shower, some TV and sleep. But my best-laid plans were soon thwarted. As we passed through the lobby on our way to the elevators, a forty-something man in a business suit jumped up from a bench beside the fountain and approached us.

"Are you Sandy Fairfax?" he asked.

He didn't have a convention nametag, so he wasn't a fan seeking an autograph. Did one of my recent girlfriends have a husband I didn't know about? Or was this someone I beat up during one of my drunken blackouts? The convention might end before it began.

"Yes, I am," I answered warily.

The man broke into a smile and shook my hand. "So it really was you!"

"It was?"

"We spoke on the phone earlier today. I'm Clyde Danvers from Channel 14, programming director. When you called, I thought you were a kid pulling a prank. I hadn't seen you in pictures for so long I thought you were dead."

Shows you how badly my career had bottomed out. "No, I've just kept a low profile."

"After you hung up I called the hotel and they confirmed that you were here for the Swingin' Sixties convention. I'm glad I caught up with you."

"Hello, I'm Bunny McAllister," my sidekick blurted. "I watch *Buddy Brave* every day. Thank you for running it."

"It's a popular show, especially in the 'tween demographics. Mr. Fairfax, the reason I'm here, could you come to the station and tape an interview for us? I know this is short notice, but we didn't know you were in town and the hotel said you were only staying for one night."

"An interview? You mean right now?" So much for my peaceful evening.

"I know it's asking a lot, but our viewers would appreciate it so much."

"Go on, Sandy," Bunny urged. "You're free for two hours before the party starts."

"But I was planning on—"

"Now's a perfect time," Danvers said. "The camera crew's free until the ten o'clock newscast."

"Stay as long as you want," Bunny said. "The mixer runs to eleven and you can drop in any time."

My body needed rest, but my ego craved attention. No entertainer worth his salt could resist a chance to get his name out and I needed all the positive publicity I could scrap up, even out here in the bland Midwest.

"All right, but give me a minute to go to my room and change clothes."

"You look fine the way you are. We need to go, I'm double parked out front."

I started to follow Danvers to the main doors and Bunny called, "Sandy! Room key!" We swapped keycards so each of us could get into our new rooms, although the way things were going, I might not see my lodgings until late tonight.

Danvers drove me to the TV station—at least his sedan had air conditioning. Now when someone says "studio" to me, I think of a full-fledged Hollywood complex sprawling across dozens of acres. My show used two soundstages, each building the size of an aircraft hanger. At this station, the "studio" consisted of a tiny room with a desk for the news anchors, a weather map and two chairs on a platform in the corner for a morning interview show.

Still, a camera is a camera and as soon as I walked in I felt an adrenaline surge. Nothing wakes up an actor like an audience.

Danvers and I sat in the interview chairs while the two cameramen adjusted the lighting and locked down a stationary camera for a wide shot of the set. They used two side cameras for the close-ups. Turns out Danvers was a fan of my show. He asked intelligent questions, not the usual fan fluff, and soon I was laughing and ad libbing jokes. The engineer cued up videotapes of the upcoming shows and I talked about certain scenes. Danvers wrote trivia questions on the teleprompter for me to ask the viewers (good thing he knew the answers because I didn't).

Once we got rolling I had a good time reminiscing about the dippy boy dick, so much so that I didn't notice the time. At a quarter to eight Danvers asked if I had to leave and I said no, I'd stay and do whatever he wanted. I recorded intros and outros for the commercial breaks, "coming up next" teasers and station identifications: "Hi, I'm Sandy Fairfax and you're watching WFIE-TV, Channel 14, the tri-state's home for *Buddy Brave, Boy Sleuth* at 4 p.m. weekdays."

After we finished Danvers drove me back to the hotel and dropped me off at the drawbridge at about nine o'clock. I figured I could bypass the party and sneak into my room for a well-deserved rest. All of the elevators were occupied, so I punched in my floor number and waited. One of the cab doors opened and discharged a horde of people with convention nametags. Apparently they assumed I was headed for the mixer because they offered to show me the way. I couldn't say no, especially since they outnumbered me and would probably rat to Bunny if I didn't show up. I figured I'd knock off a quick meet-and-greet at the party and head back to my room.

The mixer was in the Lancelot Room, but most of the convention guests made a detour into the Mead And Ale Lounge next door. Fans were leaving the bar with plastic cups of wine and mixed drinks. The sight and smell of the alcohol trigged a strong reaction in me. I knew I shouldn't have even one drink, but my gut wanted liquor in the worst way. I didn't know how to socialize at a gathering without a drink in my hand. I'd get back on the wagon again—right after I had one teeny, tiny drink.

Inside the lounge I bellied up to the bar and asked the female bartender for a strawberry daiquiri. As I waited, a familiar voice greeted me. Bunny stood at my elbow, holding a large wet plastic sack in her arms.

"What's in the bag?" I asked.

"I came in here to get more ice for the mixer. I didn't expect to see you here."

"I'm getting something to drink."

"There're plenty of soft drinks in the ballroom."

"Thanks, but I want something else."

She looked at me as if I'd announced that her pet hamster had died. "Mr. Ellis told me you gave up alcohol. I told everyone in my fan club that you don't drink any more."

Marshall's not only my manager but also my surrogate mother. He probably expected the fans to keep me in line while I was out of town. I considered telling Bunny I was old enough to make my own decisions, but as I opened my mouth, some female fans showed up to order drinks.

"Hi Sandy!" one of the gals said. "We think it's wonderful that you don't drink."

"Yeah, Sandy, we're all behind you one hundred percent," another one added.

I started to tell them to mind their own business when in the back of my mind I heard Buddy Brave, that carefully crafted image I'd kept buried for years, scolding me. Back in my heyday, no matter how badly I behaved off stage, my handlers made certain nobody ever saw or photographed me with a cigarette in my hand or a glass of anything stronger than Coca-Cola. Even though my show was cancelled years ago, the fans still thought I was as innocent and clean-cut as Buddy.

The bartender set a napkin and a plastic glass on the counter in front of me. "Your daiquiri, sir."

The women stared at the drink as if it contained rat poison.

I told the bartender, "I changed my mind. Can you make it a virgin?"

A few minutes later I carried my alcohol-free drink into the Lancelot Room, with Bunny and her ice bag in tow. On a stage at the far end of the dimly lit room was the deejay's station where a young Asian-American man dressed in canvas pants and a University of Southern Indiana T-shirt sat behind a table and loaded CDs into a player. A mirror ball hung from the ceiling and reflected rays from the colored spotlights. Red Hardiman was busy blowing up balloons with helium tank and launching them up to the ceiling. Couples gyrated on a portable dance floor set up in front of the stage. Grant stopped dancing long enough to introduce me to his wife, Prudence. Art was waltzing with an older woman who enjoyed the attention. A cluster of unescorted ladies danced together as "Tell Me Why" blasted over the loudspeakers. Scott and Dana were not in the room.

A row of tables was set up along the wall. Unlike the bare pantry of the hospitality suite, these tables nearly buckled under the weight of the platters of cookies, cupcakes, candies, donuts, finger sandwiches, fresh fruits and veggies as well as a bowl of green apples. A plastic bin full of ice held an assortment of canned soft drinks and fruit juices. As Bunny dumped her ice into the bin, we discussed my interview at the TV station. I asked her about the deejay.

"That's Alexander Watanabe, our local Beatles expert. We call him 'Magic Alex.' He's got every Beatles bootleg and recorded interview that exists. On Sunday afternoons he produces the 'Beaucoups of Beatles' show at the campus radio station at USI. I'll ask him to give you some tapes of his shows. They're really good."

A man in a short-sleeve shirt and tie strolled into the room as if he owned the place. He had heavy jowls, prominent beer gut and a bad comb over. The man didn't have a convention nametag, so he had somehow managed to slip past Elmer at the door. He spoke with Bunny, but I couldn't hear their conversation over the music. After he left, Bunny looked unhappy and I asked if the man had upset her.

"That's Mr. Bluefield, the hotel manager. He says the music's too loud."

As loudness goes, the volume was up but not unbearable. I've been inside L.A. clubs where the speakers shook the walls harder than an earthquake. If Bluefield thought this was loud, he should have heard the fans and their ear-busting screams at my '70s concerts.

"He said if we don't turn it down, he'd stop the party." Bunny frowned. "What a mean guy. He's a Blue Meanie, like the creatures in the *Yellow Submarine* movie who hate music."

She scampered off to talk to Alex about the music as I began working the crowd. My old public relations skills bubbled up after a long hibernation. With the nametags I could greet people by name and of course everyone knew me. Keeping myself busy with fraternizing helped to keep my mind off booze. And I relished the experience of walking all the way across a large room without falling down drunk. The fans welcomed me with genuine warmth and fondness. They also asked why I hadn't been touring or recording for so long. Trouble is, I didn't have a good answer, so I smiled and said I "have some projects in development," a show biz term that means "nobody's given me a job lately."

One middle-aged woman introduced me to her husband and told how they met in 1977 when she walked into a record store to buy a new record, *Donald Clark Osmond,* and the clerk talked her into purchasing my newly released *Stars In My Eyes* album instead. (I have nothing against Donny. We're friends but business wise at the time we were competing for the same audience). The girl bought my record, loved it, and ended up marrying the clerk. They played my songs at their wedding and her hubby is now the proud owner of a chain of music stores across the state.

Bunny took a camera out of a leather pouch hanging around her waist and snapped numerous pictures of the proceedings. As "Another Girl" played over the speakers, Valleri stood in a corner, grumbling to her cohorts. I thought fans came to conventions for a good time, but despite the food, music and my esteemed presence, Valleri seemed determined to stay miserable. Over the years I'd developed good instincts about people and, with apologies to Brian Wilson, from Valleri I was picking up bad vibrations.

A man standing by the food tables picked up an apple and tossed it to me. "Here, Sandy, have a snack."

"Thanks." I snagged the flying fruit with my left hand, poised to take a bite and then stopped as some mischief crossed my mind. "Throw me two more, will you?"

The man obliged and as I caught each apple I tossed it up until I had all three apples spinning in the air. The onlookers oohhed, aahhed and clapped. I couldn't believe I remembered this trick. Amazing the things one can do when sober.

"That's great!" the man said. "I didn't know you could juggle."

I fixed my baby blues on the airborne apples. "I learned this for my show. The studio brought in a professional juggler to teach me."

As always, Bunny filled in the information. "That was on 'The Billowing Big Top Caper' episode where you go undercover as a circus performer."

I let the apples fall into my hands and replaced them in the bowl. Three female fans snatched up the apples I had touched and tucked them into their purses for safekeeping until they could go home and press them into their scrapbooks.

The music ended and the dancers slowed down. Alex raised his hand to punch up the next tune on the CD player, but his finger froze as the hallway door opened. The conversation among the fans faded into excited whispers.

The crowd watched in awe as John Lennon sauntered into the room.

❖ CHAPTER FIVE

I Don't Want To Spoil The Party

NOT THE *REAL* John Lennon, of course, but this young man with a yellow nametag ran a close second. Same height and build, similar facial features, shoulder-length brown hair cut in bangs and granny glasses. He wore sneakers, red pants, a psychedelic multicolored Nehru jacket and love beads—an exact replica of Lennon's outfit from the "I Am The Walrus" segment of the *Magical Mystery Tour* movie. The kid had an acoustic guitar slung over a shoulder. He waved and greeted the crowd with, "Hello, Beatle people."

I asked Red if the kid was from a celebrity look-alike agency. In L.A. one can hire actors who portray Lucy Ricardo, Laurel and Hardy, Spider-man and any number of icons for parties and movies.

"He lives for the fan events. He shows up at all the conventions around the country and the big one in Liverpool each year. That's Winston O'Boogie."

Lennon used that pseudonym on a couple of his albums. This joker with the guitar must be playing a few mind games of his own. The kid approached me.

"If it isn't the great Sandy Fairfax." He didn't try to duplicate Lennon's exact voice, but he spoke in the delightful rhythmic cadence of Liverpool speech. I could listen to him for hours. "I love your show. I never miss it when it's on."

"Thank you, Winston. Do you live around here?"

"I live here, there and everywhere. There's no bed for Beatle John."

Was this kid crazy or just putting me on? I challenged him. "I've met the real John Lennon. I used to drop in on him and Yoko whenever I had business in New York."

I wasn't prepared for his reaction. Winston's gaze bore into me, his eyes smoldering behind those glasses. "John was murdered when he started recording again."

"Yes, it's a terrible loss."

"They should fry the man who killed him."

That uneasy feeling swept over me again and I glance around for a polite way to get away from this nut case.

Someone across the room shouted, "Winston, sing us a song, will ya?" I detected an undertone of mocking in the request.

The Lennon wannabe pulled a folding chair to the center of the room and perched atop the chair back with his feet on the seat. He strummed his guitar and sang Lennon's "Imagine." Imagine my surprise that the kid could sing. He didn't sound like Lennon, but his passion carried the song and his voice soothed the ear. The right management could easily mold the kid into a teen idol.

"What a jerk! He's not half as good as he thinks he is!"

I smelled Dana before I saw him. I nearly choked on the combination of tobacco smoke and liquor fumes as he sided up to me. Apparently after he'd left the hospitality suite he spent the afternoon in the lounge for a few smokes and more than a few drinks.

He shouted again. "Shut up, you amateur impersonator!" Winston stopped playing and gazed at Dana with languid eyes as the heckler continued. "I can do a hellava better John Lennon than you can!"

Silence fell over the room as quickly as a flop song falling off the music charts.

Winston snapped back, "Why don't you shut yer gob, you big fat git!"

"Make me, you sorry-sounding wimp!"

Winston stepped off the chair, set his guitar on the seat and balled his fists as he approached Dana. "I'll smash your face in, I will! I'll *kill* you!"

I stood directly between the two antagonists. If they lunged at each other, I'd go down with them. I grabbed Dana's elbow. Unfortunately, I picked the arm holding the glass of gin and the contents sloshed all over my shirt. Now I smelled as badly as he did.

"C'mon, let's get out of here."

"I don't wanna go." Dana pointed at the singer. "I want *him* to go."

The fans began shouting, some for Dana and some for Winston, and the escalation scared me. The convention didn't need to kick off with a slugfest, especially not with me stuck in the middle.

I waved at Alex until I caught his eye. "Play some music!"

The student took the hint and punched up "Can't Buy Me Love" at full blast. To my relief, the familiar tune diffused the situation. The people on the dance floor began moving again and the bystanders resumed their conversations. Winston picked up his guitar and left the room.

Red stepped up to me. "Thanks, Sandy. The fans were getting out of control."

"Somewhere I'd heard an old wives' tale that music can sooth the savage beast."

"I think you're right."

As Red and his wife returned to the dance floor, I realized I had just quoted a line from my TV show. I must be more tired than I realized. I started heading for the exit, but I didn't get far because Dana was shouting again, only this time at a different foe.

"What's *he* doing here?" Dana waved his gin glass at Hank, who was gorging himself on cream puffs at the food table.

"That's Hank Belcher," I said.

"Yeah, I know."

"You know this guy?"

"Hey! Hey, you!" Dana stomped over to Hank.

At the sound of his name, Hank froze in mid-bite, with bits of frosting stuck on his lips. "Mmmpphh?" He swallowed. "Hey! Dana! Great to see you! I'm looking forward to your really big shoe tomorrow night." Yes, he mispronounced the word "show" as "shoe" in a bad attempt at mimicking Ed Sullivan.

"Get out of here, Hank," Dana screamed. "You know you're not allowed at our shows."

"What do you mean?" I asked.

"When we play in Indy, this idiot disrupts our shows. Stands up while we play so nobody can see us. Yells so nobody hears our music. Makes stupid requests like 'Revolution No. 9.' His favorite's 'Rocky Raccoon.' Always harping on us to play 'Rocky Raccoon,' don't cha, Hank?"

"I like that song," Hank said.

"He's banned from our shows. You know that, Hank, so scram."

The fan held up his yellow nametag. "Hey! I paid for this convention. Long as I got this here nametag, I get in to see all the stuff. And that means the concert too."

Dana raised his voice. "You're not coming to our show!"

"Oh yeah? Yeah? You try to stop me and you'll be sorry!"

In only five minutes upon entering the room, Dana had come close to fisticuffs with two guys. This hothead needed to cool down. I squeezed his arm. "Let's go outside and get some fresh air, Dana."

I dragged the man to the nearest exit sign. As we passed by a trash bin, I chucked my half-finished drink and Dana's gin glass as well. He protested, but I didn't care. I pushed open the fire door, stepped into the hotel courtyard, and regretted my decision to come outside. First, all the smokers attending the convention had gathered here to light up. Secondly, I wasn't in Southern California where the night air cools down to a comfortable temperature. In the Midwest, the heat lingers on day *and* night. The hot air threatened to cook my guts, but I wasn't ready to release Dana back into civilization. I guided him to a stone bench beside a hedge, beneath a streetlight shaped like a lantern, as far away from the smokers as I could manage.

Trouble is, I didn't know Dana smoked. As soon as we sat, he pulled out a pack of Marlboros and a lighter. He lit one for himself and offered the pack to me. I shook my head. Dana reached under his leather vest and stuffed the pack back into his shirt pocket. He pulled a puff on the cigarette and I swear he deliberately blew the smoke right in my face. I started to leave, but he clutched my arm.

"Look, I'm sorry about that blowup earlier. You know, in the hospitality room."

"You don't need to apologize to me. I'm not in charge of the convention."

"I don't want you to think I'm a bum. Scott says I am, but I'm a decent guy."

"I'm sure you are." Truth be told, I agreed with Scott's description of his bandmate, but I didn't argue. I knew the futility of attempting a coherent conversation with a wino. "If you'll excuse me, I have to—"

"Scott thinks his little band in the only thing in the world. Wants the rest of us to spend the rest of our lives playing for him."

"Yes, I'm sure." I couldn't figure why he wanted to unload on me, except that I was the only fool dumb enough to sit here and listen to his babbling.

Dana leaned in closer and the booze on his breath nearly knocked me off the bench. "I respect you, Sandy Fairfax. I do. You're the greatest. That stuff you did with Shipwreck. Far out! I played *Black Wave* dozens of time."

My eyebrows shot up in amazement. "You heard that record?"

In the '80s after my divorce I played guitar with a hard rock band named Shipwreck. The name sums up the experience. Between my drinking and the various addictions of the other bandmates, we all played as badly as we felt. We released one album, *Black Wave*, which received almost no airplay and didn't chart. All total we sold about a hundred copies of the record to people who bought it just so they could burn it.

Dana kept rambling. "Can't remember where, but I saw you guys play some joint somewhere."

That's possible. Shipwreck had one badly managed cross-country tour of college campuses and back alley dives, playing for audiences even more smashed than I was at the time.

"You were good. The other guys with you, they stunk." Dana punched my arm. "But *you*, you maniac, you blew everyone away."

"Thanks." I knew better than to believe most of what a sot says, but I'd take an ego massage any way I can get it.

"I got an idea." Dana shoved his face in mine. "Come and play in my John Lennon band. You and me together—that'll kill Scott for sure. What'd you say?"

"Let me think about it." I didn't have to consider this offer at all. I'd rather make my living doing Elvis impersonations at a retirement home than play in any band Dana headed up.

His bloodshot eyes squinted at me. "You're not thinking of joining the Marvels, are you?"

"No, of course not."

"'Cause if you did, I'd haffa *kill* you."

His eyes locked onto mine and he didn't blink. I scooted back on the bench and was ready to jump and run, until Dana's vest fell open, revealing a handgun tucked into the waistband of his pants. I stopped moving—and breathing.

"Dana." I spoke softly and slowly. "Are you packing a piece?"

He slapped his knee and broke into howls of laughter. I didn't. "Do you think I meant that about killing you? Just a joke, man."

I couldn't take my eyes off the weapon. "No, seriously, is that a gun?"

He straightened up and tugged his vest closed. "I got a permit for it."

"What the hell do you think you're doing? You can't walk around a crowded hotel with a loaded gun. Somebody'll get hurt."

"I have to, man. I've had threats."

"Threats? What threats?"

Dana swatted at a gnat flying around his head. "Some jerk who hates me."

"Who threatened you?"

"Nobody's gonna mess me with. If they do—" Dan stuck his arm straight out and extended his finger and forefinger as if firing. "Kapow! Kapow!" He laughed as he staggered to his feet. "I need a drink."

I stood up with him. "No, you don't. You need to put that gun away right now. I mean it."

If he heard me, it didn't register. "Have you seen Elizabeth?"

"Who?"

"'lizabeth. My girl. We're gonna get married."

"I don't think so. Come on." I couldn't stand any more of Dana's craziness. I walked him to the hotel door.

"Where're we going?"

"To your room so you can put that gun to bed. Then you better go to bed and sleep it off."

"Where's 'lizabeth? I haffa find 'lizabeth. If she turns up while I'm gone, please let me know."

I don't know why he wanted to find her. In his condition, Dana couldn't make whoopie to Elizabeth even if they were on their honeymoon.

"What's your room number?" I asked.

Dana dropped his cigarette and ground it out with the toe of his cowboy boot. "I dunno. Something on the third floor. Three sixty-four. That's it. Like the song, 'When I'm 64.' That's how I 'member."

I took a deep breath before we reached the smokers' huddle and I didn't inhale until we stepped inside. I pushed open the door and the sudden blast of air conditioning felt like heaven after my time in the outdoor sauna.

"There you are!" Valleri charged towards us like a bull ready to gore a matador. "I've been looking everywhere for you." She spoke to Dana, not me. "I called you last week about the records you're selling." Dana blinked at her incomprehensibly. "The ones you advertised in *Music Outlet*," a monthly magazine with a classified section for people selling used records. "Remember? I'm Valleri."

"Yeah, yeah, sure, I remember," Dana said. "You left a message on my machine."

"Did you bring the records?"

"Yeah, but somebody else called me about them first."

Valleri's face scrunched up and turned red. Her eyes narrowed to slits and her fingers formed fists tight enough to break through a wall. Her whole body shook as she thundered about how he'd betrayed her, lied to her and cheated her out of the records that rightly belonged to her alone. Before I could jump in and restrain the volcano, Alex cranked up Wings' "Ballroom Dancing" on the sound system.

Bunny hopped up to me. "Ummm, Sandy, would you . . . would you like to dance with me?"

I wanted to take Dana to his room, but Valleri seized his arm and dragged him away as she continued her rant. If I attempted to pry him away, she'd probably beat the stuffing out of me. Besides, I wanted to dance. My feet had started twitching the minute I came in the room. My ex and I had spent many happy hours tripping the light fantastic in the finest clubs before alcohol became more important to me than my marriage.

"Sure, I'd be happy to," I said.

I brushed the cowlick out of my eyes and placed Bunny's left hand on my shoulder. I took her right hand in my left and slipped my right hand around her waist. I waited a moment to catch the beat and stepped off with my right foot. So did Bunny.

"Let me lead," I said.

After a few bars we fell into step. I felt her back muscles loosen up as she got in the rhythm. Soon we covered the dance floor like a couple of pros. A quick learner, this girl.

"You're a terrific dancer," she praised.

"I had some excellent teachers."

Indeed I did. Professional choreographers trained me for my concerts. In my shows I covered about five miles across the stage each night with almost non-stop movement. Actually the dancing was more for self-preservation than artistry. The girls in the front rows loved to throw things at me to get my attention and they couldn't hit a moving target.

As the song wound down, I told Bunny I was going to dip her. I supported the small of her back and leaned her backwards and down. She squealed in delight. I brought her up as the song ended. Bunny pushed her glasses up on her nose and thanked me profusely. I looked for Dana, but as "One After 909" kicked in, a brunette asked me to dance. That did it. Now all the female fans wanted me on their dance card. As the evening wore on, so did my stamina. I tried to leave the dance floor to rest my dogs but the DJ played a trick on me. Over the speakers came a song never recorded by the Beatles or anyone else with taste—my hit single "Meet Me At The Disco" from the *Dancin' Sandy* album.

"How did *that* get in here!" I roared. "Who requested that one?"

I glared at Alex, who grinned and held two fingers to his forehead in a salute. Of course the fans wouldn't let me escape that number.

It's Friday night, the end of the day/Time to dance those old blues away
If your life has dragged you down/Come on now, there's no need to frown.
Girl, put on your prettiest gown/And hurry down fast to old downtown
And meet me at the disco/Where the groovy people go
Meet me at the disco/Let the music ebb and flow
Meet me at the disco/Forget about your woes
Meet me at the disco/Dance and don't say no
Let your feet go, go, go, go, go

The party ended at eleven p.m. with "Twist and Shout." Alex switched on his table microphone and announced that "A Hard Day's Night" would be screening next door in the Guinevere Room in ten minutes "for those of you who need another Beatles boost before bedtime." I thanked my last dance partner and searched for Dana. He was gone, along with Grant, Art, Winston, Hank, Valleri—and Bunny. As far as I knew, Scott never showed up.

"Sandy, are you coming to the movie?" Red asked.

"I've had a long day. I'd like to get some rest."

"Sure, I understand. Thanks for showing up tonight. A number of people told me how much they appreciate you being here."

"I had a great time." I meant it. "Where's Bunny?"

"One of her friends arrived late and she's carrying in their luggage."

"She could get one of the hotel clerks to do that."

Red laughed. "You know Bunny. She likes to help. Anyway, Sandy, is there anything we can do for you before you turn in?"

"No, I'm good. What time do you need me tomorrow?" I'm sure Bunny had told me, but I'd forgotten.

"You're on at two in the Guinevere Room next door. But the convention opens at ten. We have several other guest speakers and panel discussions lined up. You're welcome to sit in on any of the programming."

No way. I was planning a lazy morning of sleeping in late, a leisurely brunch from room service, perusing a newspaper, showing up at two to turn on the charm and beating a fast retreat out of town. With the time difference, I should end up in L.A. in time to watch *Saturday Night Live* from the comfort of my own bed.

"By the way, do you know if the hotel has an overnight cleaning service?" Between Dana's spilled gin and my sweat, my clothes smelled as badly as the three-week-old pile of underwear in my laundry hamper at home.

"I don't know. Do you want me to check with the front desk?"

"Never mind." On second thought, if the clerks couldn't handle my room reservation correctly, I doubt they could clean my clothes without shrinking them three sizes.

I said good night to Red and got into an empty elevator. I started to push the button for the fourth floor, but hit "three" instead. I'd make a quick stop by Dana's room to make sure the fool had stored his gun safely. I'd sleep better know the lush hadn't shot himself in the foot.

On the third floor the torch-shaped sconces on the wall cast a faint glow. The thick carpeting muffled my footsteps. The air smelled like the sprayed-in freshener that's supposed to make the air smell cleaner but it doesn't. I was alone in the corridor. Up ahead the passageway ended in a T-junction. I stopped to consult a wall chart of the room layout to figure out which way to go to find room 364.

The sound of a gunshot echoed through the hallway.

❖ CHAPTER SIX

Happiness Is A Warm Gun

MY EARS WERE still ringing from the pumped up dance music. Did I imagine hearing a gunshot? I dismissed the thought and started walking again. Two more shots rang out. No mistaking the sound that time. So Dana shot himself in the foot as I feared. Maybe if the wound wasn't bad I could call for an ambulance. I jogged to the T-junction. Dana's room was down the left wing, so I headed that way. Three rooms ahead of me, a door opened and I stopped.

An elderly man stepped out into the hall. From inside the room, the sound of *The Tonight Show* blared from the TV. "Hello. Did you hear a strange noise just now?" He mumbled a little as if he had taken out his dentures for the night.

"Yes, I did."

"Any idea what it might be? Thought maybe one of these air conditioners exploded. They're grinding away hard in this heat. Had to run this one full blast all day to cool the place down."

"I don't think it was an air conditioner. Sounded more like a—" Maybe I shouldn't alarm the guests with suspicions about gunshots until I knew for certain what had happened. "Perhaps you're right."

"I don't hear it now. Guess it's gone. Good night."

"'night."

The old man closed the door and I moved on. The passage ended in a sharp turn to the left, leading into another corridor. This new hallway was empty except for a young couple meandering along, cooing and kissing, each one with a hand on the other one's butt. They were so engaged in their lovemaking they would have missed a Mack truck roaring by.

Maybe the gunshots came from a TV set. Crazy Dana had me worked up over nothing. I should forget about the tipsy musician and go to my room. Let's see, where *was* my room? I was on the fifth floor, no, I moved to the fourth. Maybe I should sleep in this little lounge off the corridor. Sounded like less work than tracking down my room.

Across the hall from the lounge was number 364—Dana's room. I pressed my good ear against the door. All quiet inside. Maybe Dana was asleep, or not in. I rapped gently on the door and, to my surprise, it swung open a few inches. Odd. Surely Dana had enough sense to know an unlocked door was an open invitation not only for thieves but also eager groupies—unless he was expecting someone to show up. Or else he was so drunk that he didn't close the door shut. I knocked again and called his name. No reply. I pushed the door open and called a second time.

Somebody moaned.

I stepped inside and couldn't see a thing. A faint trickle of moonlight seeped in around the drawn curtains. I reached for the light switch beside the door. Wait. Dana might be entertaining a lady friend in bed and I wouldn't want to cut in on that. But I didn't hear any noises that might suggest that scenario.

"Dana? Are you in here? Are you all right?"

I flipped the wall switch beside the door but the overhead light didn't come on. I fiddled with the switch. Maybe the bulb was burned out. If this room layout was identical to my room, a floor lamp should be standing a few feet ahead of me. I took a few steps and felt something crunch beneath my sandals. Another step and I stumbled over something large. I reached out my arms to steady myself. I groped around until I found the chrome metal pole of the lamp. I twisted the control knob and a pool of light washed over the scene. I'd tripped over Dana, who lay face down on the floor. I sighed, remembering the days when people found *me* passed out drunk on the ground. I kicked the glass ashtray out of the way (why was this on the floor and not on the table?) and leaned over him.

"Dana, wake up. Let's get you in bed, okay? You'll feel better sleeping on a mattress instead of the floor."

I shook his shoulder and he cried out—not the slurred grunt of inebriation but a painful wail for help. I rolled him over on his back—and gasped. His vest fell open. Blood dripped from a small hole in his chest and down the front of his shirt. One side of his face sported a purple bruise. A puddle of blood soaked into the carpet underneath him. The smell of gunpowder hung heavy in the air. I stared for a moment, not wanting to believe what I saw. I grabbed a white hotel towel from the bathroom, knelt beside him and pressed the cloth to the wound. I felt I had to do something, although deep down I knew the effort was futile.

"Dana? What happened? Did you shoot yourself?"

His eyelids cracked open and he gazed up at me, a vacant, nearly lifeless stare. I didn't know if he could see or hear me, but I jabbered anyway, mainly to keep myself from screaming.

"Dana, it's me, Sandy Fairfax. Remember? We met earlier today."

He kept staring, which unnerved me even more. I grabbed his hand with my free hand while I kept pressing on the wound. His breathing became more labored.

"You're gonna be fine, Dana. I'll call an ambulance. We'll get you to a hospital and fix you up. Just relax now. Take it easy. You'll be all right."

His lips twitched once, then again. His mouth opened slightly and his tongue rolled around, as if fighting to reveal some deep secret.

"Are you trying to tell me something?" I took my hand off the bloody towel and lifted his head off the floor. I bent over, my good ear close to his mouth. "What happened to you, Dana? How did you get shot?"

He wheezed. "Rocky. Rocky Raccoon."

I raised my head and looked at him. "What did you say? What does that mean?"

He repeated the words—and never spoke again.

I rested his head on the floor and released his hand. I sat back on my heels, picked the blood-soaked towel off his chest and dropped it on the floor beside me. I couldn't take my eyes off those enormous blind pupils. What should I do? Buddy Brave never dealt with corpses. The TV censors said murder was too violent for a kiddie show, so the teen gumshoe never encountered anything worse than a bump on the head. I closed Dana's eyelids because that's what movie characters do when they find a body. I sat for a moment—until a crash startled me. I fell back and stared at the doorway.

Stupid me, I'd left the door open. The young hotel employee standing in the hall had dropped a serving tray. The contents, sandwiches and drinks, were splattered on the carpet. I don't know which one of us looked more shocked.

"Room service?" The clerk stared at the body and then me.

"Go get the manager." She didn't move. "Go on, scram!"

She ran, leaving the tray debris where it lay. People in the corridor stopped and gawked through the doorway. I sprang to my feet and slammed the door in their faces. I leaned back against the closed door and panted. I brushed back my cowlick, picked up the telephone and dialed 911.

"I want to report a shooting. I think he's dead." The dispatcher asked who I was—I gave her my real name—and my location. I rummaged through the desk drawer until I found a phone book cover with the hotel's name and address. The dispatcher hit me with a barrage of questions. How did she expect me to know how the musician intercepted a lethal bullet? I was just an innocent bystander.

When I hung up the phone, my hands were shaking hard enough to play the maracas. I was too wound up to sit quietly and wait for help to arrive. I stripped off the bed quilt and spread it over Dana. It seemed like the decent thing to do. I paced the room, looking at anything except the lump under the cover. I almost stepped on a sheet of hotel stationery and a hotel pen, both on the floor near Dana's body. I'm not a tidy person, but I needed something to occupy my mind, so I picked up the piece of paper. Someone had scribbled on the page, apparently with the hotel pen: 28IF GEORGE. What did that mean? Was Dana trying to write a note about someone named George? Or did George himself scrawl the note? Who was George? It didn't make any sense.

I sat in the desk chair and studied the scene. Something didn't look right. Was Dana distraught over Elizabeth and he committed suicide? If so, why was the bullet in his chest? Suicides aim for their head or mouth, not the chest. If the gun had gone off accidentally, the shot would have probably gone into the wall or ceiling. If he was cleaning the gun, he'd be looking down the barrel or have the weapon pointed away from him.

And if he had shot himself, where was his gun?

The weapon wasn't tucked in his pants or on the floor beside him or anywhere else that I could see. If he had fired, he wouldn't have time to hide the gun before hitting the floor.

Did someone else come in the room and shoot him?

And what happened to the other two shots I heard?

❖ CHAPTER SEVEN

Helter Skelter

A KNOCK AT the hall door scared the life out of me. I cracked the door an inch and peered out. In the corridor stood a fifty-something ex-Marine-type with a black buzz cut and a brown suit from Sears. His face looked as if he'd never said the word "yes." The man showed me a badge and introduced himself as Detective Braxton. I opened the door and let him into the room.

"Who are you?" he asked.

"Ernest Farmington."

"What are you doing here?"

"I'm the one who called 911. I reported the shooting."

"Were you the last person to see the victim alive?"

"Yes, I suppose I was."

Braxton shot me an "aha!" look. "Is this your room?"

"No, no, it's his." I pointed to Dana, I mean, his mortal remains. "His room. I found him like that, on the floor."

"The victim was covered with a blanket when you came in the room?"

"No, I did that. I put the cover on him."

"Why did you do that? The fibers and dust from the blanket will corrupt the evidence on the body." Braxton stood close to me and sniffed. "Have you been drinking, Mr. Farmington?"

"Drinking? No, I've been sober all day. Honest. I'm trying to quit."

"Why do I smell alcohol on you?"

I glanced down at the gin stain on my shirt. "Dana did this. He spilled his drink on me."

"Who's Dana?" I pointed to the deceased on the floor. "You shot a man because he dumped some liquor on you?"

My heart beat faster than a bass drum at a Who concert. "No! No! I didn't kill him!"

Braxton shooed me out of the room and into the lounge across the hall so I "wouldn't further contaminate the crime scene," although I'd already stomped all over the room and left my fingerprints everywhere. In the lounge, Braxton ordered a technician to give me a Breathalyzer test. Despite my insistence I'd had nothing stronger all day than a daiquiri virgin, I obliged and blew into the plastic bag. I knew the procedure well, having done this three years ago when I was arrested for a DUI.

The detective eyed me. "Sir, is that blood on your hands?"

"Is it? Oh, no. I hadn't noticed." I reached for the handkerchief in the back pocket of my khakis to wipe off my hands, but the detective grabbed my wrist.

"Have a seat, sir. This won't take long." He pushed me into a worn easy chair.

I silently fumed as a police photographer snapped shots of my long fingers. A floor lamp beside my chair dimly lit the vestibule. The darkness hung outside the lounge windows like a black curtain. A technician scraped some of the blood particles off my hands and into a paper envelope, then swabbed my ands and bare forearms with some kind of chemically treated paper to pick up the gunshot residue. The process wasn't painful but humiliating and pointless, since I hadn't fired the fatal shot. Unless Dana shot himself, which I doubted, the real killer was running around somewhere free as a bird while I suffered in misery.

Police and paramedics hustled in and out of the murder room, chattering in low voices and stepping around the splattered contents of the fallen serving tray. A uniformed cop directed the curious hotel guests away from the area. Nobody told me there'd be days like these. I glanced down at my shirt to see if any blood had spattered on it. No. Good. I'd hate to have to strip down in front of all these people and hand over my clothes as evidence. All right, so eighteen years ago I posed shirtless for all the national teen magazines, but in those days I was leaner and trimmer and besides, a photographer's studio is far more comfortable than a crime scene.

Braxton hovered over my chair like a vulture ready to pounce on road kill.

A cop stood guard beside me, no doubt to grab me in case I tried to escape. Not likely. I was two thousand miles from home—where could I run? Braxton's lips moved but with the noise in the background I didn't hear him. I twisted around in the chair to turn my good ear toward the detective and I asked him to repeat what he said.

"I don't see any cuts on your hands, sir." The detective sounded more like a hard-nosed Joe Friday than a friendly Sam McCloud. "Where did the blood come from?"

My stomach knotted up, my typical reaction whenever I speak with law enforcement officials. My past encounters with the fuzz usually ended up with me contributing my fingerprints at the county jail.

"I don't know. I guess maybe when I tried to stop the bleeding."

The technician finished with my fingers and I kneaded my hands in relief.

"What's going on here?" Mr. Bluefield's voice boomed through the corridor.

"Sir, this area's closed." The uniformed cop tried to block the man's way. "Turn around and go back the way you came."

"I'm Jim Bluefield, the manager. I can go anywhere I want in this establishment. Why are you bothering my guests?"

Bluefield had puffy eyes and the look of someone who had been asleep only moments ago. He must have thrown on his clothes in a hurry without turning on a light as not to wake the missus. His wrinkled jacket hung unbuttoned and a tie was draped loosely around his neck. One tip of his shirt collar stood up.

My interrogator stepped over to the man. "I'm Detective Braxton. I'm in charge of this investigation."

"What investigation? My night supervisor," the man gestured toward a woman standing beside him, thirty-ish and wearing a red pantsuit, "called me at home and said the police were prowling around the hotel."

"One of your guests was found shot to death in that room."

"Shot? That's impossible. We run a respectable business. Who did it?"

"That's what we're trying to find out, sir." Braxton shot me a look and I expected him to shout, "I accuse!"

"Detective, how soon can you finish up here? Your men are disturbing my guests."

"We're working as fast as we can, sir, but these things take time."

"Can you keep this out of the news? I don't need any bad publicity."

"We can't control the media, sir."

While Braxton and Bluefield verbally wrestled, the night supervisor, who clutched a clipboard in her hands, glanced in my direction and did a double take back at me. Our eyes locked and she reacted with what I dubbed the "Oh My God, It's Him!" reaction. At first her eyes squinted slightly and her mouth tightened as if puzzled. Then recognition set in, her eyes grew large and her mouth opened slightly. The woman's face lit up like a pinball machine and she charged toward me. Considering the circumstances, the last thing I wanted was to draw attention to myself. I sank back in the chair and hoped I might disappear.

She pointed at me. "I know you!" Her voice carried a Southern drawl, not surprising since the town sat right on the Indiana-Kentucky border.

After all these years, you'd think I'd have grown used to the attention, but I still feel self-conscious whenever people stare at me. I tried the innocent act. "Excuse me?"

"When I was a little girl I had posters of you all over my bedroom wall. You're Buddy Brave!"

If I had a dollar for every stranger who said that to me, I could purchase a small Caribbean island. "Sorry, no. That was a character I played on television."

One of the paramedics leaving the murder room apparently overheard us, because he changed direction and approached us. "Are you talking about *Buddy Brave, Boy Sleuth*? I loved that show. When I was a kid I watched it all the time. Were you on it?"

Busted! Back in my heyday my handlers taught me to never treat a fan rudely, no matter how tired I felt or how annoying they acted. My anonymity shot, I stood up to greet my admirers.

"Yes, I was. I'm Sandy Fairfax." I automatically stuck out my hand, since most people want to shake it, but the paramedic glanced down at my bloodstained digits and deferred.

"Yes, I remember you." His eyes glazed over with the fond remembrance of nostalgia. "My buddies and I used to watch you on Tuesday nights and the next day at school we'd act out scenes from your show. You had better stories than *The Hardy Boys* show."

I hoped he wouldn't try to flatter me by saying the show motivated him to join the police force. "That show inspired me to go into law enforcement," he said. I keep smiling but inwardly I moaned. The only reason that program existed was to brainwash teenage girls into buying my records. "Nice to meet you, Mr. Fairfax. We don't get many celebrities around here."

"Thanks," I replied. "I wish we could meet under better circumstances."

The woman ogled me, more with adoration than lust. She hesitated, and then extended the clipboard and a ballpoint pen toward me. "Can I have your autograph, Sandy?"

A murder scene didn't seem like the suitable place for autographs, but with Braxton glaring at me, I decided not to make a scene. I flashed the woman that famous toothy grin that once graced a million lunchboxes.

"Certainly. And who is this for?"

"Eloise Baker. That's me."

I took the clipboard and glanced over the note pad, cautious lest I inadvertently sign a confession to the crime. My left hand took the pen and I wrote, "To Eloise, love, Sandy Fairfax" quickly yet legibly, as I had done a zillion times before. If I ever fell into a coma and someone stuck a pen in my hand, the muscles would no doubt automatically write my signature. I handed the autograph to Eloise and she hugged the clipboard to her chest.

"I heard you were staying with us, Sandy. Is this your room?"

"No, I'm on another floor."

"Is your room all right?"

"Yes, it's fine." At least I assumed so. After switching rooms with Bunny and Trish, I hadn't spent any time at all in my lodgings.

Braxton stepped up to Eloise. "Pardon me, miss, but you're interfering with—"

"Who are you?" Bluefield referred to me, and from the angry tone of his voice he didn't wanted an autograph.

"That's Sandy Fairfax," Eloise said. "He's a TV star from Los Angeles."

"Los Angeles? Aren't you a long way from home, sonny?"

I hate people who call me "sonny." Any time a director on my show called me that, I deliberately blew the next take just to make him mad. I gritted my teeth. "I'm here on business."

"Excuse me," Braxton interjected. "If everyone could please clear the area—"

"He's the guest speaker at the Beatles convention," Eloise said to her boss.

"Beatles, huh?" Bluefield snorted. "Hate that rock and roll racket. It's the devil's music, y'know. Gets the young people all riled up. Give me Lawrence Welk any day. Now that's good listening."

"If everyone would move along—" Braxton said.

The manager glared at me. "Are you the one responsible for this mess?"

Before I could reply, Eloise leaned in close to me and said softly, "If there's anything you need, Sandy, anything at all, just let me know, okay?"

Bluefield continued his rant. "I've heard about you L.A. crackpots. You better not cause any more trouble while you're here."

"Hey!" Braxton shouted. "I'm interrogating this man! Everybody shut up!"

The hotel employees stopped blabbering. The detective consulted a page in his notebook, and slapped the page against his palm. A tall man himself, he stood almost nose-to-nose with me.

"I need to clear up something. You told me your name was Farmington, not Fairfax."

"That's right. Stanford Ernest Farmington *Junior*." I emphasized the suffix so this corn town Barney Fife wouldn't confuse me with my respectable father who would throw a fit if I dragged him into this mess. My father goes by his first name, so I grew up as Ernest. "Sandy Fairfax is my stage name."

The dragnet dumbbell's dark eyes narrowed. "An alias? Are you trying to hide something, Mr. Farmington?"

I let out a deep sigh. I better come clean. No doubt this eager beaver cop would check up on me and find out the truth soon enough.

"No, not at all. I served time for a DUI, and for disturbing the peace, public intoxication and destruction of property."

"Yes, I remember when you were arrested." Eloise wasn't helping my case at all. "I heard about it on *Entertainment Tonight*."

"Tell me about the disturbing the peace charge."

"I was in a bar fight and broke some of the furniture."

"Did you start the fight?"

I swallowed. "I'm not a murderer."

Bluefield turned to his employee. "Eloise, go back to the front desk. If any late guests show up, don't put them on this floor."

"Sure, Mr. Bluefield." She whispered to me, "Sandy, before you check out, can you give us a photo to hang in the front lobby?"

"What? Yeah, I'll see what I can do." I vaguely recalled someone telling me earlier today that my manager had sent over some headshots. Now if I could remember who had them . . .

"Thanks awfully much." Eloise stole another peek at the autograph and skipped away.

Braxton ordered the manager not to allow the maids to clean the room and then told him to leave. As the Blue Meanie stomped away, I asked the hot shot cop if I could go too.

"No. We need your fingerprints, Mr. Farmington."

"You can get a copy of my prints from the L.A. County Sheriff's Department." My reply sounded more belligerent than I intended, but I wanted to go to my room and hide under the bed covers instead of taking a trip to police headquarters.

"We will. You can count on it."

Braxton turned over a fresh leaf in his journal. I had a feeling he wouldn't let me go until he filled every stinking page in that stupid notebook. "How well did you know the victim?"

Exhausted, I sat in the easy chair and clasped my hands. "Not well. I only met him today."

"Why did you come to the room?"

"Earlier this evening he wasn't feeling well and I wanted to stop by and see if he was okay and . . ." I stopped. The more I said, the lamer I sounded. Braxton crossed his arms and shot me a disapproving look that spoke volumes. "It's not what you think."

"Uh huh. Just checking up on him. Is that *all* you had in mind?"

I tried to give the Sherlock Holmes wannabe an outraged scowl, but with my pretty boy face the best I could muster up was a peevish frown. Damn my good looks. In school the girls I dated didn't take me seriously because they thought I looked like a kid brother and the boys beat me up because they said I looked like a sissy.

Before I could say something to the detective that might land me on the wrong end of a police baton, Bunny screamed. She had sneaked past the police and now stood outside the door of the crime scene. She stared through the open doorway at the body, her hands over her mouth. I jumped up and pushed my way past the cops to reach her. I grabbed her shoulders and turned her away from the unpleasantness.

"Don't look at it, Bunny," I said.

"Is he really dead?"

"I'm afraid so. I'm so sorry."

I handed her my linen handkerchief. She gripped it in a fist as the tears kept flowing. She cried so hard that I wrapped my arms around her and patted her on the back.

"Shhhhh, now. It's all right. Everything will be all right."

She hugged my waist and rested her head on my chest. Her tears dampened my shirt. "Sandy, what are we going to do?"

Her words trigged something deep in my subconscious. I answered her loudly, full of confidence. "Don't worry! I'll think of something!"

Bunny gazed up at me and grinned through the tears. "That's your catch phrase from your TV show!"

My frazzled brain must have checked out for the night without leaving a forwarding address. And I can't explain why I did what I did next. Maybe I felt sorry for Bunny as she gazed at me with those sad eyes. Or perhaps old habits are tough to break. Whenever Buddy found himself in a tight jam, he always kissed the girl before pulling off a fantastic escape. So I leaned over and bussed Bunny. A gentle peck on the check. A stage kiss.

From a few feet away a camera shutter clicked.

I raised my head and stared straight into a telephoto lens. The photographer snapped off another pix.

"Stop that!" I yelled. The only paparazzo in the Midwest and he'd found me.

The man lowered the camera and held up a laminated press pass. "*Courier* newspaper."

I pushed Bunny's arms away from my midsection. "Let's get out of here."

"Don't leave, Mr. Farmington." The devil detective blocked our path to the elevator. He jabbed his notebook at Bunny. "Your girlfriend?"

"She's a friend, yes, and she's a girl. But no, she's not my girlfriend." I touched her arm. "Bunny, go to your room now."

She took off her glasses and wiped her eyes with my handkerchief. "Will we have to call off the convention?"

"We'll talk about that later. Get some sleep."

"What about you?"

"I feel fine. Go on now."

I turned to face the formidable flatfoot as Bunny slipped away. Braxton pounded questions at me as I rubbed my bloodshot eyes. I couldn't concentrate.

"Look, detective, I'm exhausted. I've had a long day that started before sunrise three time zones ago." I glanced at my wristwatch: nearly 1 a.m. Pacific or Central time? I couldn't remember if I reset my watch after my flight landed. "Can this wait until tomorrow? I mean, later today? The body can't get any more dead than it is now."

Braxton glowered at me so hard that if looks could kill, he'd have a second stiff on the floor. "You claim the victim was still alive when you came in the room?"

"Yes, sir." I squeezed against the wall so the paramedics could carry out a stretcher with a black body bag strapped to it. As much as I wanted to look away, I couldn't peel my eyes off the corpse.

"Did the victim do or say anything that might identify the murderer?"

"Yes, sir."

Braxton waited, his pen poised over his notebook page. "Well? What was it?"

I licked my dry lips. I felt terribly thirsty. I knew Braxton would hate my answer. "He said, 'Rocky Raccoon.'"

Sure enough, he frowned at me. "Is that a joke?"

"No, sir. That's exactly what he said."

"Is that the name of the murderer? An animal? What's a Rocky Raccoon?"

"It's a song." Bunny stepped up beside us as she closed the zipper on the pouch that hung from her waist. "By John Lennon and Paul McCartney. Paul sings lead. It's on disc one, side two, track five of The Beatles' 1968 double record 'White Album,' which isn't the name, but everyone calls it that because it was issued in a plain white cover with no artwork. I have a 1978 French import reissue with the records in white vinyl."

Braxton stared at her, too stunned to take notes, but I took it in stride. Fans possess encyclopedia knowledge of the minutest trivia.

"Thanks, Bunny," I said. "Please go to your room now. Everything will be all right."

Bunny nodded and plodded towards the elevator. By now the crowd of investigators had cleared out, leaving the hallway eerily silent. A cop shut the door to the tainted room and taped yellow "do not cross" tape across the doorway, which was guaranteed to attract more attention from the guests than simply locking the door.

"That's enough for now, Mr. Farmington." Braxton tucked his little black book into his shirt pocket. I nearly leapt for joy at the thought he might finally leave me alone until he added, "But don't leave town."

"What do you mean, don't leave town? In a few hours I'm booked on a flight back to Los Angeles."

"Why are you in such a hurry to leave?"

"No reason, I . . ."

"All right then. Stay put."

"What am I supposed to do in the meantime?"

He gestured at the walls around us. "This is a hotel. You've got a place to sleep." With that he darted for the elevator before I could slip in a parting shot.

Alone in the hallway, I stared at the yellow-ribboned door for a moment. I didn't want to ride the elevator with the dopey dick, so I trudged up a flight of stairs to my room. Once safely inside, I locked the hallway door and the windows and switched on all the lights as if the brightness would keep the killer away.

The dried blood on my hands irritated me and I stepped into the bathroom to wash it off. I turned on the sink tap and tried to unwrap a tiny cake of stinky perfumed complimentary hotel soap sitting atop the faux-marble vanity. I fumbled and dropped the soap twice. As I scrubbed my hands, I puzzled over my predicament.

*A photo of me kissing a strange woman would hit the wire services by morning.

*A room clerk found me alone in a hotel room, kneeling over the body of a dying man I hardly knew.

*My only clue to the killer's identity was the title of a Beatles song.

I shut off the water, wiped my hands on the thin white hotel towel and scrutinized my haggard reflection in the mirror over the sink.

My television show was never this cheesy.

I went into the other room, sat on one of the twin beds, took the broken piece of pottery out of my pocket and turned it over in my hands. I had to remind myself why I'd take this job in the first place. In the comfort of my room, Dana's death didn't seem real. But I was sober, so I wasn't hallucinating. I glanced at the clock radio on the nightstand: almost three a.m. I'd been on my feet almost twenty-four hours straight and I still had one more task to do.

I dialed a phone number more familiar to me than my own. I chewed on a fingernail as I listened to the rings. Finally an answering machine clicked on and a generic voice said to leave a message.

"Marshall, pick up. I know you're home. It's me, Ernest. Wake up, I have to talk to you."

"Hello, Ernest. My wife and I just got back from a dinner party. Why are you calling so late? I'm been waiting all day to hear from you. Are you having a good time?"

I gripped the receiver in both hands. "Marshall, you've got to help me. I'm in a terrible jam. The police think I did it."

"Police? Ernest, why are you mixed up with the police? Have you been drinking?"

"No, Marshall, let me explain. Someone was murdered."

"A murder?" He thought this over for a moment. "Did you do it?"

"Marshall!"

"All right, all right, calm down. Who was killed and why does this concern you?"

My words came out in short gasps. "His name's Dana Mumford. He's one of the guys in the tribute band. They're supposed to play tomorrow night. Tonight. They're playing tonight. I met him earlier today. Yesterday. I met him yesterday. Friday." I was so upset I didn't know the day of the week. "I watched him die, Marshall. He died in my arms. I was holding him and . . ." I stopped. If I said any more, I'd burst out crying.

"Relax, Ernest. Slow down and tell me what happened."

My voice cracked as I related the sad tale. "I was in the hallway and heard gunshots and I ran to see what was going on."

"You ran *toward* the gunshots? Ernest, what were you thinking? You could have been shot!"

"And I stumbled over the body. He was bleeding all over the place and I got blood all over my hands and. . ."

"Take it easy, Ernest. You're doing fine. So I take it somebody called the police?"

"Yeah, I did. The police think I did it. They think I killed Dana."

My manager groaned. "Do you need your lawyer?"

"I don't think so."

"All right. Now listen to me, Ernest. I'll tell you what to do. If the police arrest you, call me immediately. Any time, day or night. I mean it. I'll ship out your lawyer on the next flight. And don't say one word to the police until he arrives. You hear me?"

"Yes, Marshall."

"And don't let the police search your room without a warrant. These small town cops like to harass celebrities so they can make a name for themselves."

"Yes, Marshall."

"And don't talk to any reporters. They'll hang you out to dry. Absolutely no press. Is that clear?"

"Yes, Marshall. Look, the cops won't let me leave town. I'm stuck here. I won't be coming home tomorrow. Today."

Another groan. "All right. Hang tight for now, and see what happens. Maybe this will blow over soon. Are you still doing your appearance at the convention?"

"I don't know. Right now. I don't know anything."

"Listen, Ernest. Don't let this knock you off the wagon. I know you're stressed, but don't start drinking again."

I twisted the phone cord around my fingers. "Marshall, come here. I need you."

"Sorry, no can do. I have a golf date on Saturday with a producer and another client. But you'll be fine. Keep me posted and call me if you need me. All right?" I mumbled an affirmative. "Get some rest, Ernest. You sound awful."

My agent said good night and hung up. I replaced the receiver, grabbed a handful of tissues from the complimentary box of facial tissue on the nightstand, and sobbed. Despite my exhaustion, I was too keyed up to sleep.

And if I didn't get a drink, I'd jump right out of my skin.

The craving came on so strong I was willing to leave my secured room and venture into the dangerous outdoors. I wiped the tears off my cheeks and took the elevator downstairs to the lounge. Closed. Don't these Midwesterners stay up late? I stepped out to the sidewalk in hopes of taking a taxi to a convenience store to buy beer but I didn't see a cab. Even the taxis turned in early around here. Why couldn't this convention take place in Las Vegas where the stores stayed open all night?

I took a walk around the hotel to the courtyard where Dana and I shared our almost final words together. I needed the exercise to work off my frustration. I was furious at Dana for drawing me into this quagmire. I only wanted to do my gig and go home and not get involved with these people. Even though I barely knew the man, I was sorry and angry over his death. I didn't like dealing with these emotions. I could escape my feelings if I got drunk—but what good would that do? That wouldn't change the facts. Sobriety was making a better human being out of me—whether I liked it or not.

I returned to my room, changed into my pajamas, untied my ponytail and got into bed where I tossed and turned for an hour before I fell asleep. Some time later I woke from a nightmare, screaming and sweating. I saw myself back home on my patio. The sky glowed crimson red. Dana was drowning in my swimming pool. He thrashed his arms and called for help. I tried to run to the pool to save him, but my legs felt like concrete and I moved in slow motion. I reached the edge of the pool just as Dana sank into the water. As I dove into the pool, the water turned into blood.

❖ CHAPTER EIGHT

Good Morning Good Morning

A SWARM OF bees buzzed inside my head—no, the phone was ringing. I laid on my stomach in bed, under the covers, my face buried in the pillow and one arm dangling over the edge. I cursed the fool on the other end of the line waking me up. I ignored the persistent racket until I realized Marshall might be calling with some important news. Nobody else knew my number. When I checked in yesterday I told the front desk not to put through any calls from the fans. With my eyes still shut I groped around the nightstand until I found the phone receiver. I meant to say "Hello?" but the words came out more like a muffled "Mewwo?"

"Sandy? Is that you? Did I wake you? Good morning. It's Bunny." I was wrong—one fan knew my number. She better have a good excuse for interrupting my sleep or the convention might suffer a second fatality.

"Reason I'm calling, Sandy, we're having a meeting, all the people involved with the convention. We need to talk about what we're going to do because of, you know, what happened last night." I rubbed my eyes as I thought back to the events of yesterday, when all my troubles seemed so far away. "We're meeting in the hospitality suite at seven. Can you make it?"

"Yeah, sure, I'll be there. Where is it, this hospitality suite?"

"You remember, down the hall from your room."

"Right." I couldn't even recall what city I was in.

She told me the room number of the suite, thanked me and hung up. I kicked off the bed covers, swung my legs over the edge of the bed and sat up in a futile attempt to rev up my brain. I yawned and pushed the hair out of my face. I squinted at the clock radio: six-thirty, hardly enough time to make myself presentable by seven. After years of unemployment and hangovers, I rarely fell out of bed before noon. My body didn't know how to function at this hour. Hopefully the meeting wouldn't last long and I could crawl back into bed until my stint at two o'clock.

I stumbled into the bathroom for a quick shower and shave. Shaving razor's cold and it stings. I ran the complimentary hotel hair dryer over my wet locks and tied it all back in a ponytail so I wouldn't look as skuzzy as I felt. As usual, the cowlick wouldn't cooperate and it hung in my face. I threw on an old lay-around-the-house T-shirt I'd brought with me, faded blue jeans and sandals, an outfit guaranteed to land me on the Hollywood Worst Dressed List. Before I set off I put my wallet, clean handkerchief, comb, keycard and the broken piece of pottery in my pockets.

I trudged down the hall to the hospitality suite and thought about my horrible experience of last night. Thankfully, I didn't have to pass the crime scene this morning. A middle-aged early riser dressed for a morning jog nodded as he walked by. He didn't seem to recognize me. Good. I didn't feel like wit and smiles. When I arrived at the suite I noticed I'd forgotten my nametag. When Bunny and I had switched rooms, she'd placed my registration packet on the desk. After Dana's death I was too upset to open the envelope and inspect the contents. I'd pick up my nametag later.

Inside the suite Red was setting out a tray of pastries. "'Morning, Sandy. Did you sleep well?"

"As well as I could. And yourself?"

"I was up most of the night consoling some of the fans. I don't know how they found out, but they did."

"They couldn't miss the cops and paramedics stomping around."

"I guess so. Help yourself to the donuts. There's orange juice, and the coffee should be about ready." A glass carafe of juice was chilling in a bowl of ice cubes and a silver coffee urn was bubbling away.

"Thanks, Red. You're a lifesaver." I filled a Styrofoam cup to the brim with hot coffee. I needed a pick-me-up so badly I was ready to chew on raw coffee beans.

"If you want cream or sugar—"

"Thanks." I loaded the cup with sugar. I grabbed the largest cinnamon roll off the table. Caffeine and sugar, the staples of life. Fortified with junk food, I could now face the world.

Red busied himself with arranging the chairs into a circle while I ate standing up. We passed the time with small talk while avoiding the major topic of the day. I finished the sweet roll as Art came in, looking forlorn. He came straight over to me and gave me a big bear hug. I didn't have a chance to bend over and meet his hug halfway, so I raised my arms to keep from spilling my coffee as he embraced me under my armpits.

"Thanks, Sandy," Art said.

"What's that for?"

"For what you did for Dana."

"I didn't do anything."

"Yes, you did. You stayed with him so he didn't die alone."

"Glad I could help."

Grant and Magic Alex came in together. Grant poured himself a cup of coffee while Alex helped himself to juice and an apple (smarty pants health nut).

"I can't believe it," Grant said. "Why would Dana want to kill himself? Sure, he was upset yesterday, but he always bounced back."

I blurted out, "I don't think Dana shot himself."

"Don't be crazy. Nobody else was in the room with him."

"Dana's gun was missing. And when I found him, he was on the floor. If he killed himself, wouldn't he be on the bed or in a chair? Suicides don't shoot themselves while standing up."

"But who would want to kill Dana?" Art said. "The fans loved him."

"Has anybody seen Bunny?" Red asked. "I thought she'd be here by now."

"She's on her way," Alex Watanabe said. "She's getting the morning paper, see if it says anything about last night." He shook my hand as Grant and Art talked amongst themselves. "Sandy, I didn't get a chance to introduce myself last night. I'm Alex. I'm the emcee for the weekend. I'll be introducing the guest speakers. That is, if the convention's still on."

"Did you use your own CDs for the dance last night?" I asked.

He nodded. "My CD collection is about two hundred and I've lost count of my records." Impressive accumulation for a kid his age. He must have teethed on a 45 single. "I have some of your records, too. The one with Shipwreck and original soundtracks from your movies and an instrumental recording of your songs played by the Melody Strings Orchestra."

"Melody Strings? I never heard of that one."

The others joined us. Red addressed the bandmates. "Guys, I can't tell you how sorry I am about Dana. Please give my sympathies to his family. Let me know if I can help in any way."

"There's one thing you can do for us," Grant said. "I called Elizabeth. She's coming down from Indy today. Can you look after her when she arrives?"

"Of course, Grant."

"Poor girl," Art said. "What a rotten break. She and Dana were crazy about each other."

"Elizabeth?" I asked. "That's Dana's fiancé, isn't it?"

"How do you know about her?" Art asked.

"He told me about her last night at the party."

"You talked with Dana last night?" Grant sounded suspicious. "What about?"

"Nothing much."

A young man holding an old worn backpack rushed into the room, out of breath. I hadn't seen him at the mixer last night.

"Hey, Red," the man said. "I ran into Bunny downstairs while I was checking in and she told me to come straight up here. Jeez, didn't give me a chance to go to my room or nothing."

Red, along with the rest of us, eyed the man's uncombed hair and wrinkled clothes. "Is that what you're wearing today?"

The new guy had a plain face covered with old acne scars. He wore jeans, beige loafers and a long sleeved denim shirt, which seemed out of place for summer weather, but understandable since the air conditioners kept the hotel as frigid as an ex-wife in divorce court.

"Didn't have time to iron stuff when I got home from the Laundromat." The new guy dropped the backpack on the floor with a thud.

"Make yourself presentable before the guests see you," said Red. "And why wasn't the hospitality suite stocked?"

"I wasn't here on Friday, remember?"

"You were supposed to make arrangements with the kitchen staff."

"Okay, I'll see to it. Jeez, you're always on my case about something."

"I wish you'd take more initiative, that's all."

Red introduced the band members and me to the newcomer, Billy Shears. I greeted Billy and extended my hand, which he shook with all the enthusiasm of a Led Zeppelin fan listening to The Archies.

"You did all that bubblegum stuff, huh," he said. "I suppose it's okay for the kids, isn't it, but it's not *real* music."

My mood escalated from lethargic to livid. "*Real* music? Listen, I was playing violin solos and piano duets with my father's orchestra before you were old enough to sing 'Happy Birthday.' Hand me a guitar, mister, and I'll show you some *real* music."

In my rage I unwittingly crushed the Styrofoam cup in my hand. The cold coffee ran down my hand and onto Red's old brown shoes.

Red said quietly, "Sandy, you're dripping on me."

I apologized and grabbed a bunch of paper napkins from the table to wipe off my hand. Red assured me his footwear was washable and the damage negligible. Grant and Art covered their mouths with their hands and tried unsuccessfully to hide their laughter. I threw away the cup, poured myself a fresh mug of coffee and wondered what other stupid things I'd do today.

Billy said, "While I driving down from Princeton, I heard something on the car radio about a guy getting shot here last night. What was his name?"

"Dana Mumford," said Art. "One of our bandmates."

"I guess you'll have to cancel the concert."

"That's what we need to talk about," said Red. He asked us to sit down so we could discuss the matter.

I grabbed a bear claw from the pastry tray and plopped into one of the armchairs. Grant and Art took the sofa, and Alex and Red grabbed the other available seating, which left Billy grumbling about getting stuck with a folding chair.

"Where's Scott?" Red asked.

"Let's call his room," Billy suggested. "Maybe he's sleeping."

A thought ran through my half-awake brain: Scott and Dana were both booked in the room. Scott wasn't there when I arrived at eleven o'clock last night and he couldn't get in after the police sealed the crime scene. So where did he spend the night?

"Haven't seen him since supper last night," Grant replied. "He didn't want to go to the mixer. He's probably at the casino."

Art rolled his eyes. "That means we'll never see him again."

"Casino?" I asked "Around here? I didn't think Indiana had casinos."

Shows you what a West Coast snob I am. Like many L.A. natives, I assumed civilization existed only on the two coasts and that the flyover states were barren of such inventions as museums, major universities, theaters, electricity and indoor plumbing.

"Sure. Casino Aztar, the big hotel next door," Red said. "Technically, land-based casinos are illegal in the state unless they're on property owned by an Indian tribe. Doesn't matter if the tribe lives in the state as long as they hold the deed. But floating casinos are allowed. So Aztar was built right over the river. It's connected to the shore by a pedestrian gangway. It looks like a riverboat and has 'boarding times' when people can enter, but it never moves. It's permanently anchored but it's on water, so it's legal."

That convoluted explanation made less sense than the plots on my TV show.

"Lookie here, everyone!" Bunny burst into the room with a black cardigan sweater, an armful of newspapers and a huge grin on her face. She waved one of the papers. "I got my picture in the paper! I never get my picture in the paper." She handed each of us a copy of the morning's *Evansville Courier*. "And you're in the paper, too, Sandy! You look great. You always take a good photo."

The picture covered a quarter of the front page above the fold and showed me, in living color, kissing Bunny. In the photo I looked bloated, no thanks to years of hard drinking, from lifting too many beer bottles and not enough free weights. Men usually don't worry about their spare tires until their first heart attack, but since my looks launched my career, I'm more aware of my appearance than most guys. I glanced at the caloric-loaded sweet in my hand and tossed it into the wastebasket.

"Did you buy every paper in the gift shop?" Alex asked Bunny.

"I sure did, and I drove to a gas station and bought up their copies."

Bunny's T-shirt this morning showed The Beatles making the semaphore arm signals for "Help!" as seen on the album cover of the same name. How appropriate. Right now this convention needed all the help it could get. She set the papers on the food table and put on the sweater over her T-shirt. Apparently Billy wasn't the only one feeling cold.

She stepped over to Grant and Art. "It's horrible what happened to Dana. I cried and cried when I heard about it. I'm going to ask my fan club to send flowers in his memory."

"Thanks, Bunny," said Grant. "That's nice of you."

She set up a folding chair next to me and sat down. I read my copy of the news rag. The banner headline shouted, "Hotel shooting rocks tribute band." The title above my photo screamed, "Aging teen idol comforts grieving fan."

"Aging!" I howled. "I'm only thirty-eight! I'm not *old*!"

"What does the article say?" Bunny asked. "I haven't read it yet."

I scanned the story, which didn't turn out as awful as I expected. "Doesn't say much, only that I was the one who found the body. Doesn't mention Dana's last words."

"Last words?" Billy said. "What did he say?"

"Not much. All he said was 'Rocky Raccoon.'"

"What did he mean by that?"

"I don't know. I didn't get a chance to ask him before he died."

"If I may interrupt," Red said. "We need to talk about the convention. Should we cancel or carry on?"

Alex said, "If we cancel, we need to call the other speakers right away so they don't make a trip for nothing." He told me that they had scheduled a record shop owner to talk about collectibles, and a college professor to discuss the influence of Beatles music on pop culture.

"But will the fans be safe with a killer on the loose?" Bunny asked.

"I thought the police called it a suicide," Art said.

I stated that I heard three gunshots. "If Dana had shot himself, how could he miss on the first two tries?"

"Maybe a thief broke into the room," Billy suggested, "and Dana shot at him."

"I doubt it. When I turned Dana over, I saw a lump in his back pants pocket.

He still had his wallet. And the room wasn't ransacked. Whoever killed Dana wasn't looking for money."

Art stood up and inspected the donut tray. "Anyone trying to rob Dana was wasting his time. He never had any dough on him. He was broke all the time." He selected a chocolate glazed éclair and sat down.

"I heard he was trying to sell some albums," I said. "Did he have any valuable ones?"

"Yeah, a few," Grant said. "He was trying to unload his 'butcher cover.' He needed money for something. Never said what."

"Maybe someone wanted his records," Alex said. "Some fans get pretty wacky about the merchandise. One time at a garage sale I found a Beatles' *Christmas Album* in mint condition. Another customer threatened to slash my tires if I bought it."

"So you let him have it?" I asked.

"Of course not. Are you kidding? Give up mint condition?"

Red held up his hand. "Excuse me, can we get back on track? I suggest we leave the investigation to the police."

Bunny beamed. "Sandy will solve the case for us, won't you? You always find the bad guy."

Art smiled. "That's right. Sandy knows all about clues and sleuthing."

"I'm not a detective!" I shouted. "I just played one on television!"

The others stared at me. Lack of sleep and a murder had frazzled my nerves. I stepped over to the food table. More caffeine would only make me jumpier so I went for the orange juice instead. Big mistake. At home I pluck and squeeze the oranges from the fruit trees on my property. This stuff tasted watered down. I wandered to the window and gazed out.

After what seemed like an eternity of silence, Alex spoke up, "I say let's go with the convention. Red and Bunny spent a ton of time and money setting this up. The vendors are coming in and the fans gave up their holiday weekend to come. Sandy traveled halfway across the country for us. If we quit we'll lose money and the fans will feel cheated."

Grant stepped up to the coffee urn for a second cup. "Dana was a trouper. Never missed a gig. He was looking forward to the show tonight. We were all excited to play at a fan convention. I'm sure he'll be with us today in spirit."

"Here, hear." Art raised his cup in a toast. "We're all sad about Dana leaving us, but life goes on within you and without you. Paul McCartney kept on recording the day after John Lennon was shot."

Red turned to me. "Sandy, what are do you think?"

I shrugged. "The police told me not to leave town, so I'm not going anywhere."

Red asked for a show of hands and the vote was unanimous for going on.

"Is anyone else cold in here?" Bunny walked over to the air conditioner and fiddled with the dials.

Red turned to the band members, "But can you guys play as a trio?"

Art frowned. "If Scott doesn't show up, we might be a duo."

"Be tough to find a last minute replacement," Grant said. "All the guys I know are in Indy and besides, all the good musicians are booked on Saturday nights."

Bunny's face brightened with the delirious look of someone who discovered a tape of a previously unreleased Elvis song in her attic. "Sandy, he could do it!"

"Me!" I nearly dropped my cup of orange juice.

"Why not? You sing. You play guitar."

"And you're *here*," Alex finished.

Red chimed in, "That's a great idea. Sandy, how about filling in for Dana?"

I broke out in a sweat, but not from the heat. "I haven't done a live show since . . . I can't remember when."

I lied. I vividly recalled my last catastrophic concert with Shipwreck in 1988. The day started with me tanked and I kept guzzling hooch right up to show time. Halfway through the first set I fell off the stage, plastered, and at intermission the band fired me. I hitched a ride to the nearest bar where I drank until I passed out again. The bouncer tossed me into a back alley Dumpster so I could sleep it off. I woke up in time and scrambled out as a forklift was raising the bin to empty out the garbage. Worst of all, someone from a tabloid showed up and took photos of me covered in trash. After that I couldn't pay anyone to give me a job. As much as I wanted a comeback, the thought of performing again in front of an audience terrified me.

"We'd be happy if you could perform with us," Grant said.

"I can't learn a concert in one day." My plans for a relaxing weekend were evaporating faster than my record sales after my TV show was cancelled.

"Sandy, these are *Beatles* song," said Art. "*Everybody* knows Beatles songs."

"But I can't do it. I have a contract . . ." I said the words with so little conviction I'm sure I fooled nobody, least of all myself.

"That's a shame. " Alex sounded genuinely hurt. "The concert is a big part of the weekend. Some of the fans came a long way just to hear the band."

"Come on, Sandy, please." Bunny stared at me through her thick lenses with her puppy dog eyes. "It's for the fans. If you won't do it, then I guess you don't love us."

My brain shouted, *No, no, no,* but my mouth said, "All right, I'm in." Did I really agree to this insanity? That's the last time I show up at a meeting too tired to think straight.

"Yippee! That's wonderful!" Bunny clapped her hands.

"I can't guarantee how good I'll sound."

"Don't worry," Grant said. "We'll start you on the music right away. I've got a guitar in my room you can practice on."

"So we're all set." Red smiled. He tucked his newspaper under his arm and stood up. "We open this convention in two hours. Let's get rolling."

As we all stood up, Scott stormed in, bedraggled and in a foul mood. He still wore the same clothes from Friday.

"What the hell's going on! Why can't I get into my room? There's yellow tape all over the door and my keycard won't work."

The rest of us exchanged glances. "You don't know what happened?" Grant asked.

Bunny handed Scott a newspaper. He started reading the front-page article and sank into an empty chair. The blood drained from his face. He lowered the paper, his eyes glazed.

"Dana's *dead*?" Scott mumbled. "I can't believe it. It can't be true."

"You didn't hear about it?" Art asked.

"No, I just got back from the Aztar."

"You were at the casino all night?" I said. "When did you sleep?"

"I didn't. The guys know I get insomnia during gigs. Can't sleep in a strange place. I went to the casino, played craps, had something to eat this morning and now I'm back."

"The casino's only a couple of minutes away," Billy said. "Maybe you left here during the night, came here and walked back."

"Why would I do that? Wait a minute." Scott jumped to his feet. "You're saying I had something to do the shooting?"

"How do you know he was shot?" Billy countered.

Scott threw the newspaper at him. The kid ducked and the paper fluttered to the floor. "It's in the paper, stupid. And how could I shoot him? I don't have a gun."

Bunny said, "I'm sure Billy didn't mean to imply—"

Scott shoved his face close to Billy's "Why would I want to kill one of my bandmates?"

"What about your argument yesterday?" Red suggested.

"Don't mean a thing. Dana and me, we were always fighting. The guys," he gestured at Grant and Art, "can tell you we never got along. But Dana was a terrific musician. I'd never hurt him, especially not the day before a show."

From my experience of working in bands, arguments were common but not fatal. Musicians are highly passionate people with their own artistic vision. They often clashed, but once band members vented their feelings, everyone cooled down and got back to work.

Before Scott could argue further, Bluefield and two maids entered the room. The housekeepers began clearing off the food tables.

"What are you doing?" Bunny asked.

"Since you're canceling your convention, we're cleaning the room so we can rent it again," said Bluefield. "Given the circumstances, I won't charge you the usual forfeiture fee."

"But we're using the room," Red said. "The convention's on."

Bluefield pursed his lips. "Really? I assumed that because of the shooting last night—"

"You assumed wrong," said Alex.

"I won't tolerate another incident like that," the manager huffed.

"Give the kids a break," I said. "It's not their fault. If your hotel had better security, the shooting would have never happened."

Bluefield glared at me. "You're that smarty pants from L.A. You've got some nerve, telling me how to run my business." He turned his attention to the rest of the gang. "I'll let all of you stay for now, but if there's any more trouble, you're out of here."

"Nothing else will go wrong, Mr. Bluefield," said Red. "You can count on it."

The manager didn't look convinced. "If you say so. By the way, some reporters are downstairs asking about Mr. Mumford. Get rid of them so they'll leave the guests alone."

"We'll take care of it," Bunny offered.

"As for you," the manger put his hands on his hips and squinted one eye at me. "I'm keeping my eye on you." With that threat, he and maids hurried out of the room.

"Who was that?" Scott asked.

"The Blue Meanie," Bunny said.

"You got that right," Grant quipped.

The group dispersed. Red ordered Billy to get cleaned up and man the registration table while he helped the vendors move into the dealers' room. Alex headed downstairs to set up the microphones for the guest speakers and the band guys went off to prepare for the concert.

I was about to leave when Bunny said, "I guess I'll go and see about those reporters."

I touched her arm. "Stay here, Bunny. Those news hounds will eat you alive." Bunny meant well, but she's the last person I'd send on a press junket. Those gossip gatherers would badger her to tears. "Let me go and throw them a bone."

"That's okay, Sandy. You don't need to get mixed up in this."

As if I wasn't already hip deep in murder, music and mayhem. "I'll do it. I know how to talk to reporters."

"What are you going to say to them?"

"I haven't the slightest idea."

She gave me Grant's room number so I could meet up with him later. I ducked into the suite's bathroom to check my appearance and smooth down my hair. My eyes were red from lack of sleep. Usually the camera loved me, but today I looked like death warmed over. And normally I steeled myself for press conferences with a stiff drink or two. I wasn't sure how I'd do, facing the scandalmongers sober.

Bluefield underestimated when he said "some" reporters. I stepped off the elevator and into a swarm of cameramen and reporters from the local newspapers, radio and TV filling the lobby. Why should the death of an unknown tribute musician draw so much attention? A buzz ran through the crowd as I approached and I understood. I was a reporter's dream on a silver platter—a Hollywood celebrity and murder, an awesome ratings combination.

Lights switched on and cameras stared rolling and clicking. The reporters shoved microphones in my face. They literally backed me up against the lobby wall and fired questions fast and furious as I tried to figure out which camera to face next.

"Sandy Fairfax, what are you doing in Evansville?"

"I'm making a guest appearance at the Swingin' Sixties convention here at the hotel."

"Did you come from L.A. to visit Dana Mumford?"

Honestly, how do these rumors get started? "No."

"But you were the last person to see him alive."

"Yes, that's true."

"Did he have any last words?"

A tricky question. Usually I'm forthright with the press, but the news snoopers would hound me endless on what "Rocky Raccoon" meant. Dana entrusted me with an important clue but until I figured it out, I planned to stay silent.

"No, nothing of consequence."

"Is it true that the victim was involved with a criminal gang?"

That one left me speechless. Dana might be bumped off over drugs, but he was a drunk, not a junkie. So why would he have any gang connections?

"I'm not aware of any such involvement," I said.

"Was Mumford's death a suicide—or murder?"

"That's for the police to decide."

"But you're the famous boy detective, Buddy Brave. Did the police call you in to assist with the case?"

"No! I am not Buddy Brave! He's a fictional character! I'm just a musician!"

A pretentious reporter dreaming of a Pulitzer shouted, "Mr. Fairfax, you've had several run-ins with the law in Los Angeles. And now you're found at the scene of a shooting. What's the connection?"

I blinked at the camera, astonished. Whatever happened to the good old days when reporters from the teenybopper magazines lobbed easy questions about my favorite movies, childhood pets and what I look for in a date? This time I didn't bother to hide my contempt.

"My prior arrests have no relevance to this case." The wolves shouted more accusations, but I help up both hands. "That's enough questions. Don't bother the convention goers. They're here to have a good time. Please respect their privacy. Thank you."

The reporters surrounded me and blocked the path to the elevators. I scooted past them and ran down a hallway. The herd stampeded after me like the old days when everybody wanted a piece of the world's greatest teen idol. Some things never change. The promising escape route, however, turned into a literal dead end. I turned to face the vultures as they charged towards me.

Trapped.

❖ CHAPTER NINE

Run For Your Life

MY PRECARIOUS PREDICAMENT—stuck in a narrow hallway with a hoard of hungry reporters on my tail—reminded me of a *Buddy Brave* episode in which the schoolboy shamus was stuck at the end of a tunnel with a tiger licking its chops. Buddy jumped, grabbed an overhead light (don't ask me why a deserted tunnel was wired for electricity) and swung from lamp to lamp down the length of the tunnel. I glanced up and, sure enough, the ceiling had a row of fluorescent tubes. The lighting fixture didn't look safe, but neither did the advancing army of tattlers. I crouched low, sprang up towards the light, and missed. Eighteen years ago I could handle this trick with no effort, but out-of-shape middle-aged men need stunt doubles.

I stepped up on a tall ceramic ashtray standing against the wall and from there stretched out my arms, leaped and grabbed the lighting fixture. I scrambled for a better handhold and pulled up my legs, my heels barely clearing the heads of the throng below. The fixture started to sway. The cameramen tilted their heads back and kept on shooting, capturing a doozie of a photo op of me swinging like Tarzan—or rather, more like Cheeta.

The hot metal casing heated my palms as I hurried along, hand-over-hand. At the end of the corridor I let go and landed awkwardly on my feet, panting, my arms aching. If I got out of this weekend alive I'd hire a personal trainer to whip my flabby carcass into shape. The rabble turned and headed my way, but at least I had room to maneuver. I sprinted through Ye Olde Country Inn and into the kitchen. The reporters collided with the guests and the cameramen, who couldn't see through their viewfinders, fell over the tables. In the kitchen

I and asked the chef for an escape route and he pointed me towards the employees' service stairwell.

On the second floor I knocked on the door of the Burlingtons' room. Prudence let me in. Grant and Art were seated, watching the TV.

"Interesting press conference," Grant said. "You sure know how to handle the reporters."

"You mean that went out *live*?"

Art grinned. "I like how you hung from the ceiling. Maybe we can work that into the show tonight."

I sighed. "My morning aerobics ought to keep the media entertained for a while. What else can I do today to embarrass myself?"

Prudence excused herself and left the room "so you boys can take care of business." The guys started writing out the song lyrics and guitar chords on hotel stationery so I could learn the music. Grant told me that the police had allowed Scott into room 364 long enough to remove his personal belongings. The musician was now checking into another room so he could take a nap and join us later for rehearsal. But I had other things on my mind besides the show.

"Is it true that Dana was associated with a criminal gang?" I asked. "One of the reporters asked me about that."

"Dana wasn't into anything shady," Grant said. "We wouldn't keep him in the band if he was gang banger."

"Did he owe money to anyone?"

"He gambled a lot," said Art, "but always low stakes and he wasn't in hock to any loan sharks, if that's what you mean."

I persisted. "Was Dana in the habit of bringing guns to the gigs?"

Grant glared at me. "Look, Sandy, if you're trying to imply that Dana was a cheap crook, forget it. He was a great guy and didn't deserve to die the way he did."

"Sorry. I didn't mean to sound crass," I said. "I'm just trying to make some sense out of what happened, that's all."

The guys handed me the lyric sheets and I looked over the songs. Normally I'm a quick study with music—in the studio I used to knock out a solid performance in only one or two takes. But tonight's show had me scared spitless and I couldn't concentrate, not with questions about Dana's death rattling around in my head.

In the band Dana played the John Lennon part, rhythm guitar, which suited me fine. When it comes to guitar work I'm no Eric Clapton, but I can hold my own against a session guy. I made it clear, though, that I wouldn't try to act like Lennon or wear a Beatle wig.

"And will a left-handed Lennon ruin the show?" I asked. "I'm a southpaw, you know."

"I didn't think of that," Grant said. "Would you prefer doing 'Paul' instead?" The real Paul McCartney played left handed.

"Bass isn't my strong suit."

"The fans wouldn't care if you plucked the strings with your toes," said Art, "as long as we put on a show for them."

Grant handed me a beautiful blonde wood acoustic guitar for practice and also a new set of strings so I could restring the instrument for left-handed playing. The guitar's pick guard and the cutout for reaching the high notes were both in the wrong place for a lefty. Still, I could make do. After I replaced and tuned the strings I picked out a twelve-bar walking bass line to limber up my fingers. Good sound from the ax but some stiffness in the digits. I hadn't touched a guitar in months. I ran through the tunes as the guys wrote them. As I played, I felt less moody. When playing Beatles songs, a person can't help but smile. I chugged along until my fingers throbbed with pain. Pressing down hard on the steel strings cut deep grooves into my fingertips.

As I sucked my fingers, Art said, "Lost your calluses? They'll come back."

"That better happen before the show tonight," I said, "or the fans won't be the only ones screaming."

I set the guitar on the king-size bed, stepped into the bathroom, turned on the tap and ran cold water over my fingertips until the pain eased up. When my fingers felt better I picked up the guitar again and sang. I sounded worse than a stray cat in heat.

"What are you wearing for the show?" Grant asked. "We plan on playing mostly early Beatles songs, so we're going to wear our brown suits. You don't have to match us exactly, but any kind of suit would do."

I don't think I even owned a suit. "I didn't bring anything like that with me."

Someone knocked on the door and Grant let Bunny into the room.

"Hi! How's everybody doing?" Bunny said. "Sandy, you were great at that news conference. Some of the girls and I, we watched it in the hospitality suite." Did everybody in the universe see that debacle? She nodded at my guitar. "How are you coming along with that?"

"At the concert tonight," I said, "tell the fans to scream as if they were at a real Beatles show. That way they can't hear my mistakes."

She laughed. "You'll sound great, I know it. Can everyone come down to the Galahad Room? The convention opens in a few minutes and we're going to introduce the band and the guest speakers. Sandy, please come. I know everyone's dying to meet you."

I gave my regrets and told her I needed to practice. Actually, I wasn't interested in sharing the stage with the local talent. Grant announced that the band would rehearsal at noon after Scott woke up. I agreed, and the guys left for the Galahad Room.

"I'll see you later, Sandy," Bunny said. "Anything I can get you in the meantime?"

"I need a suit for the show tonight. Are there any good men's stores nearby?" I also wanted some regular clothes to tide me over until the cops let me go home. I didn't want the reporters snapping photos of me in the same old rags every day.

"The mall has some good stores. I can drive you out there."

"No, Bunny, I don't want to put you out. You're busy with the fans."

"I don't mind. Alex can open the convention without me."

Since I lacked transportation—I should have rented a car at the airport—I accepted Bunny's offer. We stopped off at my room on the fourth floor long enough to drop off the guitar and music sheets so I could practice later. Then back down to the second floor where we took the enclosed pedestrian walkway to the parking structure where Bunny had left her clunker.

As we drove to Eastland Mall, she pointed out Roberts Stadium where she had seen my show years ago. The sight of it brought up nothing more than a vague recollection. I'd performed in so many venues that my touring days blur together. Bunny, however, named every song I sang that night and remembered all my costume changes. She also told me about the drive-in movie theater (now replaced by an indoor multiplex) where she and her girlfriends saw my two movies, *Buddy Brave and the Suspicious Spy* and *Buddy Brave and the Dangerous Demon.*

If you're wondering if I ever played a role other than a detective, no, I haven't, not even in my guest spots. On *Charlie's Angels* in 1980 I was an undercover cop working with the angels. While filming one particular scene I deliberately messed up my lines repeatedly so I could keep kissing Jaclyn Smith. On *Fantasy Island* in 1983 my character's dream was to solve a case with Sherlock Holmes. In *The Love Boat,* 1985, I portrayed a private eye hired to follow Julie Newmar on her vacation cruise to see if she was cheating on her fiancé. She wasn't, and I got to smooch her, too. With so much experience in sleuthing, I could open my own detective agency.

The mall had just opened when we arrived, so foot traffic was light. Bunny and I split up and agreed to rendezvous in an hour at Spencer's Gifts. My attitude towards shopping is to zip in, grab what I needed and hurry home so I can do something more enjoyable than comparing prices or trying on clothes—like cleaning toilets. (A trip to Guitar Center is different, however. I'd camp out for days in a good music store). Bunny ran off to buy film for her camera while I checked out the clothing stores. I feared these Corn Belt shops might only sell overalls and work shirts, but I located a couple of quality stores. I soon found what I needed — a week's worth of duds as well as a brown suit, tie and shoes suitable for the stage. I hoisted my shopping bags under my arms and set out to meet Bunny, ready to head back to the hotel.

By now half of the city's population had packed into the mall. I stood still as the mob pushed past me, too many bodies crammed into the space. People talking, shouting, laughing. Muzak blared from overhead speakers with a pounding beat. The chaos reminded me of a time when my most ardent fans nearly trampled me to death inside a mall.

I've never understood the concept of hurting the one you love, but I've experienced it. I don't know what causes sweet, shy girls to mutate into frenzied animals, or their obsession with owning a piece of their idol. I suppose this harkens back to medieval times when the pious believed a relic from a saint—a bone fragment or piece of a robe—possessed magical powers.

I supposed holding a piece of my shirt or a lock of my hair made my fans believed they were close to me.

When *Buddy Brave, Boy Sleuth* premiered in 1975, I'd spent my days cooped up in a studio, far from the public. Sure, I'd seen the newsreels of Beatlemania, the crush of girls clustered outside the hotels where the fabs stayed, the screaming and the chasing. But I never dreamed little ol' me could evoke the same reaction.

On my first concert tour when I was a mere lad of nineteen and clueless about life, I was inside a mall somewhere in the Deep South for an autograph session. My handlers were called away to check on the arrangements and they left me in the care of some young, inexperienced mall staff. The employees slipped away for a smoke and left me stranded. While I was window-shopping when I heard a clamor. A groundswell of shrieking pre-teen girls rushed towards me. I found later that the ringleaders of my fan club had posted spies with walkie-talkies throughout the shopping center, ready to signal a "Sandy sighting" to the others.

Alone, defenseless and terrified, I ran like a rocket through the mall, with no idea of the building layout or where I should go. I headed down a wing until it ended at a children's play area. They girls drew closer. I climbed up a jungle gym, a tower of metal poles. The fans gathered around the base, grabbing and screaming. Lucky for me, most of them wore their Sunday best dresses and didn't want to ruin their clothes or expose their derrieres by crawling up the tower. A few brave souls came after me. From my vantage point atop the structure I yelled at them and kicked—not hard enough to knock them off, but to keep them away.

My handlers found me by following the noise. Even after they sent the beasts home, I refused to come down. My fingers clutched the pipes in a death grip and I was too shaken to move. The mall director finally coaxed me down with the promise of extra security, a shopping spree at the mall stores and a complimentary meal topped with a hot fudge sundae (my favorite dessert). After that incident my handlers learned their lesson and during my public appearances, they always put a guard on me. Two people stayed with me at all times, even when I went to the john (*you* try taking a leak with an audience at your elbow).

Inside Eastland Mall, I forced myself to breathe and stay calm. The good people did not attack me, but went about their shopping. I steadied myself and met up with Bunny.

"It's almost lunch time," she said. "Why don't we eat here?"

Before I could say, "Get me out of here!" my stomach gurgled, "Feed me!" My food options were to either eat here or face the surly waitress and mediocre meals back at Ye Olde Country Inn. We pushed our way through the crowd to the food court, a cluster of fast food shops surrounding a dining area of bolted-down tables and molded plastic chairs. We bought our food and snagged the last remaining two-person table. I tucked my purchases under my chair. Bunny had ordered a salad and lemonade. I bought a huge sandwich stuffed with grilled steak, onions and cheese along with a large order of fries and a super size Mountain Dew. No wonder I looked like a blob in the newspaper photo. If I didn't start eating better, I'd look like fat Auntie Jessie stuffing herself with mountains of spaghetti in the *Magical Mystery Tour* movie.

I pushed the cardboard carton of fries towards Bunny's plastic tray. "Here, help yourself."

"Sandy, I can't take your food."

"Go ahead. I can't eat all of this."

She took the two shortest fries for herself. I picked up the carton and dumped most of the fries onto her tray. We hunkered down with our food. I drifted off into my own thoughts until Bunny interrupted my daydreaming.

"Are you nervous about the concert?"

"What?" Yes, I was terrified. If I didn't pull this off I'd never get back on a stage again. And if I screwed up I couldn't blame the booze. "A little. Why do you ask?"

"You looked preoccupied. I'm sorry. I shouldn't pry."

"Don't apologize. I was thinking about Dana's death. I can't figure it out. What I heard and saw doesn't make sense."

She put down her plastic fork. "What do you mean?"

"Why did he say 'Rocky Raccoon'? If somebody shot him, why didn't Dana tell me the name of the murderer?"

"Scott's last name is Rockwell. That sounds like 'rocky.'"

"Then why didn't he say 'Scott Rockwell' instead of 'Rocky Raccoon?'"

She speared a forkful of salad. "Maybe Dana was tipsy and couldn't talk right."

"Not likely. Whenever I was on a drinking binge, I never spouted off the names of Beatles songs." I'm not proud of my boozy nights, but my long-time fans knew about my sordid past.

"I have an idea," she said. "When we get back to the hotel, I'll check the registration list and see if anyone registered at the convention is named Rocky."

"That's a start."

"But what if the killer isn't at the convention? Maybe some crazy person came in off the street."

"I don't think so." I munched on the fries as I rambled. "Nothing in Dana's room looked broken or out of place. That means Dana didn't put up a fight. He was shot in the chest, not the back, so he was facing the killer. He wasn't trying to run away. He knew the person. The door wasn't kicked down, so Dana probably let the person in."

She grinned. "That's terrific, Sandy. You're starting to think like a sleuth."

"I'm not trying to solve the case. I'm just curious, nothing more."

While I sipped my soda with a straw, two pre-teen girls came up to me. "Excuse me mister," said the blond one. The other one intently sucked on a lollypop. Both wore halter tops and short shorts. "My friend says you look like someone we seen on TV."

"A lot of people tell me that." I wanted them to go away so I could finish eating in peace. I'm outgoing to fans when duty calls, but when I'm not working I value my privacy.

"You look like that guy on *Buddy Brave*," the girl continued.

"No, I don't think so."

"Uh huh!" the lolly licker said.

"I'm sorry, you have me confused with someone else."

The girls stated to leave. That's when Bunny blabbed, "Yes, you're right. He's Sandy Fairfax. He played Buddy Brave."

I wanted to strangle her.

"No way!" the blonde said.

"Yes, he is," Bunny added. "He's in town for the Beatles convention at King Arthur's Arms. He'll be talking to the fans at two o'clock. Why don't you come and hear him?"

"Yeah, cool."

The lollypop girl nudged her friend and whispered, "Ask him for an autograph."

"Sorry," I said politely. "I don't have a pen on me."

"I do! I do!" Ever-helpful Bunny to the rescue. "Wait, I got one in here somewhere."

She dug around in her Yellow Submarine tote bag until she produced a ballpoint pen and a journal with blank multi-colored pages. She tore out two pages and, while my food cooled, I dutifully scribbled my moniker for the kids. They grabbed their priceless treasures and scampered away. I resumed eating my sandwich but watched the girls. A few yards away they huddled with six other young lassies, showing off the autographs and pointing in my direction. The girls gazed at me with hungry eyes and I lost my appetite. The situation looked all too familiar and warning bells clanged in my head. The group started moving in my direction.

I gathered my packages. "We better get out of here."

"I want to do some more shopping," Bunny said.

I picked up my parcels and stood up. The girly gang hurried toward me. Two girls I can manage, but not a mob.

I snapped at Bunny, "We need to leave *now*."

She heaved her tote bag on her shoulder as I tried to figure out which direction led back to our parking spot. The girls sped up into a fast trot. I tucked my bags under one arm, grabbed Bunny's hand and pulled her to her feet.

"Run!" I yelled.

We bolted, bumping into passers-by and attracting unwanted attention. The girls chased us and screamed. I passed a security guard who shouted something but Bunny and I kept going. I didn't stop—a minimum wage rent-a-cop was no match for excited fans. We reached the exit door. I slammed my hip against the panic bar, pushed the door open with my shoulder and stepped outside into the stifling heat. I let go of Bunny's hand and we ran between around the parked cars until we reached her vehicle.

I glanced over my shoulder. The girls peered through the shopping center door, waving and shouting at me. Either they didn't want to run through the hot parking lot or they had simply lost interest in the chase. Bunny waved back at them.

"Get in the car," I ordered.

Bunny shot me a puzzled look but unlocked the car. I threw the shopping bags into the back seat, climbed in the front seat, slammed my door shut and locked it. I rolled down the window and, with my handkerchief, wiped the sweat off my face.

Bunny started the car and pulled out of the parking lot onto Green River Road. "Do people chase you a lot?" She sounded happy. To her, our near escape was an adventure; to me, a nuisance.

"Bunny, in future I'd appreciate it if you don't introduce me to strangers unless I want you to."

"But the girls seemed so nice."

"Girls that age can get out of control. I had the situation in hand until you butted in."

She frowned. "I wanted to make them happy."

"I'm not a collectible for you to show off."

"Sandy, listen, I want you to know something." She kept her eyes on the road, never looking at me. "When I was eleven I went to the school dance. It was a big deal and I was looking forward to going. I spent a lot of money on a nice dress. I bought myself a corsage. Mom let me use some of her makeup. None of the guys asked me out, but I went anyway. At the dance I sat by the wall the whole time. Nobody asked me to dance. None of the girls talked to me. I felt so stupid."

She blinked back some tears. "I went home and threw away the flower. I cried and cried. Nobody liked me. I got out my suitcase and packed it. I was going to run away from home. Nobody would miss me when I was gone. Before I left I wanted to play your *Soda Shoppe* album one last time. I turned on the record player in my bedroom and you know what happened? Listening to your music made me feel better. Your songs make me forget my troubles. You were my best friend in the world. I unpacked my suitcase and stayed. So you see, if it hadn't been for you, who knows where I'd be today."

She stopped at a red light. The car idled loudly.

I said, "Bunny, I'm sorry people were mean to you, but don't lay that kind of burden on me."

"I thought you were my best friend."

"I like you, Bunny, but I'm not responsible for your life."

She shot me a glance. "Why can't you be more like Buddy Brave?"

Bunny popped a cassette into the tape deck and turned up the volume. The Beatles' song "Don't Bother Me" blasted over the car speakers. The light changed and she drove on to the hotel.

For the rest of the trip, the music drowned out the silence.

❖ CHAPTER TEN

Not Guilty

BUNNY STOPPED IN the circular drive in front of the hotel drawbridge and I retrieved my shopping bags from the back seat. I thanked her for the ride, but she said nothing and drove off to park the car. I wanted to smooth things out between us except that band rehearsal started in six minutes and I had no clue where the guys were meeting. I stopped at the front desk and asked about the band's whereabouts. The clerk said she had seen the guys hauling technical equipment into the Lancelot Room, the site of Friday's mixer. She also handed me a pile of phone message slips from my manager. The way this day was going, I wouldn't have time for Marshall until a week from next Wednesday. I asked the clerk to have my shopping bags taken up to my room, tipped her and set off for the Lancelot Room. I didn't get far.

"I need to speak with you, Mr. Farmington."

Detective Braxton sat in ambush for me on the bench by the lobby fountain. He had a black portfolio in his hands. A uniformed cop stood beside him. Why did Braxton need to bring muscle? Did he plan to beat a confession out of me?

"Hello, Braxton, I'm sorry but I don't have time for you. I'm busy."

"Mr. Hardiman told me you're free until two o'clock."

"I have to get to a rehearsal in three minutes."

"I didn't know you were performing."

"I didn't know it, either. It's a last minute change of plans. I'm filling in for Dana Mumford. You know, the man who was murdered."

Braxton stood and his eyes narrowed into a "gotcha" look. "That must be convenient for you. One of the band members dies and you're available to take his place."

I frowned. "I can get gigs without killing for them."

"Is that so? I checked up on you, Mr. Farmington. Seems you haven't worked for several years."

Bystanders were staring, so I lowered my voice. "I don't need to work. I have money."

"Is that so? According to your financial records, you're nearly broke."

"How dare you look through my personal information! Is that legal?"

Legal or not, the detective was right. Between a lack of income for many years and living expenses, child support, alimony and booze, my accountant informed me that my bank account was draining faster than a beer keg at a Dodgers game. Yes, I was almost penniless, but Braxton didn't need to know that.

"It's my job to get the facts," he replied.

I glanced at my watch. "I have a job and you're keeping me from it." I started to move away.

He grabbed my arm. "Right now your job is with me. Do we talk here or at the station?"

I jerked my arm away from his grip. "Can I at least tell the band members I'll be late?"

Braxton sent the uniform cop to relay my message to the guys. The detective then escorted me to Bluefield's office, a cramped hole-in-the-wall crammed full of filing cabinets and bookshelves holding old ledgers. The manager, seated at his desk, glanced up at us.

"Hello, Detective Braxton. Any new developments in the shooting?"

"I'm working on it right now. I need your office so I can interrogate this man."

The manager glared at me. I seem to get the funniest looks from everyone I meet. "It's you again. I should have known." As Bluefield shut down his computer, he fawned over the cop. "Make yourself comfortable, detective. Take as long as you want. I'll wait outside." The Blue Meanie smiled at the cop as he walked out the door, but sneered at me.

Braxton closed the door behind the manager and asked me to sit down. I sank into a chrome-and-vinyl padded chair and crossed my arms. He grabbed an office chair, wheeled it between the door and myself and sat down facing me, effectively blocking the only way out.

Tricky dick placed the portfolio on his lap and flipped open his annoying memo book. "Did you sleep well last night, Mr. Farmington?"

"No, but not because I have a guilty conscience."

"I saw you carry in some packages. Out shopping in our fair city?"

"I used my own credit card. You can check on that. I didn't steal any money from Dana."

"Did you buy more bullets?"

"I didn't shoot Dana."

He consulted a page in his memo book. "Last night I spoke with a Mr. Clarence Ford from Akron, Ohio. Mr. Ford has a room on the third floor. I showed him a photo of you and he said he saw you in the hall at the time of the murder."

"Mr. Ford? I don't know a . . . is he an elderly man?"

Braxton nodded. That must be the man who stepped out of his room and asked if I'd heard a noise. I sat on the edge of my chair. "So what does that prove? If I had killed a man—and I said *if*—I wouldn't hang around and chat with strangers who could identify me. And did Mr. Ford say I was walking *towards* Dana's room, not *from* it? And this was *after* the gun was fired, not *before*."

"It places you in the vicinity at the time and place of the gunshot."

"Gun*shots*. I heard three separate shots."

He tapped his memo book on the arm of his chair in a steady rhythm. "I interviewed several other guests on that floor. You're the only one who heard more than one shot."

"I can't help that. Maybe their TVs were turned up or their hearing aids were turned off. I know what I heard."

Braxton's lips moved, but he mumbled too softly for me to hear. "What? Can you speak up?"

"I said you're a bit deaf, aren't you, Mr. Farmington?" He grinned oh-so-smugly.

I silently cursed myself for falling into his trap. "I can hear gunshots with no trouble at all."

"If you heard the shots, why didn't you hear anyone running from the victim's room?"

"The carpet's thick. A herd of elephants could stomp down that hallway without making a sound."Despite my innocence, my heart beat a steady staccato rhythm of panic. "Look, we went all through this last night. You have my statement."

"I'm trying to get a clear picture of what happened." Not likely. Braxton couldn't reconstruct the murder if he had three bloodhounds, blueprints of the crime scene, Perry Mason's legal staff and the killer's confession.

"Answer the questions, Mr. Farmington."

"I have a question for you. Where is Dana's gun?"

"What are you talking about? The victim didn't have a gun."

"Yes, he did. I saw it on him."

"Mr. Mumford had a firearm permit in his wallet, but my men didn't find a weapon in the room. Will you stop making up lies, Mr. Farmington?"

"I'm not lying! What happened to Dana's gun? And where did the three shots go? One killed Dana. What happened to the other bullets? Did they disintegrate in the air? Did your men bother to look for bullet holes in the walls?"

"Yes, Mr. Farmington, we look for things like that. We call them 'clues.'"

"The other two bullets are the evidence you need to crack the case," I shouted. "Now tell your lazy men to get off their butts and find them."

"Don't tell us how to do our job." Braxton didn't raise his voice but his tone dripped with venom.

I sprang to my feet. "Then do it, damn it, instead of hassling me!"

"Sit down, Mr. Farmington or I'll place you under arrest."

"Like hell you will!" I slammed my fist into the file cabinet beside Braxton's chair.

On my TV show, Buddy easily punched and kicked his way through doors and walls constructed of flimsy breakaway materials. This cabinet, however, was built to last from sturdy, unyielding steel. The pain ricocheted through my clenched fingers and up my left arm. The uniformed cop came in, saw my punch and reached for his baton.

Braxton watched me like a parent waiting for a child to wind down from a temper tantrum. "If you're innocent, Mr. Farmington, why are you so nervous?"

"I'm sorry, sir." I slowly backed up and sat in the chair. My right hand cradled my bruised fist.

The cop said, "Do you need first aid, sir?"

"No, no, I'll be all right." I wrapped my handkerchief around my knuckles and wondered how I'd play guitar with an injured hand. My throat felt as dry as the air in the Palm Springs desert. I nodded towards the automatic coffee maker sitting atop a low bookcase.

"I'm thirsty. Can I please have a cup of coffee, sir?"

Braxton nodded to his flunky, who filled a paper cup from the glass carafe and handed the coffee to me. I rested my sore hand in my lap and took the cup in my right hand. I took a sip and pondered whether prison coffee tasted this badly.

The detective opened the portfolio, removed a sheet of paper encased in plastic and held it up for me to see. "What does this mean?"

He had the sheet of hotel stationery I saw in Dana's room, the page with the cryptic note "28IF GEORGE."

"I have no idea. Why don't you ask the guy who wrote it?"

"I *am* asking. We found this at the crime scene. Your fingerprints are all over it."

"I picked it up off the floor. Is neatness a crime?"

"You walk into a room, see a body and your reaction is to tidy up?"

"I didn't write that and I don't know what it means."

"We need a handwriting sample from you."

My nemesis replaced the paper in the portfolio, flipped to a blank page in his memo book and handed both it and the pen to me. I set my coffee cup on the only bare spot on Bluefield's cluttered desk and grabbed the pen and paper. With my sore hand I hastily scribbled my signature.

Braxton looked askance. "Mr. Farmington, will you cooperate? That's not what I want."

"How was I to know? When people shove pens at me, they usually want my autograph."

He told me to write the same wording as on the stationery page. I printed what he wanted, although my hand hurt so much the letters came out in a scrawl. Braxton tucked my writing into the folder and shift in his chair.

"You say you heard three shots."

Why was he still gnawing on this?

"How much time passed between the shots? One minute? Two minutes? Less that that? Longer?"

I could have told him, but at this point I was so irritated I didn't feel like answering. "I don't know exactly. I didn't look at my watch."

Braxton wrote something in his memo book. "Did you hide the murder weapon on your person after you fired it?"

I better talk fast or I might end up playing jailhouse rock for the rest of my life. "Look, detective, I've never owned a gun in my life and if I did, I couldn't bring it with me because of airport security. A dozen witnesses can tell you where I've been every minute since I got here. They'll tell you I haven't stopped at a pawnshop or gun store. How could I shoot Dan when I don't have a gun?"

"Since you claim the victim had a weapon, maybe you used his."

That scenario made sense. Why hadn't I thought of that? As drunk as he was, Dana wouldn't have put up much of a fight if someone tried to wrestle his gun away from him. For a second I almost believed Braxton's story, but I reminded myself that I hadn't been drinking last night. I didn't black out. One nice thing about sobriety—I could account for my actions at all times.

"You can't charge me unless you find the gun on me," I said.

"You disposed of the murder weapon this morning when you went shopping. You tossed it into a trash bin at one of the stores."

I met his stare straight on. "No, sir, I did not. And I'm not hiding a gun in my room. If you don't believe me, get a warrant and look for yourself."

"Mr. Farmington, I doubt that even you are stupid enough to keep a murder weapon where the police could find it. Unless you enjoy hanging onto sick souvenirs like that. Do you?"

I didn't bother to dignify his comment with a reply. I wished Braxton *would* arrest me so my lawyer could sue him for false arrest, slander, defamation of character and bullying. But the flatfoot didn't recite the Miranda rights or even make a note in his little black book. Instead he tucked the pad in his suit pocket and rose.

"Okay, that's all my questions." I nearly jumped for joy until he added, "for now."

Damn. That meant I could expect another session in the principal's office. He thanked me for my time and told the cop to open the door. The blood pounded through my head so hard I barely heard what he said. I mumbled a goodbye of sorts and as soon as I saw a clear path I shot out of the office like an L.A. motorist trying to beat a yellow light. I ran like the devil for the Lancelot Room, hopeful I might find some safety and comfort amongst friends. Instead, I pulled opened the door and stepped into an inferno of eighty-five-plus degrees.

"The air conditioner's broken," Grant said, stating the painfully obvious. He squatted on the stage, taping the set lists on the floor beside each microphone stand.

"Did anyone call maintenance?"

Art was adjusting the lugs on his drum kit. "We sent Billy to find someone."

"Can we use another room until this one's fixed?"

Scott was setting up one of the monitors. He looked groggy from his morning nap, but at least he had changed clothes. "Only if you want to haul all this gear yourself to another room. But you're probably used to having roadies do the work for you."

True enough. Living inside the limelight left me terribly spoiled, but I didn't relish the thought of rehearsing and possibly performing in this heat.

Grant finished with the set lists and stood up. "Why don't we prop the doors open. Maybe we'll get some air from the lobby."

We pushed open the hall doors and knocked down the kickstands to hold them in place. A breeze gushed through the openings, although much of the coolness dissipated by the time the air reached the stage on the far side of the room. With the room lights on, I had my first clear look at the venue. The mirror ball was gone and the dance floor was replaced by rows of fabric-covered metal chairs. The instruments and stage equipment filled the tiny stage. The room was more suited for corporate meetings than concerts. I could hardly wait to hear how badly the sound would echo off the hard walls and high ceiling.

The four of us gathered in front of the stage. "Are you all right, Sandy?" Grant asked. "You look like you walked in from a haunted house."

Braxton had that effect on people—five minutes with him and you're scared senseless. "The detective's trying to pin Dana's death on me."

"Why does he think you did it?" Scott asked.

"He doesn't have a lead and he's fishing for a scapegoat. Just because I was the last guy to see Dana alive, he thinks . . . I don't know what he thinks."

Scott's eyes burned into me. "Did you kill Dana?"

"No, I did not." I met his gaze with equal fury. "Did *you*?"

He grabbed the front of my T-shirt and threw a punch.

One thing I learned from the rehearsing the fight scenes on my TV show was how to dodge a punch. I ducked and Scott's fist swished past my head. I brought my left hand down hard on the crook of his elbow while my other hand grabbed his wrist and twisted the skin to force him to release me. When Scott let go I stepped back and raised my hands to avoid a follow-up punch.

Grant grabbed my attacker's shoulder. "Cool it, Scott. We need to practice."

I extended my right hand to Scott. "I know you didn't do it. No hard feelings?"

He shook my hand and gave me a wry smile. He grabbed the edge of the stage and jumped up on it. Even if he didn't kill Dana, from the look in his eye a moment ago, I knew Scott could pound the life out of somebody if he wanted to.

"What happened to your hand?" Art said

The bruise on my left hand was turning black and purple. I flexed my fingers and they hurt so much I almost screamed. "Nothing. Let's get started."

I walked around the stage to get a feel for the space. Whenever my feet hit a stage I get a tingly feeling, the sense that I'm in a magical place and something special is about to happen. The fondest memories I have of my touring days are the moments when I left the darkness of backstage for the bright lights of the stage and the audience erupted in an awesome roar. I love connecting with the fans from the stage. That's what makes performing worthwhile, not the glamour or paychecks.

The Mersey Marvels' instruments were authentic replicas of the original Beatles gear—Hofner bass for "Paul," Gretsch guitar for "George," "Ringo's" Ludwig drums and, set up beside its own mic stand at stage left, a Rickenbacker guitar for "John."

"Where did you get the instruments?" I asked.

"Took us some time to track 'em down," Art replied. "Music shops, antique dealers, friends of friends. Got me drums from another tribute band that broke up."

I picked up the Rickenbacker with my sore hand and winched in pain. I needed a miracle and a potent painkiller to survive this show. I strapped on the ax; the strings were already in place for a left-handed player. How considerate of the guys to prepare the instrument for me. I strummed some chords and it sounded sweet.

The guys took their places. Art sat at the drums on a raised platform behind Grant, who stood center stage with his guitar. Scott had his own mic stand stage right. He held the bass left-handed like McCartney, even though he was naturally right handed. I admire performers who are willing to make the extra effort for a good show.

Jumping into an established group is like going to a new school and trying to join in the playground games already in progress. The guys were used to working with Dana and I tried to fit in as best I could. My head ached from trying to learn so much music so quickly. And my left hand hurt so much I almost quit, but I forced myself to continue. I needed to prove that I could still put on a show, that I wasn't a fallen star.

Leaving the hall doors opened meant that passers-by could stop and watch us practice. Most of them only gave us a glance, but one particular young man stopped in the doorway and watched us.

"You're a disgrace!" Winston wore a Lennon-esque white pants and jacket, straight off the *Abbey Road* album cover. "How dare you pass yourselves off as the greatest band that ever existed!"

We stopped playing. "What's the problem, Winston?" Grant asked.

"I hate tribute bands!" One thing I could say about Winston—just like the real John Lennon, this guy spoke his mind. "You're making a mockery of the music!"

"That's not fair, Winston," Grant replied. "We've worked hard to get the arrangements as close to the originals as possible. We sound a little off today 'cause we've got a substitute."

"Better watch out. That bad karma you generate is gonna get you." With that remark, Winston slipped away as quietly as he appeared.

"Well!" Art exclaimed. "What was that all about!"

Grant shook his head. "Can't please all the people, I guess. There's one in every crowd."

I said, "Guys, if Winston hates tribute bands so much, do you suppose he might have shot Dana to keep the band from playing?"

"That's crazy," Scott scoffed. "That kid's peculiar, but he seems harmless enough."

Harmless. That's what people said about Mark David Chapman before he shot and killed John Lennon in 1980.

The band started playing "Baby's In Black" and I tried to concentrate on the music, but another thought ran through my mind. Since I was now part of the band, standing in a dead man's shoes, would Winston come after *me*?

As Grant was picking out the opening guitar lick to "Ticket to Ride," Hank waddled into the room and plopped down in one of the middle rows. His clothes consisted of too-tight jeans and a food-stained T-shirt with an almost completely faded picture of The Beatles. He rested his forearms on the chair in front of him and watched. He bobbed his head off beat, waved his hand as if he was conducting and, worse of all, sang along off key.

After a few bars of the distraction, Grant motioned for us to stop. "What are you doing here, Hank?"

"Hey, Grant, how're ya doin'! Just stopped by to listen in."

"This is a closed rehearsal, Hank."

"But ya got the doors open."

"We're trying to keep cool." Art said. "The air conditioner's on the fritz."

"Ain't that a shame," Hank said. "But I still wanna hear you guys."

"You can hear us at the concert," Grant said, "but for now you have to go."

"Ah, come on, why're you always picking on me?"

Scott took off his guitar. "Hank, get lost before we call security."

"Hey! That's no way to treat your biggest fan!"

Scott stepped to the edge of the stage. "Don't make me come down there and haul your hinny out of here."

Hank stood and waggled his finger at us. "You don't sound so good without Dana. Nobody's gonna like the show with Dana gone. I'm gonna tell everyone you guys stink. I'll see to it nobody comes to the show."

Hank toddled out of the room, but his departure left me more anxious than relieved. "Do you think Hank will make good on his threat?"

"Don't pay any attention to that creep," Scott said. "He's been making dumb threats ever since we banned him from our shows."

Last night Dana told me someone was threatening him. Did he mean Hank? Would a vindictive fan make sure that if he couldn't see the band, neither would anyone else?

"Hank isn't bright enough to hurt anyone," Art said.

"Doesn't take brains to kill," I said. "Just a strong trigger finger."

Grant suggested we get back to work and I agreed. I was getting too wrapped up in this murder. Let the police handle it. I tried singing the vocal for "In My Life," a gentle ballad by Lennon that suits my voice. If I ever recorded another album, I'd love to cover that tune. We ran through the song several times and took a break. Art picked up a new pair of drumsticks from his stick holder while Scott and Grant tuned their guitars. I tilted my head back and rubbed the nape of my neck—my shoulders ached from the tension.

I saw something move overhead along the catwalk.

Since the stage lights were off, the person moved in shadows, their head and face hidden by a hooded sweatshirt. The mystery person pushed a large box to the center of the catwalk, stopped, and tipped the container. A bunch of small objects tumbled out of the bin and hurdled downward—straight toward me.

"Get out of the way!" I shouted.

I shoved Grant aside and almost knocked Scott over as dozens of hard, round objects plummeted around us. One object hit me on the top of my head. Scott, Grant and I stood upstage as the objects smacked into the wooden stage. Some made squishy noises and others rolled across the floor. We waited until the deluge stopped.

"What was that!" Scott exclaimed.

Bunny came in from the hall and headed straight for the stage. "Sandy, it's time for—"

"Be careful, Bunny!" I rubbed the sore spot on my head and pointed at the small green spheres. "Don't touch those things! They could be dangerous!"

Some of the objects rolled off of the stage and onto the main floor. Bunny picked one up, studied it—and bit into it. "It's not dangerous. It's an apple! See?" She held it up to show us.

As strange as it sounded, she was right. The stage was buried beneath a mound of green Granny Smith apples.

Grant picked up one of the edible missiles. "What a crazy thing to do. Why would someone dump a load of apples on us?"

Bunny's eyes grew large. "It's an Apple Bonker! You know, like in the *Yellow Submarine* movie. The Apple Bonkers were the bad guys who dropped apples on the good people of Pepperland and turned them into stone."

Scott kicked some of the apples, which sent them rolling beneath the drum platform. "So who would want to bonk us?"

Art laughed. "Maybe it's a music critic."

I inspected one of the felonious fruits. Someone had carved the words GET BACK, a Beatles song title, into the skin. I showed the inscription to the guys.

"Get back? Get back where?" Art asked.

"Get back to Indy?" Scott said. "I bet Hank did this. He wants us to leave town and forget about doing the show."

"Maybe somebody wants Sandy to go back to L.A." Bunny suggested.

I looked up at the now-empty catwalk. I wished I could go back home. Hopping on the next crop duster headed west sounded better than sticking around this crazy town and risking another pelting by a horrifying harvest.

"Somebody doesn't want us looking into Dana's murder," I said.

As if we didn't have enough interruptions, Bluefield stormed in the room. "Excuse me, Miss McAllister, but there's too many people in the dealers' room. You need to clear out some of them before the fire warden—"

We never learned what the fire warden might do because Bluefield stepped on a pile of apples and his feet slid out from under him. He waved his arms in an attempt to regain his balance, but he cried out and fell flat on his back.

Bunny ran to his side, reached out her hand to pull him up and apologized.

Sputtering, Bluefield grabbed one of the aisle chairs and pulled himself up. "What's going on here?"

"Are you hurt, Mr. Bluefield?" Bunny asked.

"Fortunately, no. I doubt that workman's comp will cover this." The manager dusted off his clothes. "What are all these apples doing all over the floor?"

"They sure ain't baking up in a pie," Scott quipped.

Grant pointed to the catwalk overhead. "Someone went up there and dumped the apples on us."

"You expect me to believe that?" the manager said.

"Yes, because it's the truth," I said.

Bluefield squinted at me. "Is that guy from L.A. here?"

"Yes, I am, Mr. Bluefield," I answered pleasantly.

"I should have known that long haired weirdo was responsible for this mess."

"Sandy didn't do anything," Bunny protested.

"She's right, Mr. Bluefield," I said. "We don't know who dropped the fruit."

"But I know who's going to clean it up," said the Blue Meanie. "I want every last apple picked up within ten minutes or this room's closed off for the rest of the weekend." He straightened his tie and hurried out into the hallway.

Bunny ran off to get help with the cleanup while Art crashed his sticks onto his cymbals. "That's it. I can't work with fruit dropping from the sky and Blue Meanies shouting at us."

"I agree," said Grant. "Let's call it quits for now."

The guys and I shut off the instruments and the sound system. Bunny returned with Alex, Billy, a maid and a pile of plastic garbage bags. All of us pitched in and filled the bags with the apples in record time. As I worked, I wondered if either Hank or Winston caused the fruity attack. Neither one of them was in the room at the time. And both of them were such avid Beatles fans that posing as an "Apple Bonker" didn't seem far-fetched at all.

Alex stared at the stuck of overstuffed bags. "So what are we going to do with these apples?"

"Let's donate them to the city food pantry." Bunny glanced at her watch. "Look at the time! Sandy, we gotta go. It's time for your appearance."

Two o'clock already? Where did the time go? I excused myself to the band members and left the room with Bunny. First I needed to run upstairs and change into more presentable clothes. I may dress like a slob off stage, but when I'm working I want to look my best. In the lobby, Bunny got on an empty elevator. I pushed the "up" button with my left index finger and cringed in pain.

"Is something wrong with your hand?" Bunny asked. The bruising had spread across my knuckles and the back of my hand. "Will you be able to sign autographs?"

"Of course I can still write. I gave Braxton a handwriting sample today."

"Why did the detective want a handwriting sample?"

We reached the fourth floor and the cab door opened. As we walked down the hall, I told Bunny that Braxton wanted to compare my writing to the paper found in Dana's room. "Some bizarre note with the number '28' followed by the word 'IF' and the name 'George.' Makes no sense at all."

Bunny stopped so short I nearly bumped into her. "Sandy! It makes all the sense in the world! That's a Beatles death clue!"

❖ CHAPTER ELEVEN

I Want To Tell You

"DEATH CLUE?" I asked. "What are you talking about?"

"Sit down and I'll show you."

We stepped into a small hallway lounge, identical to the one where Braxton grilled me the night before, and sat in the two easy chairs. Bunny set her Yellow Submarine tote on the round table and removed a record from the bag.

"I bought this in the dealers' room this morning. Isn't it beautiful? When I get home I'm going to frame it and hang it in my memorabilia room."

"Aren't you going to play it first?"

She gave me a skeptical look. "Play it? I didn't buy this for playing!"

Her prize was a picture disc version of The Beatles' *Abbey Road.* A full-color photo from the original album cover was embedded directly into the circle of vinyl. The record reminded me of the picture disc versions of my own *Castles In The Air* and *Walk In The Park* albums. When the discs came out, I got stoned and watched the colors on the record as it spun round and round on my turntable until I fell over.

Bunny explained the death clue to me. "Back in 1969 a rumor started that Paul McCartney had died in a car accident and an imposter had replaced him. According to the rumor, The Beatles themselves had placed 'death clues' in their songs and album covers to prove it. Look here." She pointed to the picture on the record that showed John, Ringo, Paul and George striding across the pedestrian crosswalk on the Abbey Road thoroughfare in London. "Look at their clothes. John is dressed in white as an angel. Ringo is in a suit, like an undertaker. George is in jeans as the gravedigger. Paul's walking out of step with the others and is barefoot, a symbol of death. And see this car parked along the curb behind the guys? The license plate says '28IF,' like what you saw on that note."

"I see it."

"If Paul had lived and not died, he would have been twenty-eight years old when the record came out. Dana was twenty-seven. His birthday's next month and if he lived he'd be twenty-eight. Pretty spooky, isn't it?'

"How many people know Dana's age?"

"Probably not many."

"Wait a minute. The note I saw also had the word 'George.' Dana played 'John' in the band, not 'George.'"

"That's true. Maybe Dana was trying say that someone named George shot him?"

"But if that's the case, what's the point of '28 IF'? Why would Dana write that instead of the person's last name?"

Bunny gasped. "Grant is 'George' in the band. Do you think Grant shot Dana?"

"What's his motive? From what I've seen of Grant, he seems to like Dana. I can't think of a reason why he'd want the guy dead."

Bunny frowned and placed the record back in her tote. "I don't know either."

"And how does '28 IF' fit in with 'Rocky Raccoon'? Unless the killer wrote the note and not Dana. Maybe the death clue is supposed to throw us off the track."

"But doesn't this prove the murderer is someone at the convention? Apple Bonkers don't know anything about the death clues."

"You mean the apple bonker who dropped the fruit on us?"

"Yeah. Apple Bonkers are people who hate The Beatles." Naturally. That made sense.

I placed my elbows on my knees and rested my chin on my fingertips. "Why would the murderer leave such an incriminating note when he knows another Beatles fan would figure it out? Wouldn't the killer try to hide that he's here at the convention?"

She shrugged. "I can't figure it out. Maybe you should tell Mr. Braxton about the clue."

Not likely. I'd rather play tuba with a polka band than attempt to explain anything Beatle-ish to the dingaling detective.

Bunny looked at her Sandy Fairfax watch. "Oh no! It's five after two! You're late!"

I told Bunny to wait for me in the lounge. I ran to my room and in my haste almost collided with an older couple. In my room I made a quick pit stop and changed into the clothes I'd brought from home: a long-sleeved black Western-style shirt, black pants and black boots.

I'd also brought with me a gold neck scarf, similar the one I wore on the TV show. Marshall and I argued about it before I left home. He demanded that I wear it for my presentation and I insisted I was not appearing as "Buddy Brave." Marshall said the fans would love it and I said the fans should get a life. Back in my heyday the studio demanded I wear that damned scarf for every episode, concert and photo shoot. By fourth season it felt like a noose choking the life out of me. I threw the scarf on the bed, but at the last minute picked it up and stuffed it into my pants pocket. If Braxton arrested me, I could use it to hang myself in the jail.

Back in the lounge I found Billy waiting for me, all alone.

"What happened to Bunny?" I asked. "She was here a minute ago."

"She sent me to fetch you. Bunny's downstairs telling the crowd that you're on your way." As we walked to the elevator he said, "A policeman came around this morning looking for you."

"Yes, we met," I said tersely.

"How's the investigation going? The police, have they caught anyone?"

"Not yet." We stepped into the elevator, the door shut and we headed down. "Did you know Dana?"

"Me? No, I didn't know him. Why should I know him?"

"No reason. Just asking. I thought you might have seen the band before."

"No, I live in Princeton. That's a long drive from Indy. I don't get over there much."

"Do any of your friends know Dana?"

"I can ask around. Are you trying to solve the case? Like Buddy Brave?"

The next person who compared me to that cheeky boy detective would have his head removed and tossed around in a beach volleyball tournament. "No, not at all."

The elevator bell dinged and the door opened. As we walked through the lobby, Billy said some people had left the convention because of Dana's death, but most of the fans had stayed on and a few more showed up after seeing me on the morning newscast. I guess my escapades had given the event a publicity boost, although I hoped none of the fans expected to see me swing from a chandelier.

"Do you know anybody named Rocky?" I asked. "Maybe as a nickname?"

"There's a Rocky Raccoon on the Internet chat rooms. But she lives in Oklahoma and she's not here. And there's Buster. He lives in Rockford, Illinois. That sounds like 'Rocky.'"

"Do you know him?"

"Sure. That's Buster over there."

Billy pointed to a young man attempting to stuff a crumpled dollar bill into a vending machine. The device spat the currency back at him. After the third attempt Buster kicked the machine.

I pulled a crisp new dollar bill from my wallet, eased it into the slot and asked the kid what he wanted. I pushed the buttons and a jumbo-sized chocolate bar dropped off the rack. I handed the candy to him and he offered me the wadded up bill in exchange.

"No, keep it," I said.

His eyes brightened. "Hey, you're Buddy Brave! Hi, Buddy!"

"No, I'm Sandy Fairfax. Enjoy your snack."

"Thanks, Buddy!"

I gave up. Trying to fight an image is too much work. "My pleasure." Buster of Rockford, Illinois didn't seem like a suspect.

Billy took me through a door that led to the backstage area of the Guinevere Room. He mumbled something about wanting to hit the hospitality suite and hurried off before I could object. The "backstage" consisted of an unlit narrow space between the back wall of the room and a movie screen that hung from the ceiling. On the screen the tag scene from "The Different Drummer Caper" played out, the *Buddy Brave* episode in which Ringo had guest starred. Bunny was no doubt running the show for the benefit of the fans that hadn't seen it before and to get them warmed up for the fantastic guest speaker to follow.

Red and a woman I hadn't seen before entered through the backstage door. He spoke softly as not to talk over the film soundtrack. "Glad you're here, Sandy. The fans are excited to see you. Here's someone I'd like you to meet. This is Elizabeth Brown, Dana's finance."

When Dana told me his girl was gorgeous, he was badly underrating her. This lass was drop dead (pardon the cliché), head turning, fantastic. Her blond hair flowed down her back like a waterfall. Her thick eyelashes framed eyes that sparkled like the Hope Diamond. Her creamy white skin looked like something in a TV commercial. Her tight crop pants and tank top showed off more curves than Lombard Street in San Francisco. She flaunted a balcony one could perform Shakespeare from.

I held out my hand. "Hello, I'm Sandy Fairfax. Pleased to meet you."

She slapped my face.

Women often slapped me after we've dated, but never when we first meet. Her long painted fingernails scratched my face and I flinched. I raised a hand to my burning cheek.

"Excuse me?" I said.

"How could you let Dana die?" she said. "Why didn't you help him?"

"I did everything I could."

Red touched her arm. "Elizabeth, keep your voice down."

"You let his murderer escape!"

"Come on, Elizabeth," Red said. "I'll take you down to the police station. Sorry I won't be able to watch your presentation, Sandy. Good luck."

They left as the *Buddy Brave* theme music blasted over the loudspeakers and the closing credits scrolled down the screen. The applause sounded weak. Was anybody out there?

Alex appeared at my side. "Sandy, do you want to stand up or sit down?"

"Sit down? Where? Here?"

"On stage, for your appearance."

"Sit down, I guess."

The screen went blank and, without the light from the projector, I couldn't see a thing.

"Gotta go," a voice said in the darkness. "You stay here and come out after I introduce you."

Alex slipped away and left me all alone in the dark, an easy target for the murderer who could easily sneak in backstage and snap off a couple of slugs. Where was security? Why was Elizabeth angry with me? And did I have time to run to the lounge for a drink to steady my nerves? I'd never had a bad case of stage fright before, but right then I panicked at the thought of facing a crowd of strangers without my liquid crutch. How the devil would I survive the next hour? I took a deep breath and tried to forget the craziness of the last twenty-four hours so I could focus on what I had to do.

Alex's voice thundered over the speakers, startling me. The microphone volume was turned up far too loud. "Beatles fans, we have an incredible treat for you today. Our special guest star has traveled all the way from Los Angeles to share his memories of the Fab Four with you. Some of us have met him already and I think you'll agree he's a funny, delightful, wonderful guy. Please give a warm Hoosier welcome to musician, actor and the world's greatest boy sleuth—Sandy Fairfax!"

I groped my way around the heavy stage curtain until I stumbled onto the stage. The only light was a single spotlight searing into my baby blues. I shielded my eyes with my hand and gazed into the black void from whence came faint clapping and a few feminine screams. Alex stood center stage next to a barstool. He handed me a microphone on a long chord and jumped off the front of the stage onto the main floor.

When the brief clapping died down I spoke into the mike. "Can I please have the house lights up? I like to see the people I'm talking to." After a few seconds of dead air, every bulb and fluorescent tube in the room shot on at once in a blaze of light, causing me to blink. A wave of feedback whined through the speakers. "Can someone please tune down my mike? It sounds hot."

With the lights on, I could see clearly now. The stage had a low ceiling that cleared my head by only a few inches. Behind me, the movie screen was rolling up into the ceiling. I perched on the stool, hooked the heel of a boot over a rung and inspected the troops. The space was half the size of the Lancelot Room. If I had expected a sell-out crowd, I was sadly mistaken. The audience numbered about a hundred, scattered throughout the room. Either the dealers' room was offering some fantastic bargains to draw the fans or my popularity rating had dipped below zero.

Prudence sat in the front row. Billy Shears stood in the back, working the controls on a portable soundboard. Beside him stood a tripod with a video projector for the *Buddy Brave* episode. In the center aisle, Alex was setting up a microphone stand where the audience members could ask me questions. A solid row of mostly middle-aged women and a few young girls who knew me from the TV reruns stood in front of the stage and gazed up at me. During my '70s concerts, teenage girls likewise crowded beneath my feet. I called them my ringside girls. Among these gals was Bunny, who set a portable tape recorder in front of one of the stage speakers and pushed the play/record buttons to capture my golden words.

Valleri rushed in from a side door, fumbling with numerous shopping bags from the dealers' room. She elbowed her way through the ringside girls. The gals who had waited on their feet for more than an hour for their choice spots shot her dirty looks, but moved aside to accommodate her. Valleri dumped her bags on the stage and pulled a record from one sack.

"Look what I got," she bragged to those standing beside her. "A 'butcher cover!'"

"That's nice." The woman next to her was only mildly impressed. "Did you find that downstairs at one of the vendors?"

"I got it last night." Valleri propped the record against her bags so the audience could see it. How dare she upstage me?

I stepped over, picked up the album and handed it to her. "You better put this away. I wouldn't want to step on it accidentally." I offered her my biggest smile.

She glared at me, but obliged and shoved the record back into the sack.

Working without a script or a rehearsal always unnerved me and as I settled back on the bar stool, I realized I hadn't a clue of what to say next. Some people shuffled in their seats and whispered, the kiss of death for a performer. How could I have bored them before I even started? And the crowd wasn't entirely friendly—Braxton stood on the main floor by the wall to my left, jotting notes into his memo book. I'm sure he wasn't planning to write an article for a fanzine. I tried to ignore him as I fumbled forward.

"Hi, it's great to be here. I want to thank Red and Bunny for inviting me. I'm sure by now you've all heard about what happened last night to Dana Mumford. I don't want to dwell on it except to say if you saw anything suspicious or have any information, come and talk to me and maybe I—maybe *we* can solve the mystery." Good lord, the first words out of my mouth and I'm talking about murder. And why was Braxton staring daggers at me? Did he think I was planning to silence the witnesses? "Or you can talk to Detective Braxton. He's right over there."

I pointed to the detective, which made him scowl at me. Someone sitting in the front row yawned. I needed to kick-start my act and fast, before the crowd demanded its money back. I scanned the room for someone to rescue me.

"Bunny, where would you like me to start?"

She stepped over to the standing microphone and leaned in too close, causing her letters to pop. She shot me a sour look. "I lost a bet with Trish. I told her that you'd be wearing your scarf today and she said you wouldn't. So I owe her a free dinner."

She sounded hurt, not at losing the bet but because I had, once again, unwittingly pricked holes in her image of me. The crowd laughed and Bunny squirmed with embarrassment. I could tolerate Bunny's angry towards me—I'd developed a tough hide from dealing with critics—but she didn't deserve to have the fans turn on her.

Time for some mischief.

I stood, put the microphone on the stool, took the scarf from my pocket, rolled it up and tied it around my neck in a square knot. I picked up the mike. "I knew I'd forgotten something. Is this better?"

The crowd went wild with applause. The ringside girls took out their cameras and snapped photos.

"Bunny, you tell Trish to take you out to someplace nice."

I sat down and flashed that famous grin at the fans and then I gritted my teeth as pain shot through my left hand. I'd forgotten about my bum hand and what a bum I was to smash my fingers the way I did. I shifted the mike to my right hand and kept smiling.

Bunny beamed at me with so much ardor I expected her to bronze me on the spot. "Sandy, you look so much better now that you're dressed!" The fans roared with laughter. She put a hand to her mouth and blushed. "Oh! I didn't mean that the way it sounded!"

I laughed out loud, partly because Bunny was in on the joke, but mostly to relieve my own anxiety. I felt a shift in the crowd's vibes. They'd come to see the boy sleuth, and as long as I played into their fantasy, they loved me. As they say in the biz, give the public what it wants. With the crowd in a good humor, I could relax and put on a good performance. A teen idol show is all about having fun with the audience.

"In case you don't know, the scarf thing started by accident. We were shooting the first episode of the show on location and my neck got sunburned. I burn easily. I open the curtains in the morning and get sunburn." Some laughter from the audience, a good sign. I plowed ahead with confidence. "The wardrobe mistress found a scarf to cover up the burn. When the producers watched the dailies they loved what they saw and wanted to keep the scarf as my trademark, like Mike Nesmith's wool hat. And that's how I was stuck with this. I suppose it could have been worse. At least I wasn't in drag that day." A stupid joke, but the fans responded with a hearty chuckle. "So, Bunny, what would you like me to talk about first?"

"Why don't you tell us about working with Ringo on your show?"

"Sure thing. Ringo had moved to Los Angeles while my show was on the air. About that time he had his own special on American TV." One of the ringside girls yelled something at me. "What did you say?"

"1978!" the woman shouted back. "Ringo's special aired April 26, 1978."

"Yes, of course." Who am I to argue with an ardent Beatlemaniac? My cowlick fell into my eyes and I jerked my head sideways to flip it out of the way. "I've always been a huge fan of The Beatles, and when I heard Ringo was in town I begged, threatened and cajoled the producers to get him on my show. The writers had a script ready about a gangster who was a drummer but the character was an evil psychotic and we couldn't have Ringo play that.

I mean, Ringo's Ringo. The writers changed the script as we shot to fit his personality."

I scanned the room as I talked, giving a few seconds of eye contact here and there, with a tad more attention to the ladies down front. "When I met Ringo on the set, I was nervous. I mean, he's a *Beatle*. I shook his hand all formal like. 'Good morning, Mr. Ringo, very pleased to meet you, welcome to the show.' And he said, 'Relax, I'm not the queen of England. Got a cup of tea somewhere?' After he had his tea, Ringo asked me about the music scene in L.A. and before long we were having a good time. Too good, in fact. When we started shooting, I flubbed a line and Ringo made a joke. We ad libbed and upstaged each other and ruined the takes. The director said if we didn't behave he'd put us in separate rooms and shoot nothing but close-ups. We settled down and finished the scene, but I'm sure someone somewhere has a great blooper reel from the outtakes."

"I do!" one of the ringside girls shouted.

"What?"

"I have the *Buddy Brave* blooper reel on video. I bought it from a mail order vendor in Missouri."

Nothing surprises me these days. A fan somewhere in the world probably has my third-grade report card. While I continued my spiel the women standing beside the fan asked her for the name of the vendor.

I went on to say that despite our joking around, Ringo was pleasant to work with, very professional, down to earth and a hard worker who never complained. After we finished shooting he invited me to his house for a party with some musicians and we jammed all night. I also told the fans how I met Paul and George during my British concert tours, and spent time with John and Yoko at their apartment in New York City.

When I start jabbering, my brain doesn't always keep up with my mouth and I made a near fatal blunder. "I asked Ringo if he'd play drums on my albums. He was interested but obviously it never happened. More's the pity. I would have *killed* to record with one of the Beatles." Braxton scribbled furiously in his memo book. "I mean that figuratively, of course."

Too late. Braxton gave me a knowing look and left the room. His actions flummoxed me so much I lost track of what I wanted to say. While I pulled myself together, the fans lined up behind the mike stand to ask questions and gush about how much they loved me. We began with the usual inquires about how I started in show biz and making the records. I trotted out the same pat replies I'd honed through countless interviews.

Someone asked about *The Hardy Boys Mysteries* that ran on the ABC network during the last two years of my show. The suits at ABC felt their show would give mine some stiff competition, but Buddy always tromped the Hardys in the ratings. The *Hardy Boys* actors—Parker Stevenson and Shaun Cassidy—and I were friends. We often had dinner together on Friday nights after we finished shooting for the week.

Shaun had a music career, too. We both wanted to sing together but my record label, SuperTonic, nixed the idea. One day Shaun and I were both recording in different studios in the Capital Records building. I sneaked Shaun into my session and just for kicks he laid down some backing vocals. We never told the suits and he wasn't credited on the liner notes, but you can hear him on my Christmas record, *Sandy Rings In The Holidays*.

I asked for the next person in line and a large lump plodded to the standing mic. "Hey, Sandy! Remember me?"

As hard as I'd tried to forget him, how could I? "Hello, Hank. What can I do for you?"

"I dig your show. It's the best show on TV. Why aren't you making more episodes?"

The trick with question-and-answer sessions is to keep a straight face and not sound condescending towards incredibly stupid statements. "Remember, Hank, Buddy's always been a teenager. If I made the show now, we'd have to call it *Buddy Brave, Senile Sleuth*."

The crowd laughed, but Hank wasn't fazed. "Your *Buddy Brave* movies are awesome. Think you'll ever make another one?"

If I can only scrap up a hundred people for a personal appearance, how will I ever attract millions of people to see a film with me in it? If I wanted a career again I might have to start pounding the Hollywood streets like all the other struggling actors in town.

But I said to Hank, "I'm looking into some possibilities with my agent."

My answer pleased him because Hank smiled, nodded and returned to his seat. I made a mental note that soon as I got home I better start looking into some job possibilities for real so I wouldn't feel like such a heel for lying to the fans.

Winston, still in his white suit, stepped up to the mike, his humorless eyes staring at me through the granny glasses. "Where were you on the night John Lennon was shot?"

The crowd gasped and the ringside girls lost their smiles. I shifted in my seat. I couldn't believe someone would bring up such an unpleasant topic, but I couldn't berate Winston in front of the fans. I decided to answer him quickly and move on.

"Becka and I—we were still married at the time—were at a party at a beach house in Santa Monica. Everyone was outside dancing on the patio. I remember the song on the record player, 'Ready Teddy/Rip It Up' from Lennon's *Rock 'n' Roll* album. A woman came out of the house and told us that John had been shot. She'd heard it on the radio. After that nobody wanted to party and we all went home.

"Becka and I watched the late night news reports on TV and cried. The next day I called Yoko and offered my condolences. It's a terrible loss to the world, but we can be thankful that John left us such a rich legacy of music and art we can still enjoy."

The last remark generated some applause and a few smiles. I wanted to steer the crowd back into a happy mood, but the kid wouldn't budge from the mike.

"It's disrespectful for tribute bands to imitate John Lennon, and if you play with a trib band you're insulting the man yourself!"

I placed Winston at the top of my suspect list.

❖ CHAPTER TWELVE

Photograph

MOST FANS ARE well-adjusted people who channel their Beatlemania into a healthy hobby, but a few let their obsession overpower their grip on reality. Winston's morbid curiosity about Lennon's death didn't bode well. Maybe he thought anyone who dared to mimic his hero deserved to die in the same manner—by a gun. The detective might find such behavior hard to believe, but I didn't.

"I'll have to disagree with you on that, Winston. Since the four Beatles will never play together again, tribute bands are the only way fans can hear the songs live. As long as the music's played right, I think tribs are a good way of keeping the spirit alive."

My remark generated some enthusiastic clapping, but Winston wouldn't quit. He clutched the mike stand with both hands. "No musician can ever play or sing like John! He was the greatest musician, ever!"

I waved at Billy Shears and when I caught his eye, I drew my finger across my throat and pointed at Winston. I hoped he'd understand my message and, fortunately, he did. In response to my gesture, Billy "killed" Winston's microphone and the audience could no longer hear the kid's ravings.

I wiped the sweat off my forehead with my sleeve. "Okay, can we have the next person in line?"

Alex jumped up on the stage, grabbed the mike from me and spoke to the audience. "I'm sorry, Sandy, but that's all the time we have."

"Let me have one question more, please," I begged him. I wasn't about to let

Winston have the last word. I wanted the people to leave on a happy note.

Alex relented and handed his mike to one of the younger ringside girls who wanted to know if I had a favorite *Buddy Brave* episode. I did, "The Sultan's Silver Caper," because during filming I met the woman I later married. Becka was hired as an extra, a serving girl in the sultan's court, and I was smitten with her on the first take.

When I finished talking, Alex told the crowd we had to stop because the convention had fallen behind schedule and the next guest speaker was waiting.

I grabbed Alex's wrist and pulled the mike back to me. "I want to say you've been a lovely audience and I had a wonderful time."

Another wave of applause came and went. Alex announced, "And if you'd like to see Sandy again, he'll be playing with Hoosierland's best Beatles tribute band, the Mersey Marvels, in the Lancelot Room at eight o'clock tomorrow night."

The crowd gasped and cheered. The ringside girls screamed. Apparently the organizers had kept quiet about the substitution.

I tugged on Alex's sleeve and whispered, "The concert's tonight."

He covered the mike with one hand and said to me, "Grant talked to Red a few minutes ago. He wanted us to move the show so you'd have more time to practice."

Best news I'd heard all day. I breathed a deep sigh of relief. I needed more practice time.

Alex turned his attention to the audience. "Sandy will be next door in the Camelot Room to meet each and every one of you personally and sign autographs. But before he leaves, let's give him one more round of applause!"

Instead of granting me the appreciation I richly deserved, the fans shot out of the doors to stake out a good spot in the autograph line. The ringside girls grabbed their belongings and nearly crushed each other in a rush for the exits. Alex kept blabbering into the microphone about the next speaker, but fans were no longer listening. I know I wasn't. I made my way into the wings, a silly thing to do since I had no idea where I was going.

Bunny, my guardian angel, showed up to rescue me, with her ever-present tote bag hung over her shoulder and her tape recorder in hand. "You were wonderful, Sandy! I'm going to make copies of this tape and send them to everyone in my fan club!"

"I'm glad I pleased you." Apparently she'd forgiven me for our disagreement in her car earlier today, since I was back to behaving like a proper Pop Star. "Can you take me to the Camelot Room? I have no idea where it is."

"Yeah, sure."

Inside the Camelot Room, the signing table was set up along the far wall and nearly everyone who attended my talk was waiting patiently in a line that stretched across the room. The table was equipped with bottled water, a handful of ultra-fine point black Sharpie markers (good, because I didn't have a pen on me) and a pile of headshots of me from the 1970s (when I get home I *must* get some new photos made). I didn't see Alex, Billy or Red, but I figured they were busy elsewhere in the hotel. Elmer sat on a folding chair beside the table, glowering at the crowd.

"What's he doing there?" I asked Bunny.

"Elmer will protect you against any unruly fans," she said.

His presence didn't give me much comfort. What would he do if someone acted up— blow cigarette smoke in their face? Bunny stood beside the table to navigate the line and collect money for the headshots.

I sat down, opened a bottle of water and took a long swig. The talk left me parched. I picked up a Sharpie and smiled at the first woman in line. She asked me to sign her *Sandy Sings Live For You* LP cover, which showed remarkably little wear for its age. She also introduced me to her two young daughters who faithfully watched my show on the local channel. The older one looked about ten years old, the same age as my own little sweetheart, Robin Joy Farmington. The girls smiled shyly and hid behind their mom. I asked them about school to set them at ease and soon they warmed up to me. Mom wanted to take a picture of the girls with me, so I had them stand one on each side of me. Everyone smiled big for the camera.

Most of the grown-up women wanted photos as well, so I stood and put my arm around their waist (they love that). I cheated my face to the side to hide the scar on my cheek. I chatted with the ones who wanted to talk. Many of the gals asked for hugs and kisses, which I obliged. Some of the women were so excited they either couldn't speak or they gushed endlessly about how much they adored me. I never saw so many happy, giddy, silly people in my life.

I have the best job in the world.

A number of men showed up too. Guys liked me for the action and adventure in my TV show, not for the lovely-dovey music. I chatted with them and shook their hands. Some of them told me about their favorite *Buddy Brave* episode or childhood memories of racing through their homework so they could watch the show.

One boisterous young gal who had a couple of beers for lunch leaned over the table and asked me to sign the ample bosom spilling out of her tank top. Her friend stood by, ready with a camera. I hesitated. I didn't need a picture of me fondling a pair of hooters to show up in a fanzine or, even worse, in the tabloids.

"Tell you what," I said to her. "If I sign here, it'll wash off the next time you bathe. I'll sign your shirt so you can keep it." Before she could argue, I hastily scrawled my mark across the hem of her top. The gals giggled and left, apparently too loaded to care one way or the other about the signature.

As the line moved along, I noticed two women whispering conspiratorially among themselves. They acted as if they were planning something devious. One of them kept glancing at me with an evil glint in her eyes, as if she intended to spring something on me. I nudged Elmer's leg with my foot. He glanced at me and I nodded toward the women. I wanted him ready in case they attacked.

The women stepped up to the table. One of them pulled a full-color glossy magazine from a manila envelope and slapped it on the table in front of me.

"Sign this for me, Sandy," she purred.

I glanced at the magazine and felt so embarrassed I wanted to slide under the table. I looked at the woman in shock. She licked her lips and smiled oh-so-sweetly.

On the table was the October 1989 issue of *Buzzword*, a now-defunct Southern California monthly publication that once covered the steamy side of L.A.'s nightlife—the one piece of merchandise I refuse to sign.

Bunny leaned over my shoulder. "What's that, Sandy?"

I pushed the magazine away from her, my voice shaking. "Oh, nothing."

The woman opened the magazine. "I'd like you to sign on page thirteen."

I smacked my hand down hard on page thirteen to keep Bunny from seeing it and then closed the periodical. I grabbed one of the glossy headshots stacked on the table, signed it, slapped it on top of *Buzzword* and handed it all back to the woman.

"No charge for the photo." I didn't give her a smile. "Thanks for coming,"

The woman protested but I turned my attention to the next person in line and ignored her until she finally gave up.

As she left the table, the girlfriend said to her, "I *told* you he wouldn't sign it!"

Almost two hours later I greeted the last fan in line and signed my final autograph of the day, my overworked left hand throbbing with pain. Bunny offered to drive me to an urgent care clinic for medical attention. The nurses shot X-rays (no broken bones, thankfully), taped up my hand and gave me an ice pack and pain pills. The cool pad felt great on my hand, but I held off taking the pills. Medication makes me drowsy and I needed a clear head to keep track of everything going on this weekend.

As we rode back to the hotel, Bunny asked, "What was the magazine that woman wanted you to sign?"

"What magazine?" Of course I knew what she was talking about.

"You know, the one you didn't want me to see." She shot me a knowing glance before returning her eyes to the road. "I have every single magazine with your picture on the cover or an article about you and that one didn't look familiar."

I pursed my lips. "You really want to know?"

"Sure. If it's got something about you, I want it."

"Pull over."

I had a feeling Bunny might be upset over my story, and I didn't want to risk her veering off the road in shock. She parked in an empty curb spot and smiled at me, expectantly.

I took a deep breath and told the tale.

❖ ❖ ❖ ❖ ❖

In early 1989, when I was divorced, an acquaintance invited me to a gallery in L.A. for an exhibition by a young up-and-coming photographer who called herself Desiree. The impressive display consisted of moody black-and-white portraits full of shadows and atmosphere. Desiree and I met over a glass of wine and she took my breath away. She was a tall, thin waif dressed in a black leather jumpsuit and matching boots, with one eye peeking out from beneath black bangs. She expressed a burning desire to photograph me and, flattered, I readily agreed to a photo shoot. I figured the exposure might jumpstart some career opportunities.

She wanted to shoot in my home instead of a studio for a more "natural presence." Desiree came over one night and set up her lights and camera while I fixed us both a light supper. She brought along a bottle of wine, which we soon finished, and I procured a second bottle from my own stock. After we drained it she offered me a joint "so you'll feel more relaxed and open." She was right about that—after the wine and pot, I was so relaxed I could barely stand up.

We shot some poses outside and in various rooms. When we ended up in the den, she asked me to remove my shirt. No problem, as the teen magazines often ran pix of me bare chested (the young girls loved that). I took off my shirt and draped it over the back of the sofa. After a while I felt chilly with my shirt off and I started to build a blaze in the fireplace. Actually, Desiree ended up lighting the fire. I was so stoned I'd have probably burned down the house.

She placed a sheet of paper on the coffee table, fluttered her eyelashes and asked for my autograph. Feeling light headed, I signed.

She brushed back the hair off my face. "Please sign your real name."

"What for?"

"I like it. Ernest. Has such a virile sound."

"Oh, I don't think so."

She walked her fingers down my chest. "Come on, Ernest, you tiger you." She made a growling sound in my ear. "It'd make me happy."

After a little (very little) persuasion, I scribbled my legal name as well as I could manage. The paper had some fine print on it, but my eyes couldn't focus enough to read it.

She slipped the paper into a slim briefcase with a lock on it. "I'll treasure this always."

"What was that other writing on the paper?"

Desiree pushed me down on the sofa, snuggled in on top of me and kissed my nose. "Now don't you worry your handsome head about that, you beast."

"Are we finished with the pictures?" With Desiree's warm breath on me, my mind was drifting off onto doing something else besides modeling.

"No, let's do a few more. You're so photogenic." I reached for my shirt, but she snatched it first. "Baby doesn't get this until after we're done."

"Come on, Desiree."

"I have a very nice reward for baby if you're a good boy and do what I want."

I raised my eyebrows. "And what might that be?"

She nibbled my ear and ran the tip of her tongue down my neck. She knew just how to drive me crazy.

"All right." I grinned like a kid eager to please. "What do you want me to do?"

Her nimble fingers started to unbuckle my belt. "Take off your pants."

I'm no prude, not with my reputation among the crew of my TV show as the Don Juan of the dressing room, but I never wanted the type of reputation that comes with nude photos, no matter how "artistic." I'm not ashamed of my body, but the thought of having my posterior preserved in pictures for all posterity for the public to gawk at gives me pause.

"No, I don't think so." I moved her hand away from my pants.

"Come on, be a sport." She rested her forearms on my chest. "It's all for fun. Don't you like me?"

The pot made me feel goofy. "Only if you take off your blouse."

Damn the woman—she called my bluff. Desiree sat up and stripped off her black blouse, revealing a skimpy black lace bra holding up two magnificent mounds of flesh, the sight of which charged me up for the next round of photos. We both got off the sofa and I disrobed. There I stood in all my glory, Mother Nature's son, naked as the day I bounced into the world. Desiree returned to her camera. The light from the fireplace cast a sexy glow on her face and chest. She shot a whole roll of film until I announced I was feeling hot and not because of the fire. She turned off the camera and we made passionate love right there on the shag rug (which has since been replaced by more sensible flooring).

Desiree coaxed me into fetching another bottle of wine and the next thing

I remembered was waking up in my bed, buried under the covers and still naked, with the entire lineup of The Rockettes tap dancing across my brain. How I managed to drag myself up the stairs or what happened in the wee hours of the morning, I never found out.

"Good morning, tiger." Desiree opened the window curtains and the sunlight scaled my eyelids. I hid my head under the pillow and muttered obscenities at the sun. "Did you sleep well?" I peeked out from beneath the pillow. She was showered and fully dressed. "It's time to get up."

I wasn't sure if she wanted me to get up out of bed or get *it* up, but in my condition, I wasn't capable of either action. "No," I mumbled. "Don't wanna get up."

"Suit yourself, but I must leave."

I pushed the pillow aside and lifted my head as far as I could without causing more pain. The dancers in my head were stomping around in golf cleats. "Don't go." I grabbed for her, but she stood just past my reach.

"I have an appointment." She kissed me. "You were fantastic last night. Thanks for all you did."

"Yeah?" I couldn't recall exactly what I had done for her, but apparently she had no complaints. "Call me?"

"Sure, of course." Another kiss. "'Bye now, tiger. I'll see myself out."

I'm glad she said that, because if I had tried to walk to the front door I'd have fallen down the stairs. I sank my face back into the pillow and spent the rest of the day sleeping off a monster of a hangover.

Desiree never called. I phoned her work number several times (she never gave me a home number), but I always reached an answering machine and she never returned my calls. I finally forgot about her and moved on to other women.

About six months later I received a frantic phone call from Marshall. "Ernest, I heard a nasty rumor and you better me it's not true."

I laughed. "Marshall, you know this town. Hollywood thrives on lies."

He didn't return the chuckles. "I heard from a reliable source that *Buzzword* magazine is planning a nude photo spread on you."

"Don't be crazy, Marshall. You know I'd never pose in the buff for—"

Then I remembered Desiree.

I unleashed string of profanities about the girl that almost melted the phone line. I called my lawyer and he tried to submit an injunction to stop the presses, but the magazine was too close to deadline. I sued the publisher but the judge, obviously not a fan of mine, ruled that I had signed a legitimate release form with my legal signature—the "autograph" that Desiree seduced from me—and if I hadn't bothered to reading said form before making my mark, tough luck.

When the issue hit the streets, Marshall discretely bought up as many copies as he could so I could burn them in my fireplace. Despite my efforts, the rag sheet still found its way into the sweaty hands of the drooling curious. Not only did *Buzzword* feature my photos as the main spread, but ran the front cover headline of "Sandy Fairfax: Boy Sleuth Works Under (the) Covers," above a shirtless shot of me grinning stupidly at the camera and wide eyed from the pot.

The photo spread resulted in job offers, but not the kind I wanted. One of Desiree's artist friends asked me to pose for his live drawing class and adult film producers wanted me for starring roles—I turned them down. Worst of all was the fallout when my prim and proper parents found out. My father nearly disinherited me. I hid in my house for months and drank, too ashamed for the public to see me (they'd seen enough already). I also grew a beard so people wouldn't connect me with the clean-shaven idiot in the dirty pictures.

❖ ❖ ❖ ❖ ❖

As I expected, Bunny exploded. "Sandy! You posed for naked photos? How could you!"

"Desiree promised me she'd keep the photos private. How was I supposed to know she'd lie?"

Bunny stared out the windshield. "I never thought you'd do anything like that."

"I'm only human. I made mistakes. Maybe Buddy Brave is perfect, but I'm not."

Without saying a word she put the car in gear and started back for the hotel.

After a few minutes Bunny said, "You must have looked pretty good in those photos if you got job offers."

She looked at me, grinned and we both laughed.

❖ CHAPTER THIRTEEN

Whatever Gets You Through The Night

BACK AT THE hotel Grant caught up with me in the lobby and asked if I could squeeze in another rehearsal right away before the evening programming began in the Lancelot Room. I agreed, but only after I changed out of my Buddy Brave clothes. With all the madness going on, I'd forgotten to take off the scarf—no wonder the nurses at the clinic gave me peculiar looks. I stopped at the front desk and a helpful clerk handed me another pile of phone messages from Marshall. In my room I put on one of the shirts and pants I'd bought that morning at the mall and phoned my agent.

Marshall and I go way back. We connected through default in 1984 when the agency representing me had no clue what to do with a faded pop star and so unloaded my file onto the flunky at the bottom of the company food chain—a brash, ambitious twenty-year-old intern working on a business degree at UCLA. One day Marshall came to my house to plan my future. At the time I was going through my divorce and far as I was concerned, without my wife and kids I had no future. He started talking about me getting new headshots and we ended up looking at my family photo albums. Marshall never found me work that year but he gave me a shoulder to cry on.

After he graduated from college magna cum smarty-pants, Marshall set up his own stable of clients and kept me on. Why, I don't know. On most days he claims I'm more of a problem than a profit—like today.

"Ernest! Where have you been! I thought you'd jumped bail! I've been calling all day!"

"Good afternoon to you too, Marshall. Look, I've been on the run since six-thirty this morning. I haven't had time to piss, let alone call you. I just got back from the urgent care clinic and—"

"What's wrong? Are you sick?"

"No, I hurt my hand."

"What did you do to your hand?"

"Nothing, I—at least I didn't punch out the cop."

"Why are you beating up the police? Are you trying to get arrested?"

I sighed. I was too tired to explain my day, especially since I didn't understand most of what had happened myself. "Skip it, everything's all right. What's up?"

"What were you doing at that ridiculous news conference this morning? I told you not to talk to reporters. Didn't I tell you not to talk to reporters?"

"Reporters?"

"And why were you swinging from the ceiling? I send you out to a nice quiet town for a simple guest appearance and you end up looking like a fool!"

"How do you know about that? I only talked to the local press."

"Those were network affiliates, Ernest. They broadcasted the feed to their sister stations across the country, including the L.A. channels. One of the local reporters contacted Helen and she talked their ears off."

I sank onto the bed. After my divorce I dated a string of girlfriends and Helen Wheeler was the least emotionally stable of the bunch. "Good lord, what did she say?"

"She said, quote, 'If he's found guilty, it wouldn't surprise me.' And your mother saw the interview." I groaned. "She called me when she couldn't reach you. She's upset. She wants you to talk to her."

"Not now, Marshall."

"Ernest! Call your mother!"

I rubbed my temple. I felt a headache coming on. Dealing with family issues always made me cross. "If I do, I know what will happen. My father will get on the extension and give me his usual lecture on how much I've disappointed him *again*. Right now I don't have the energy to deal with them."

"Are you ever going to make peace with your father?"

Good thing I didn't have a bottle handy or I would have drained it. "I'll think about it when I get home."

"Ernest, have you been drinking?"

"No, Marshall, I swear. I've been stone cold sober since I've arrived, although the weekend might go better if I wasn't." He started to chide me further, but I cut him short. "I'd love to sit and chat, Marshall, but I have a rehearsal to go to."

"Rehearsal? What rehearsal? Didn't you finish your appearance?"

"Yes, but I need to practice for the concert tomorrow night."

Even from two thousand miles away, I could visualize Marshall's veins popping out in his neck. "Concert! What concert?"

Why did I feel like the child telling his mother he broke a window with a baseball? "The concert with the tribute band. I'm filling in for the murdered man."

"Ernest! You don't do concerts without negotiations, a contract and a retainer fee! Have you gone crazy!"

I picked up the phone and paced the room. "Yes, Marshall, I think I've gone stark raving bonkers. Must be something in the water out here."

"How much are they paying you? Did you even talk about payment? Or were you too busy jumping around on the chandeliers to discuss important matters like money?"

"This is my first gig in years. I *have* to do this."

"Don't you dare play one note without a contract. I won't let you."

Saved by a knock on my hall door. "I have to go, someone's at the door. Yes, I'll have someone call you about a contract. I promise. I have to go now. Goodbye, Marshall. Good bye." I hung up the phone with my agent still in mid-rant.

I opened the door and Prudence smiled at me. She said the guys had sent her to fetch me so we could get started. We made small talk as we rode the elevator to the ground floor. When I stepped inside the Lancelot Room, streams of cold air washed over me. Some wonderful mechanic had fixed the air conditioner. We could practice in blessed coolness and also keep out the obnoxious fans. Prudence headed off to Ye Olde Country Inn for dinner with some old friends while the bandmates and I got to work.

Rehearsal went well enough, and the tape on my hand helped considerably. After a while Alex and Billy arrived to set up a karaoke machine with Beatles songs for the evening's entertainment to replace the concert. Grant invited me to join the guys for dinner at a local seafood restaurant. At last I could enjoy my first decent meal of the day without interruptions from fans, killers, Blue Meanies or Apple Bonkers. As we passed through the lobby on our way to the parking structure, we saw Elizabeth. Her eyes were red from crying. Grant invited her to have dinner with us.

"Go on without me," she said. "I'm not good company."

"Are you sure?" Grant insisted. "Can we bring back something for you?"

"I'm not hungry." She shredded a paper tissue in her hand. "The police won't release Dana's body until the autopsy."

"An autopsy?" Scott asked. "Why do they need to do that? Everybody knows what happened to him."

She shrugged. "It's standard with cases like this. That's what the police said. Bad enough Dana was shot, now they want to chop him up like a slab of beef. Damn it, he's human being. He's not a *case*. To the cops he's nothing more than a file folder."

"That's tough, Lizzy." Art gave her a big hug. "You look beat. Don't try driving home tonight."

"I know. I got a room here. I'll leave in the morning."

Grant gave her hand a squeeze. "If you need anything, let us know, okay?"

The guys went on, but I hung back so I could talk to her alone. "Elizabeth, I want you to know that if I did or said anything to upset you, I didn't mean it." She looked at me, puzzled. "When you slapped me earlier. I thought you were mad at me."

She wiped her eyes with the remains of the tissue. "I don't know why I did that. I'm so angry about Dana. I had to take it out on someone and there you were. I'm not myself today. I'm sorry."

"I understand. You've had a terrible shock." Elizabeth's tissue had smudged her mascara, so I used my thumb to remove a black blot.

"What are you doing?" she asked.

"Excuse me. Your makeup was smeared. Elizabeth, can I talk with you tomorrow?"

"What for?"

"I want to help the police find Dana's killer. If you know anything that might help, I'd like to hear it." What was I saying! Here I was, acting like the gallant knight in shining armor out to rescue the maiden. A pretty face always makes me lose my mind.

"I already talked to the police. I don't know what else to say. I don't know happened last night. I wasn't here."

"I know, but—"

Scott called from the lobby door. "Sandy, hurry up! We're leaving!"

"Be right there!" To Elizabeth I said, "Did Dana have any enemies? Somebody who might want to hurt him?"

"I don't know—yes, there's one guy."

"Sandy! Are you coming or not!" Scott hollered.

I smiled at her. "Let's meet for coffee in the morning, okay?" She offered a half-hearted nod and a faint, "we'll see." My fans would pay a year's salary for the chance to have coffee with me but Elizabeth didn't seem to care. I've never understood women.

The guys and I piled into Grant's SUV and we took off. When they said "seafood restaurant," I assumed they meant a high-class sushi place like the ones I frequented in L.A. No such luck. Grant drove us to a Red Lobster franchise. The hostess, dressed in a colorful outfit with a large lobster name tag pinned on her shirt, led us to a booth next to an aquarium set in the wall. The brightly-lit place was decorated with kitschy fishing nets, buoys and stuffed swordfish. Somehow all the fake nautical doodads were supposed to wet one's appetite.

Scott got into the booth first, and I scooted across the vinyl-covered bench right away so I could sit next to him. Grant squeezed in beside me and Art plopped down on the other side of Scott. The setting offered me the perfect opportunity to question the three guys closest to the murder victim.

But first I had to wrestle with temptation. Grant ordered a pitcher of beer for the table to share. He poured a glass of brew and set it down in front of me. I started at the frothy glass. The aroma titillated my nose, like a beautiful woman enticing me. I reached out to grab it—until I remembered something.

"Guess what, guys. Today's my anniversary. I haven't had a drink for one whole week."

"Let's drink to that." Scott grinned as he raised his own beer.

I shook my head. "I can't touch the stuff. If I start I'll end up drinking that entire pitcher and you'd have to carry me back to the car."

"That's very admirable of you, Sandy." Grant took my glass for himself. "Sorry I gave this to you. I didn't know."

"That's all right. I never thought I'd make it past one day, let alone a whole week."

If I tried hard, maybe I could stay sober for another week. Or even an entire month—no, that sounded too scary. Better concentrate on getting through this one meal with a clear head.

While the guys enjoyed their beer, I ordered an iced tea. When my drink arrived, I proposed a toast. "To absent friends." We all clinked glasses. The waitress took our orders and left a basket of warm cheddar biscuits. Art grabbed a biscuit before the basket hit the table. I asked the guys if they planned to carry on with the group or disband.

"We don't know yet," Grant said. "We haven't talked it over."

"Be tough to find someone like Dana," Art said between bites. "He was the best."

I turned to Scott. "Is it true that Dana was involved with gangs?"

He eyed me and chugged a big swallow of beer. "Where'd you hear that?"

"This morning at the press conference. One of the reporters brought it up."

"I don't know how anyone got wind of that. Yeah, Dana was a bad boy. But that was back in high school." Scott fiddled with his silverware as he talked. "We all went to high school together, although we didn't know Dana that well. He hung out with some jerks that called themselves the Red Tornadoes. They acted tough, but they were nothing but a bunch of punks. They mostly got drunk on weekends and cruised around and made noise. After graduation Dana ditched those clowns and got serious about his music."

"Would one of those guys want to hurt Dana now?"

Art started chewing on his second biscuit. "What about Ralph?"

"Yeah, Ralph," Grant nodded.

Scott sighed. "Oh, him."

Art waved his biscuit at me. "You ought to try these, Sandy. They're fantastic!"

"Are you going to fill up on those?" Grant said.

"Don't worry." Art patted his stomach. "Plenty of room in here for the crab legs."

"Anyway, about Ralph," Scott continued. "Most of the Tornadoes eventually went straight, but not Ralph. Last I heard he was busted for running a meth lab in a shack out in the country."

Grant added, "People called him 'the raccoon' because he lived in the woods. Had a big barn where he kept stolen property."

"Raccoon?" I said. "Do you think that's what Dana meant? Right before he died he told me, 'Rocky Raccoon.'"

"Possibly," Scott said. "Ralph showed up at some of our gigs and pestered Dana about something. Wanted Dana to get in on some scams he was running."

"Ralph was jealous because Dana made good and he didn't," Grant said.

"Would Ralph be at the convention?" I asked.

"Could be. Our schedule's no secret," Grant said. "We advertise in the paper and Prudence sends out a newsletter with our concert dates. Ralph might be on the mailing list, but I don't know."

The guys said that they hadn't seen Ralph at the hotel, which meant nothing. He could be hiding in one of the rooms or he might have left town after the shooting. They gave me a description of Ralph: medium height, scrawny, stringy hair, not what one would call handsome. Those features resembled any number of characters I had seen around the convention in the past two days.

Scott pointed out a flaw in my theory. "If Ralph wanted to kill Dana, he wouldn't drive all the way to Evansville to do it."

"Unless he wanted to cover his tracks and make it appear like a local person did it," I suggested.

The waitress arrived with our food and Grant asked about my recording career. He seemed eager to change the topic, so I gave my sleuthing a rest. I'm sure the guys were as tired and stressed as I was with the busy weekend and needed a rest. Besides, I'm always happy to chat about my favorite topic—myself.

After dinner we returned to the hotel and everyone scattered. Alex and Billy ran the karaoke machine for the fans and Art left with his local friends who were providing him housing for the weekend. In the Guinevere Room, Red screened "The Beatles At Shea Stadium" for those not in the mood for karaoke. Grant and Prudence drove off to the mall's multiplex to catch a movie. Bunny commandeered the Galahad Room to throw a private party for her fan club members. I didn't want to sit in the lounge and drink or watch TV in my room, so I walked with Scott to the casino.

Compared to the huge razzle-dazzle resorts in Las Vegas, this joint was definitely small potatoes, just a few tables and slots in plain, nondescript rooms. I played a few hands of blackjack but lost. My mind kept mulling over the murder and I couldn't focus on the game. I left the table and wandered through the gaming rooms, casually asking the dealers and drink servers about Scott. They remembered seeing him the night before. Hard to miss him, they said. He either cheered or complained loudly, depending on his luck. But nobody could definitely alibi him at the exact time of Dana's death, since casinos have no clocks. This avenue of sleuthing proved inconclusive.

My watch said midnight and I was exhausted. Scott was going strong at the craps table, so I returned to the hotel alone. I went to my room, changed into my jammies and swallowed a pain pill. As I emptied out my pants pockets, I found the broken piece of pottery I carried with me. I sat on the bed and held the jagged ceramic chunk in my hand, thinking about what the object meant to me and how it had landed me in this bizarre murder mystery on the Ohio River.

Exactly one week ago last Saturday I went to Becka's house in Ventura County, west of L.A., for my visitation day with the kids. Once a month I was allowed to see my son and daughter, but I hadn't done soon in months because I was seldom sober enough to remember. This time Becka informed me she was fed up with my neglect of the kids and I couldn't see them again until I'd cleaned up and started working an honest job.

I returned to my home in the Hollywood Hills, which stood too empty and too quiet. I missed the sound of my old friends who used to hang out in all-night parties and the noise of my kids running through the halls. I parked the car in the garage and headed into the kitchen to handle my despair the way I always dealt with my problems—with a bottle of scotch. In my haste I didn't bother to pour the firewater into a glass but drank straight from the bottle, much like a baby sucking the nipple of a milk bottle. Booze gave me the same feeling of contentment.

I wandered into the sunken den and almost tripped going down the stairs, careful not to drop the booze. I started to take another drink when I stopped and stared at the bottle.

Was this hooch more important to me than my kids?

I threw the bottle against the wall.

I meant to toss the flask into the stone fireplace, but in my rage I didn't aim well and the missile struck a small homemade ceramic pot sitting on a shelf. The artwork shattered. The pieces fell to the floor. The scotch dripped down the wall and the room reeked of alcohol. I rushed over to rescue the clay pot.

A few years ago, around the time of my DUI arrest, my boy Chip made the piece on a potter's wheel in his school art class. (His full name's Stanford Ernest Farmington III, but he looks so much like me that we call him Chip, as in "chip off the old block"). After the teacher fired the clay piece, Robin painted flowers on the pot. The kids were proud of their work. They wanted to present it to me on Father's Day, but they had to wait until I finished my stint. Some father I was, spending my time in jail instead of with my kids and breaking something they had made special for me.

Now I scooped up the pieces, sat on the sofa and spread out the chunks of clay on the coffee table. I tried to reassemble the pieces but the pot was broken beyond repair. The sharp edges of the pieces cut my hands and my palms bled. I sobbed as I stared at what was left of the irreplaceable gift of love. No amount of glue would ever patch up the mess I'd made of my life.

That's when I quit drinking.

❖ CHAPTER FOURTEEN

Do You Want To Know A Secret

THE PAIN PILL I took packed a punch, because I dozed off the moment my head hit the pillow. I slept soundly until the phone rang. I peeked at the clock radio. Eight a.m. Tonight when I go to bed I'm going to unplug the phone so I can get some sleep. I picked up the receiver.

"'Morning, Sandy," Red said. "I trust I didn't wake you."

"No, no, I was just getting up."

"I was wondering if you'd like to join us for breakfast in the dining room. The hotel serves a great Sunday brunch buffet."

"Thanks, but no. I'm not hungry."

"That's too bad. Grant thinks he found a clue about Dana's death."

My appetite immediately improved.

I stumbled out of bed and into the bathroom. My injured hand didn't ache as much as it did the night before, although trying to keep the bandage dry while I showered proved challenging. I shaved, went through my usual morning bathroom routine and put on a new polo shirt and khakis brought in yesterday's shopping spree. As I dressed I tried to figure out the unusual but pleasant sensation I felt. In the last few years I hadn't experienced many Sunday mornings without a hangover. Sobriety was starting to agree with me.

I trekked down the hall to the hotel ice machine to refill the ice bag. Back in my room, I placed the bag on my sore hand for a few minutes as I surfed the TV channels for news. Nothing about Dana or myself, which meant both of us had passed into the realm of *old news*. That suited me fine. Maybe I could do a little sleuthing today without the reporters annoying me. Was I crazy?

Let Braxton do the detective work. I needed to spend my time rehearsing for the concert. I set the ice bag in the bathroom sink, put what I needed in my pants pockets (including the piece from the broken pottery jar) and headed for the elevator. Between floors I realized I had, once again, forgotten my nametag. But after my exposure on TV yesterday, I doubt that anyone would forget my face.

The hostess of Ye Olde Country Inn directed me to a private party room where the usual crew—Alex, Red, Billy, Art, Grant and Prudence—ate breakfast at a large round table. Scott was probably either still on his craps hot streak or sleeping off his winnings. Everyone else, of course, had *their* nametags. Red and Grant scooted their chairs to make room for me at the table. Alex carried in a chair for me from the main dining room and set it between the guys.

"Don't get comfortable yet," Red said. "Get yourself a plate from the buffet and help yourself to the food."

"Unlimited refills!" Art mutter between bites. From the empty plates stacked up around him, he must be on second helpings already.

Usually I don't eat a big breakfast, but when I wandered into the dining room for a cup of coffee the bouquet of the spread lured me in. The tables were loaded with steam trays and platters offering rich, artery-clogging foods such as pancakes, waffles, French toast, biscuits and gravy, bacon, sausage and donuts. Not much in the way of yogurt, granola or fresh fruit for a health-conscious West Coaster. But I wasn't into health fads and if today turned into another madhouse of activity, I better load up. Who knows when I'd get a chance for another good meal. I filled a plate with meat and pancakes, picked up a cup of coffee and rejoined the others at the table.

I placed a napkin on my lap and poured syrup on the pancakes. "Where's Bunny?" I was getting used to seeing her at my side.

According to Red, she had forgotten the prizes for the afternoon trivia contest and made a quick trip to her apartment to pick them up. Grant asked how my hand felt. I flexed my fingers— sore, but I wasn't writhing in agony. I ate a couple of bites and asked Red about the "clue" he mentioned on the phone.

"Grant found something in the pocket of Dana's jacket," he replied.

"What jacket? I thought the police had confiscated his belongings."

"Only what he had in the room," Grant said. "This morning I found his jacket stuffed under the back seat of my van. He rode with us down from Indy. He was always leaving his stuff in the van."

"Why was he wearing a jacket in this weather?" I asked.

Prudence spread jam on a slice of toast. "Because Grant likes the air conditioner freezing cold, don't you, darling?" He frowned at her as she bit into the crunchy toast. "Why don't you show Sandy what you found?"

Her husband handed me a small, fat manila envelope with Dana's name and address neatly printed with black ink in plain block letters. The mailer was covered in cancelled stamps, but provided no return address. The postmark was obscured except for "Ill."

"Looks like someone mailed this from Illinois," Grant said.

I studied both sides of the package and asked if the writing looked familiar to anyone. A resounding "no" from around the table. "Has Elizabeth seen this? She might recognize the handwriting."

"Haven't seen her this morning." Art muttered through a mouthful of scrambled eggs.

Prudence said, "I was going to invite her to come downstairs for breakfast, but she had a rough day yesterday and I didn't want to bother her if she was sleeping."

Nobody cared about waking *me* up early in the morning.

The flap on the package had been secured with clear packing tape, the tough kind a person couldn't rip open with a finger. Someone had cut the short end open with scissors. In response to my question, Grant said he found the envelope already open. I squeezed both sides of the package, tipped it over and a small plastic reel of audiotape dropped into my palm. I asked if anyone recognized it.

"I haven't seen it before, but maybe it's a demo reel," Art said. "I bet Dana was auditioning guys for his John Lennon band."

"I don't think so," I said. "A demo reel would come with a resume and headshot. And a tape bought from a vendor would have a return address and receipt. This meant something important to Dana or he wouldn't carry it around with him."

"Should we give it to the police?" Red asked.

"Not with our fingerprints all over it."

Some detective I was. Buddy Brave knew better than to contaminate a clue with his grubby mitts. With my prints all over this, Braxton would assume I recorded the tape in my home studio.

I held up the tape reel and examined it. "We need to hear this."

"How you gonna do that?" Billy gulped a spoonful of Fruit Loops cereal and talked with his mouth full. "Nobody plays tape on reels anymore. Everything's on cassette." He wiped his mouth on his sleeve.

Alex raised his fork. "I own a reel-to-reel player."

"You do?" Fans never cease to amaze me.

"Sure. I collect old-time radio programs. Some of them are only available on reels."

"How soon can you play this?" I felt jittery, the way I got keyed up as a boy reading the *Hardy Boys* hardcover mysteries in bed and staying up all night to solve the case.

"I'm opening the convention at ten, but after things get rolling I can dash home and get the player."

"Why don't you set it up in the hospitality suite?" Red said. "Let's all meet there at eleven. Alex, will that give you enough time to set up?"

Alex flashed him a thumbs up. He reached out to take the parcel, but I held on tightly. I didn't want an important clue to leave my sight. Who knows, Alex might accidentally brush up against something magnetic and erase the tape.

"I'll keep this, if you don't mind," I said.

"Why not?" Alex grinned. "You're the boy sleuth."

Everyone laughed except me. Before I could think up a snappy comeback, Bunny burst into the room. She wore blue jeans and a white T-shirt with a picture of the animated Beatles from the 1965 American Saturday morning TV series. Right now my life felt like a cartoon.

"Hi, everybody!" she greeted. "Sorry I'm late. Good morning, Sandy! Glad you could join us. Did you sleep well?"

"Hi, Bunny. Actually, Red woke me from a pleasant dream in which I was filming a movie with Bo Derek. Are you going to get something to eat? Assuming Art left some food?"

Art set down his fork for the first time that morning. "I need my energy for the show tonight!"

"Art, the concert's twelve hours away," Grant chided. "You'll have plenty of time to snack."

Bunny said she ate breakfast earlier, but she left the room to get some fruit juice. The band members and I agreed to rehearse right after we listened to the mystery tape. Prudence excused herself to go swimming in the indoor pool while Grant and Art went to the gift shop. They were off to buy a Sunday newspaper and check on any developments about the murder. Alex left to open the last day of the world's strangest fan convention. And Red asked to Billy to cover the registration table.

The kids talked around a mouthful of bacon. "I'm not through eating."

"Hurry up. You've had as much time to stuff your face as the rest of us." Red turned to me. "We've gotten a few calls about the concert tonight from people who heard you were playing. We'll sell them one-day tickets at half price."

"I guess my antics up on the lights paid off," I said.

"Billy, are you still here?"

"Work, work, work! Jeez, can't a guy have some fun?"

"You volunteered to help. Nobody made you."

I ate my sausages and pretended I didn't hear the squabbling.

"Yeah, but I didn't expect nonstop slavery," Billy fussed.

"I have to open up the dealers' room, so I need you at the registration table."

"Why can't Bunny do it?"

"She's working on the trivia contest." Red lowered his voice. "Don't embarrass me in front of Sandy. If you don't want to help, pack up your things and go home."

Billy scrapped his chair back across the tile floor and stood up. "All right, but I want to hear the tape when it's played."

"I'll come and get you when it's time," Red said.

The kid left the room without excusing himself. Bunny sidestepped to keep from bumping into him. She carried a glass of apple juice and a plate with melon slices, a bran muffin and donut holes.

Red eyed her food. "I thought you said you already ate."

"It's a snack to tide me over until lunch." She sat in the empty chair beside me. "Did you get enough to eat, Sandy?"

"Yes, I'm fine, thanks."

"There's plenty of food out there. Have all you want."

"No, I'm full, thank you."

I wiped my mouth with my napkin and pushed away my empty plate. One thing about Midwest cooking—it's hearty and filling. I might not need to eat again for three days.

Red brought Bunny up-to-date with a summary about the morning discussion and the tape reel.

"Ooooo, a clue. That's so exciting." Her eyes danced. "Do you think the tape will tell us who the murderer is?" She sank her teeth into the muffin.

"I hope so," I said. "Once the convention's over, the killer will go home and we'll never learn the truth."

Red stood up and pushed his chair under the table. "If you need me, I'll be in the dealers' room. Bunny, do you have the trivia questions ready?"

"I forgot! I'll do that right away."

I asked Red to call my agent about the concert tonight and he agreed. After he left, Bunny explained that they were hosting a Beatles trivia contest that afternoon.

"If enough people play, we'll have elimination rounds for the championship. You can play if you want, Sandy. I'm going to throw in some *Buddy Brave* questions too."

"No, thanks. Everyone here could beat me on that."

"How's your hand today?" She slid a melon slice into her mouth.

"Better, but I could use a fresh bandage. This one looks like it's been through a war."

"Tell you what, I'll go and find Roberta. She's here at the convention and she's a registered nurse. She can help you."

"You don't need to do that. I don't want to put anyone out."

"She won't mind at all."

Speaking of good health, Bunny's eyes looked bloodshot, which surprised me. I didn't label her as the drinking type. "You look tired."

"I am." She rubbed her eyes and yawned. "I haven't slept in two days."

"Not at all?"

"The only way to enjoy a convention is to stay up all night. This is the first time I've seen some of my pen pals and we have so much to talk about. We spent last night in Michelle's room, playing videos and talking and looking at all the collectibles we brought from home. It's fun."

"How are you going to get through the day with no sleep?"

"I'm so wound up. There's so much going on. I don't want to miss anything, especially with you investigating the murder."

"I'm not investigating, I'm only—"

"Here, this is for you." She opened her ever-present tote bag and took out a sheet of lined paper, which she handed to me. "I went through the registration forms and made a list of the people who were watching 'A Hard Day's Night' on Friday. Red helped me with the list."

I took the page from her and glanced over it. "So these people have solid alibis?"

"Uh huh."

"Red told me you were helping a friend check in at eleven."

"That's right. I didn't get to the movie until the part where George is showing John Junkin how to use a safety razor."

So Bunny didn't have an alibi for the time of the murder.

If I tried to confirm her story, any one of her many pals would say she was the "friend" checking in late that night. I hate to think of sweet, naïve Bunny as a suspect but she had a strong motive—she desperately wanted me to perform. She might have killed Dana on a gamble that I'd fill in. After all, Bunny was the one who suggested me as the substitute. And she was out of the room when the Apple Bonker struck. She knew where I'd be at all times . . .

"Sandy? Is something wrong?"

"What? No, I was thinking."

Shame on me for even imagining a girl like her could shoot a man in cold blood. The murder was messing with my mind—I suspected everybody.

Bunny continued. "I also looked for names that sounded like Rocky Raccoon. All I came up with was Rachel Rabbit and John Rockerfellow. John was at the movie and Rachel didn't check in until Saturday." She rested her elbows on the table and leaned in close. "So how's your investigation going?"

"I hadn't thought much about it, but I could use some more information."

"Like what?"

"I wish I could see the police photographs of the crime scene. Might help me figure out exactly what happened that night."

She said nonchalantly, "Oh, I have photos."

❖ CHAPTER FIFTEEN

Cry Baby Cry

I NEARLY FELL off my chair with amazement. "You do? How did you get the photos from the cops?"

"Not the real police pictures. The ones I took." She patted the camera pouch hung around her waist. "Remember? Friday night when you were talking to the detective, nobody was looking and I took out my camera and sneaked a few shots. I shot from the hallway, so the angle is kinda weird."

"Bunny! You're wonderful! Whatever made you think to take pictures?"

"I don't know. Habit, I guess. I take pictures of everything so I don't miss a thing. I got five scrapbooks full of concert photos of you I took years ago. I've shot three rolls of film so far for the convention."

"How soon can you get the film developed?"

"I know a drug store with one-hour photo service. I'll go there right now." Bunny gulped down her apple juice and grabbed her tote bag.

Ever the gentleman, I rose when she did. "Good girl. I'll see you in the hospitality suite at eleven."

"No, you come with me so we can find Roberta and she can fix your hand. This way."

We left the dining room together. For a first time detective, I was catching some incredible breaks. Lucky for me Bunny was present Friday night, nosing around with her camera. As we passed through the lobby, I saw Dana's fiancée checking out at the front desk. Another stroke of good fortune. I excused myself to Bunny, stepped up to Elizabeth and turned on the charm.

"Good morning, Elizabeth. Can I buy you coffee?"

"Hello, Sandy. No, I don't have time. It's a long drive to Indy."

"Did you eat breakfast?" She shook her head. "You shouldn't start a long trip on an empty stomach. C'mon, let's get you something to eat. My treat."

I touched her arm and she agreed, although reluctantly. The dining room was filling up with fans, including Hank, who waved at me from one of the tables. I needed someplace quiet and private, so I steered Elizabeth to a small coffee cafe tucked behind the gift shop. We ordered at the counter and I carried our food to a small table at the back of the empty café—apparently the other guests were filling up at the endless buffet. Elizabeth poured milk into a plastic bowl full of oatmeal and ate while I nursed my coffee.

When she finished eating, she scrapped the bottom of the empty bowl and licked the spoon. "I was hungrier than I thought. Thanks, Sandy."

I wrapped my hands around my paper coffee. The warmth felt good in the air-cooled room. "How are you doing today?"

She sipped her coffee. "About the same."

"Do the police have any leads?"

"They won't tell me anything. All they say is, 'the investigation is continuing.' What does that mean? They aren't even trying. Doesn't this place have security cameras? Didn't anyone see something suspicious? The cops don't care. Dana means nothing to them." She sniffled, took a travel packet of paper tissues from her handbag and blew her nose. "I'm sorry."

"Have a good cry. Everyone at the convention feels as frustrated as you do.

"I didn't." put on makeup this morning. Can't drive home with mascara running down my face."

"You look great, Elizabeth. I want to ask you something. Right before Dana di—when I was with him, he said something to me. He said, 'Rocky Raccoon.' Do you have any idea what he meant by that?"

"Rocky Raccoon?"

"It's the name of a Beatles song."

"I know that, but I have no idea why Dana would say it."

"Did he ever refer to anyone by that name?"

"Dana talked about his music, but I don't believe he ever mentioned that song." Her eyes took on a faraway look and her voice softened. "He used to call me his 'Lovely Rita.'"

"I know that song."

"At home we played a game called 'Lovely Rita, meter maid.'" Elizabeth blushed. "Sorry. That's personal."

I smiled. "Did Dana owe money to anyone? On Friday night he was trying to sell some valuable records. Did he need to raise money?"

"Dana had maxed out his credit cards and I told him I wasn't starting our marriage deep in debt. He was working hard to pay off his cards. If he was selling records, I'm sure that's where he planned to put the money."

"Yesterday you said someone wanted to hurt Dana. Tell me what you know."

She twisted the engagement ring on her finger as she talked. "Last year I briefly dated a guy named Jason Wilcox. I didn't like him but he pestered me so much that I went out with him once to shut him up. I thought he might leave me alone after that, but he didn't. After I met Dana, Jason kept sending me love notes, flowers, gifts. After I told Jason about my engagement, he left threatening messages on Dana's answering machine. I told Jason if he didn't stop bothering us I'd call the police."

"Do you think Jason killed Dana?"

"That measly worm? He doesn't have the guts. And he's such a klutz. He'd end up shooting himself." Elizabeth finished her coffee and stacked the empty cup into the plastic bowl. "It's time I left. I promised Dana's parents I'd see them today. And I have to call around and find a replacement for Tuesday. I'm taking the week off from work."

"That's a good idea. What's your job?"

She swung her purse strap over her shoulder. "I'm a teacher's assistant at a preschool."

We tossed our trash in the bin by the door and left the café. When we reached the lobby, I said, "I have one more question. Does Jason live in Indianapolis?"

"He used to when we dated, but not now. At the time Dana and I announced our engagement, Jason's boss fired him. He can't hold a job. I heard he moved out of town, but I don't know where and I don't care." Her eyes smoldered. "Dana's killer is probably long gone by now. I don't think anyone will find him."

As she headed for the lobby doors, I watched her shorts-clad hips sway as she balanced on the high heels of her open-toed sandals. Now I know why hard-boiled single guys go into detective work. If a string of attractive female clients passed through my office every day, I'd hang out a P.I. shingle myself.

After Elizabeth left the building, Bunny and a sweet-looking young lady approached me. "Sandy! There you are! I found Roberta. You remember Roberta?"

"Yes, right." Who the heck was Roberta? I needed a playbill to keep track of all the people parading and in out of my life this weekend.

"Roberta, this is Sandy Fairfax."

"Hi, Sandy. I'm a big fan of yours." She smiled shyly as I automatically shook her hand. "I liked your talk yesterday."

"Thank you." I stared at her stupidly, at a loss for words.

"Roberta's a nurse," Bunny prompted in response to my blank stare. "She'll get your hand all fixed up." She handed the woman a metal box with a red cross on it. "I told Red last week we needed a first aid kit in the hospitality suite. I knew it'd come in handy. Sandy, I'm leaving you in Roberta's capable hands. See you at eleven." Bunny waved and ran off.

The woman and I looked at each other awkwardly. "Bunny said you're hurt."

"Nothing serious. I sprained my hand, that's all." No point in giving her the details of how I whacked my hand on a filing cabinet.

We headed for a secluded lounge near the coffee café. I sat in a padded chair and rested my left arm on the table. Roberta took my hand, hesitantly at first, and peeled back the bandage. The skin had turned several shades of purple.

"It looks worse than it feels," I said.

Once Roberta overcame the initial shyness of touching her idol, the nurse took care of the matter professionally and expertly. She removed the old tape and wrapped a fresh Ace bandage around the palm, snug but not too tight. I wiggled my fingers—I could easily play a guitar with the fresh wrapper. Roberta packed up the first aid kit and I thanked her profusely for her help. I also stuffed the used bandage into my pants pocket so she wouldn't swipe it as a souvenir.

My watch said ten o'clock, time for the convention to open and an hour before the grand debut of Dana's mystery tape. I should retire to my room and practice the songs, but with thoughts of Dana's murder swirling around in my head I couldn't wrap my mind around music. I asked Roberta how to get to the convention. If I had bothered to open my registration packet I'd know where to find the rooms. After she pointed me in the right direction, I sauntered off to brave the wilds of fandom and maybe solve a mystery.

A flight of stairs led to the basement and opened into a long, narrow hallway, with the huge Merlin Ballroom to the right and smaller meeting rooms along the other side. The fans, all with nametags, mostly wore Beatles T-shirts or tie-dyed shirts. Two ladies were decked out in flowing East Indian caftans, complete with colorful headbands and love beads.

Beneath the stairwell four women huddled in a circle, playing guitars and softly singing Beatles songs. I asked a passerby about the songbirds and he said the girls had been playing nonstop since yesterday morning. Why would anyone pay money and travel a long way to hide away and miss the convention activities—even an appearance by yours truly—when one could stay home and sing in the shower for free? But enthusiasts express their devotion in various ways and for some, making contact with fellow fans is what they need after spending the rest of the year surrounded by Apple Bonkers. As their singing continued, I moved on.

The first door on my left was closed. A sign taped to the door declared, "Video Room. PLEASE Keep This Door Shut At All Times!" A second sign announced the 24-hour schedule of film screenings in the room: Beatles (group and solo) and Wings music videos, concert clips, interviews, Beatles cartoons and a couple of *Buddy Braves* thrown in for good measure. The next room housed an art show, with paintings, drawing and sculptures of the fabs created by fans: some low-grade quality, most passable and a few decent pieces, but all made with love. Each piece had a tag on it with an identification number.

"All of the artwork's for sale," said a woman seated at a folding table.

I turned to face the speaker and she gave me the "OMG It's Him!" look. "Oh! Hello, Sandy. I didn't expect to see you here."

"Hi. What were you saying about the artwork?"

"It's for sale, unless you see a 'sold' sticker on it. Half of the money goes to the artist and the rest is donated to a nonprofit charity that works to stop handgun violence. The artist who earns the most money wins a prize, a reproduction of a John Lennon drawing."

I continued browsing. Most of the mediocre pieces sported a "sold" sticker. I assumed the fans bought the art more to help their friends win the prize than for any aesthetic value. On my way out the door something caught my eye—a series of four large pastel pencil sketches, matted head and shoulder poses of John, Paul, George and Ringo, each in his respective Sgt. Pepper uniform. Next to the portraits hung a huge drawing of Buddy Brave, circa 1976, complete with neck scarf, remarkably lifelike and finely detailed. The craftsmanship awed me. The five pieces were far superior to the other items. And none of them had sold.

"Are there any professional artists in the show?" I asked the woman at the table.

"No, everyone's an amateur."

A neophyte couldn't create such work. Maybe a ringer had sneaked in under a pseudonym. Then I read the signature: Beatrice McAllister. I couldn't believe it. When did that silly girl develop so much talent? She must have worked hours on each drawing, yet the fans ignored her beautiful portraits. Bunny deserved some respect for her talent.

Time for some mischief.

I said to the woman at the sales table, "I'd like to purchase one of the pieces, please. Number nine, the Buddy Brave picture."

She opened a small tin box full of index cards that listed the entries. "The one by McAllister? It's fifteen dollars."

Bunny shouldn't give away quality work at bargain basement prices. "Can I make it an even hundred?"

The woman stared at me. "One hundred dollars?"

"It's for charity, isn't it?"

"Yes, I suppose it is." She started writing on the card. "Your name? You don't need to tell me. I know who you are."

"Can I make this an anonymous donation?"

I pulled two fifty-dollar bills from my wallet, part of the "emergency fund" Marshall had given me in case I got stuck somewhere. He'll give me an earful about throwing away good money on a picture, but I didn't care. I tossed in a few more bucks to have the picture shipped to Marshall's office so I wouldn't have to carry the portrait on the plane trip home. I left the room with a smile. Not only did I do something nice for Bunny, but I finally had something to fill the empty space on a wall in my house where my ex-wife used to keep a hideous avant-garde oil painting. The first thing I did after she moved out was to throw away that monstrosity.

I moved on to the busy dealers' room inside the Merlin Ballroom, the heart and soul—and the real moneymaker—of any fan convention. Nearly all of the fans make a pilgrimage here at least once and few leave empty-handed. The musty smell of vinyl records and old magazines filled the room, along with the sound of people talking and shoes clattering across the tile floor. From the ceiling speakers played piped-in music, "Rain," one of the more obscure Beatles tunes. Long folding tables were stacked with every type of Beatles merchandise imaginable as well as original collectibles from the 1960s. Other tables sold records, books about the fabs, videotapes of films and concerts. Beatles business is big business. My own merchandise output looked mighty puny against this onslaught.

Some dealers were appraising collectibles brought in by fans; others sold or bartered their goods. One fan balked at the high price of a particular record and the vendor offered to throw in a free poster to sweeten the deal. Three women compared their purchases.

"Look what I found!" Woman No. 1 proudly displayed her catch of the day. "A 1978 Rutles record with the original 12-page booklet inside!" The Rutles were the brilliant and affectionate parody created by comedian Eric Idle and featuring spot-on faux-Beatles songs composed by British musician Neil Innes.

"Oh yeah?" Woman No. 2 challenged her by producing her own prize. "A twelve-inch Rutles EP in yellow vinyl, give out to DJs and never sold in stores!"

"That's nothing," Woman No. 3 smirked. "Look at this. Neil's first solo record, 'How Sweet To Be An Idiot.' Released only in England, never in America."

As the women continued to argue about the merits of their respective records, I moved on and found some tables with my merchandise, no doubt brought in special when the vendors heard I was coming. I glanced through the old tour programs, bubble gum cards with scenes from my TV show, official fan club membership packets stuffed with goodies and the world's greatest kid cop on the cover of a 1976 *TV Guide*, sporting a shoulder-length shag haircut. Although I never earned a penny for loaning my likeness to this billion-dollar bonanza and the items looked a bit silly, I still felt proud. How many people can boast of having their very own action figure?

A vendor tucked back in a dimly-lit corner sold autographed records, including some of mine. Back in the day I signed anything that didn't move out of the way. My handlers constantly shoved stuff at me to sign so they could give it away as a prize in a contest or promotion. The dealer, with his tiny, narrow set eyes, pinched cheeks and hunched shoulders, reminded me of a weasel. He was busy in making a sale to a fan, so I quietly picked up some records and stepped over into better lighting to examine the covers.

I remember the day we shot the cover photo of the 1978 *Knight in Shining Armor*, with me suited up in full armor and sitting on a horse. Some wise guy insisted on using authentic armor, which weighted a ton and kept in body heat like a slow cooker. We did the photo shoot in a park on the hottest day of the year. I sizzled inside the tin can like a steak on a barbecue grill. With the armor on I couldn't move—or breathe. The session lasted forever and I complained about the heat but, as usual, nobody listened to me. "Just one more shot, Sandy," they'd say. The photographer always wanted "one more shot." The producer finally called it quits after I fainted from the heat and fell off of the horse. In case you're wondering, landing on the ground while encased in a full suit of armor *hurts*.

The signatures on the records looked wrong. On one sleeve, the slant on the capital "S" in my first name leaned too far to the left. As a lefty, my writing tends to slant to the right. On another record, the bottom loop on the "y" didn't close all the way. One cover was signed "Stanford Fairfax." I never used my first name, not even before I became famous.

The autographs were fakes.

❖ CHAPTER SIXTEEN

You Never Give Me Your Money

I DON'T MIND someone making an honest buck off my name, but I'll be damned if I let thieves rip off my fans. Fraudulent autographs are not only a lazy and tacky way for vendors to make a profit, but it misrepresents my integrity and cheapens the value of the real thing. I approached the table with my teeth on edge and my rage simmering.

The vendor didn't recognize me. He nodded at the records in my hand. "You wanna buy those?"

I played innocent. "I haven't seen Sandy Fairfax records in a long time. Where did you find these?"

"I got good suppliers."

I'll bet you do. "Are these real signatures?"

"Absolutely. All my stuff, it's authentic."

Authenticated in your garage, no doubt. "Really?" I set the records on the table, picked up a pen and a blank paper sales receipt and wrote my name. I dangled the slip of paper in front of the vendor's face. "*This* is an authentic signature."

His beady eyes glanced at the paper, darted down to my photo on the album sleeve and back up at my face. His ugly puss contorted with fear. He grabbed for the records, but I snatched them first. With my other hand I seized the front of his shirt and pulled him halfway over the table.

"Get your crap out of here now or I'll beak these records over your head."

"Hey! Hey" He squeezed my wrist and dug in his broken fingernails. I let go of his shirt. For a scrawny guy, he packed a wallop. "You can't make me leave. I paid good money for this table."

"Do I call the police?"

"Go ahead. I ain't broken no law. Who's gonna stop me?"

The scoundrel was right. The local police had more important crimes to handle than to waste their time ticketing a guy for hawking a bunch of old records. Fans gathered around to watch our battle. I wanted to punch the weasel in the face but a couple of people reached for their cameras. I lowered my fist. With Braxton dying to nail a murder charge on me, I didn't need photos of me starting a fight.

Red walked up, holding a clipboard full of documents. "Is something the matter, Sandy?"

"Darn right." I showed him the albums. "This joker's selling fake autographs."

"I'm terribly sorry. I had no idea."

"I can sell whatever I want," said the weasel. "Free enterprise, y'know."

I used the one piece of ammunition I had left—myself. "Either he clears out or I skip the show tonight."

Red looked startled. "Don't do that, Sandy. I'm sure we can work it out."

I pushed the cowlick out of my face. "If he's not gone in five minutes, I walk."

"I don't leave without a full refund of my table fee," the vendor huffed.

Red whispered to me. "Sandy, our bank account's busted. I can't afford to reimburse the man."

As much as I wanted the swindler gone, I didn't want to hurt Red and Bunny. But I couldn't back down from my threat or let this crook get away with stealing. The bystanders stared at me, which gave me an idea. If I couldn't physically remove the worm from the premises, I could at least put him out of business.

I turned to the people standing next to me. "Spread the word. This dealer is selling fake merchandise." I showed them the records. "Anyone buying from this guy is getting cheated."

As I expected, my warning spread among the fans faster than first-day sales of Paul McCartney concert tickets. The crowd dissipated and the fans browsing the table moved away.

The weasel glared at me. "You chased away my customers! That ain't fair!"

"I suppose they decided to shop elsewhere." I stuck the forged albums in the back of the vendor's record bin. "It's the free enterprise system, y'know."

Red and I left the table. "Is everything all right now, Sandy?"

"As long as he doesn't make any sales, I'm happy. And if you ever plan another convention, keep him out."

"I suppose I should have screened the dealers better. It never occurred to me that someone might take advantage of us."

"Tell the fans if they want anything signed to bring it straight to me. I'm always happy to oblige. They don't need to buy forgeries on the black market."

"Right, I'll do that. Thanks, Sandy. If that's settled, I'll see you later." Red moved on to chat with some fans.

Valleri and her entourage stood court nearby. Her screechy voice cut through the other noise in the room. She waved her "butcher cover" record like a battle flag.

I walked over to Red and grabbed his arm. "Red, I need your help."

He sounded exasperated. "What is it now, Sandy? Another crooked vendor?"

"No, nothing like that. I want you as a witness. Don't say anything, just listen."

I dragged Red over to Valleri. I greeted her with a cheery good morning.

"Hi," she replied flatly. Most fans faint when I say hello, but she eyed me as if to indicate I had no business intruding upon her royal presence.

"Valleri, I'd like to speak to you for a minute if you don't mind."

"About what?"

"Something important. I'd appreciate it. Let's go some place private." She and her gang started to follow me. "No, just you alone."

Her mood brightened. She said to her crew, "Sandy wants to speak to me *alone*. Guess that makes me special!"

Only you don't know how special.

The queen bee tucked the "butcher cover" into one of her brown paper shopping bags. As we left the ballroom, she held her head high and talked loudly so everyone would notice us. Red directed us into an empty meeting room across the hall. I closed the door and asked Valleri to sit down. I pulled up a folding chair and seated myself facing her.

Red whispered, "Sandy, what's this all about?"

"Just stand by the door and don't let her leave."

He shook his head, bewildered, but stood guard anyway. Red probably thought his special guest had flipped out. Perhaps he was right—I wasn't certain I knew what I was doing.

I smiled at my prisoner. Some friendly small talk might start a conversation. "How's the convention going for you?"

"All right, I guess. I've been to better cons. This one's the pits."

I was wrong about the small talk. "Are you finding some good bargains from the vendors?"

"Yeah, a few things. What about it?"

"I notice you have a 'butcher cover.' May I see it?"

She lit up like Times Square. I finally hit the right nerve. A collector loves nothing better than to show off her loot. Valleri retrieved the prize from her bag and handed it to me. I grasped the album by the edges between my palms as not to mess up such a fine collectible—or to leave my fingerprints. "Where did you get this?"

A look of suspicion crossed her face. "Ummm, from one of the dealers."

"I heard you say that you picked this up Friday night. Is that right?"

"Yeah, so what? Why are you asking me questions? What's going on?"

I turned to Red. "Was the dealers' room open Friday night?"

"No. The vendors didn't set up until Saturday morning."

I placed the record on a chair so I wouldn't damage it. "Valleri, where did you get this record?"

Her expression turned so sour I could have made lemonade. "I don't have to talk to you. Doesn't matter where I got it. This is stupid. I gotta go." She stood up and Red moved in front of the door.

"Would you rather talk to the police?" I asked.

Valleri plopped down in the chair, crossed her fat arms and made a "hmmppphh" sound. "I bought it from someone here at the convention. Okay?"

"Don't lie to me, Valleri. We both know better than that. Most fans don't own a 'butcher cover' and the ones who do aren't about to give it up. Did you buy this from Dana Mumford?"

"Who?"

"The musician in the tribute band. The man who was shot. I saw you talking to him Friday night at the dance."

She fidgeted in her chair and started down at her hands. "Oh, him."

"Did the two of you go to his room to look at his records?"

"I didn't kill him!" She beat her fists on the side of her chair. "I didn't do it!"

I held up a hand. "Slow down, I never said you did."

"Then go pester someone else. Why are you bugging me? Just 'cause I have his record don't mean nothing."

"Valleri, I'm not accusing you of anything. I'm just trying to figure out what happened to Dana the night he died. Did you go to his room to buy his records?"

"Yeah. I looked at what he had and said I wanted them and he said I could have them."

"Dana didn't have much money in his wallet when he died. You didn't pay him for the records, did you?"

"I didn't steal them! I started writing a check and the phone rang."

Whenever Buddy Brave uncovered an important clue on my show, the background music swelled to signal the audience. If this was a movie, the studio orchestra would drown out the interrogation. I sat on the edge of my chair. "Tell me about the phone call. Who called Dana?"

"I don't know. He told me to leave 'cause someone was coming up to see him."

"What did Dana say to his caller?"

"Something like, 'Oh, it's you' and 'I'm busy' and 'if you have to, hurry up and let's get this over with.' That's all he said. Honest."

"Was the caller a man or woman?"

Her face turned red as she screamed. "I told you, I don't know! Dana hung up and told me to go. I took the records and ran out. I put them in my room so I wouldn't lose then, then I remembered I forgot to pay him. I went back to his room and the cops were there, so I left 'cause I don't want to get mixed up in all that. And anyway I figured Dana didn't need any money if he was dead."

After this last remark, I almost slapped her. "Why didn't you tell the police about the phone call? You could be arrested for withholding evidence."

A look of panic flashed across her face. "Are you going to tell on me?"

"I won't if you do something for me." I handed the record to Red, my unwilling assistant. "Red, how much would this sell for in the dealers' room?"

He turned the record over in his hands, scrutinizing both sides of the sleeve with the eye of an experienced collector. "Minimal wear and tear along the edges. The photo's barely faded, that's good. If the record has only slight wear, I'd say the going rate is about eight hundred dollars."

I rested my elbows on my knees. "Valleri, I want you to write a check for eight hundred dollars. Leave the payee line blank. On the memo line write, 'for funeral expenses.'"

She narrowed her eyes and scrunched up her mouth in an ugly frown. I stared back until she relented and took a battered checkbook from her purse. After she wrote the check, I snatched the document from her hand and checked to make sure she'd filled in the blanks correctly. I handed the paper money to my witness.

"Red, see that Dana's family receives this check right away."

He tucked the check under the clip on his clipboard. "Sure, Sandy. I'll take care of it."

"Thanks, Valleri," I said. "You've been a big help. You can go now." She rose and gathered her purchases. "A word of advice. I suggest you put away your 'butcher cover' for the duration of the convention. The police might not believe your story of how you got it."

She jerked the record from Red's hands and ran from the room so fast she almost left a hole in the door. I stood up, proud of the way I handled the situation.

"Red, thanks for your help."

"You're welcome. Do you believe what Valleri said?"

"I don't know. She might be lying about the phone call. Can you check with the front desk and find out if any calls came through to Dana's room on Friday night? And if the call came from inside or outside the hotel?"

"No problem, Sandy. But if Valleri's fibbing, why did Dana say 'Rocky Raccoon?' That song is only on the 'White Album.' It doesn't appear on the 'butcher cover.'"

He had a good point. I had so many clues they were bumping into each other.

Red glanced at his wristwatch and announced it was almost eleven o'clock, time for us to meet the others in the hospitality suite to listen to the mystery tape.

As we walked to the stairs, Red asked, "Why did you let Valleri keep the record? Technically, she stole it."

"Red, for a fan there's only thing worse than not having a prized collectible. And that's when she has it but can't brag about it."

❖ ❖ ❖ ❖ ❖

Alex set up the bulky, antique tape player on the desk in the hospitality suite's inner room. He said he purchased it secondhand and refurbished it himself. The suite was empty except for Alex, Red and myself. Nobody else was using the suite today because, Red explained, the convention had run out of money for any more guest speakers. Sunday's programming consisted of the trivia contest, the concert and a "magical mystery tour," a chartered bus trip to the nearby Angel Mounds State Park for the benefit of out-of-town guests. His mention of the concert reminded me I better stop sleuthing and start practicing if I didn't want to look like a fool tonight.

The band members joined us. Grant suggested I take advantage of the suite's free snacks since the guys planned to rehearse straight through lunchtime. Of course Art, who never needed encouragement, helped himself to the food as well. Billy had only minimally stocked the food table, so I made do with a paper plate filled with cheese slices, crackers, bagels and cookies. I also retrieved a lukewarm can of Mountain Dew from a cooler full of melted ice.

I tasted the soda. "This isn't cold."

"Sorry, Sandy," Red said. "Billy was supposed to take care of it."

Speaking of the kid, as soon as he entered the room he and Red started arguing over various things, including the lousy food supply for the inhospitable suite.

Bunny arrived and waved a packet of freshly developed photos. "Hi, Sandy! Look, I got the pictures!"

I raised a finger to my lips and she placed a hand over her mouth. Nobody needed to know about her crime scene photos.

"Are you ready?" Red asked Alex.

"Almost." With nimble fingers, Alex threaded the thin audiotape around the machine's rollers and heads.

"While we wait," Bunny said. "I want to try out my trivia questions for the contest. I wrote them while I was waiting at the store."

She removed a sheet of lined paper from her tote bag. I sat in an easy chair and munched on my snacks while the others matched their wits.

Bunny read the first question. "What rock group did Ringo play with before he joined The Beatles?"

"Rory Storme and The Hurricanes," Art said.

"What actor appeared in three Beatles movies and in what roles?"

"Victor Spinetti." Red counted the parts on his fingers. "He was the TV director in 'A Hard Day's Night,' the mad scientist in 'Help!' and the Army general in 'Magical Mystery Tour.'"

"Also in 'Hard Day's Night,'" Bunny continued, "when Grandfather's alone in the hotel room, what's the name of the record he's holding?"

"'White Satin,'" said Billy.

"Name Paul's younger brother and the groups he performed with."

"Michael McCartney," Alex said as he fiddled with the machine. "Although he performed under the name of Mike McGear. The groups were Grimms and Scaffold. I have two of their records, 'Rockin' Duck' and 'Fresh Liver.' Great stuff."

"Where and when did John and Paul first meet?"

"July 6, 1957, at a fete at St. Peter's Parish Church in Woolton," Billy said. "John and his band, The Quarrymen, were playing and Paul heard them for the first time."

"What's the name of George's estate in England and who's the architect?"

"Friar Park Henley-on-Thames," Red answered. "Sir Frankie Crisp designed the castle on the property. George wrote a song about him for his three-record set 'All Things Must Pass.'"

"Which Elton John single has a live version of a Beatles' song on the B side and where was it recorded?"

"I used to have that 45," Grant said. "'I Saw Her Standing There' was on the flip side of 'Philadelphia Freedom.' But I don't know where it was taped."

"Madison Square Garden in 1974," Scott answered. "John came onstage as part of a bet. He said he'd perform with Elton if John's single 'Whatever Gets You Through the Night' reached number one, and it did."

"How many times did the Beatles play at The Cavern in Liverpool?"

"Two hundred ninety two," Alex replied.

Bunny frowned as she placed the questions back in the tote bag. "Gosh, do you think I made the questions too easy?"

"I'm ready when you are," Alex announced.

I tossed my now-empty paper plate into the wastebasket. Red shut the office door and everyone huddled around the desk. Alex pressed the "play" button. The tape unrolled through the pathway and onto the larger take up reel. My pulse raced and I turned my head so my good ear faced the machine's speaker. Alex turned up the volume.

The tape played nothing but indecipherable gibberish.

"Is that a foreign language?" Bunny asked.

"I know Spanish and French," said Alex, "but I've never heard anything like this."

"Doesn't make any sense," Scott said.

"Maybe the tape's damaged," Art suggested.

"No, it looks all right to me," Alex said.

The tape ran until the last inch rolled off the reel. Alex clicked the "stop" button and leaned back in his chair. "That's all, folks."

"We have more of a mystery now than when we started," said Grant.

"Waste of time," Billy scoffed.

I pressed my fingertips together, held them near my face and pondered. Something about the nonsense on the tape nagged at my memory. Somewhere I'd heard a similar sound.

"Thanks for your time, Alex." Red opened the door to leave. "I guess that clue was a bust. Let's all get back to—"

"Wait a minute!" I exclaimed. "I have an idea."

"What is it, Sandy?" Bunny asked.

"Play the tape backwards."

❖ CHAPTER SEVENTEEN

Tell Me What You See

"BACKWARDS?" ALEX ASKED.

"Yes," I insisted. "Don't rewind the tape. Leave it on the take up reel, flip it over and play it."

"What a screwy idea," Billy said.

"No, it isn't. The Beatles used the same technique. Remember their song 'Rain?' I heard it a few minutes ago in the dealers' room. The song ends with a snippet of tape inserted backwards. It sounds garbled, like this tape."

Red nodded. "It's worth a try."

Alex reversed the reels as I suggested and hit "play" again. This time we heard a man's voice, distorted but audible, along with weird spooky noises in the background.

"You know who this is," the voice warned. "Drop it or you'll be sorry. Stay away from Evansville or that'll be your final concert. This is your last warning."

The tape ran out and slipped around on the reel. Alex stopped the tape and we stared at the machine. Bunny trembled and I touched her shoulder. She jumped.

"Sorry, Bunny, I didn't mean to startle you."

"That tape!" she said. "It's creepy!"

"Anyone recognize the voice?" I asked. No reply. "Alex, is there any way you can filter out the voice on the tape so we can tell who it is?"

"Sure, if I had the right equipment, but I don't."

"What did he mean by 'drop it?'" Grant asked. "Drop what?"

"Drop the gig in Evansville," Billy said. "Red and Bunny and me looked at a bunch of bands for the convention. Maybe one of those other groups got mad 'cause we didn't hire them."

"That's stupid," Scott said. "Musicians don't kill for gigs."

"Besides," Art said, "if a guy's mad at the band, he'd send a tape to everyone, not just one of us, right?"

"What about Hank?" Grant suggested. "He was furious when we kicked him out of the last show. Maybe he didn't want us taking this gig."

"Does Hank know how to record tapes?" I asked.

"Unfortunately, yes. He dreams up these terrible Beatles parodies and sends us tapes of him singing them."

I asked how Hank submitted his demos and the answer was—you guessed it—on reels.

"Who was that kid who barged in on our rehearsal yesterday?" Scott asked. "The one who thinks he's John Lennon? He said he hates tribute bands. Maybe he sent the tape."

"You mean Winston?" Bunny said. "He'd never hurt anyone. He seems like a gentle soul."

"Sometimes the quiet ones are the most dangerous," I said.

"But the tape—"

"A fanatic like Winston would have an expensive stereo system," Alex said. "He lives for the music. He probably makes tapes of himself singing along with the records."

I offered another opinion. "Maybe the voice on the tape wants Dana to drop his engagement. Elizabeth told me about a jealous guy named Jason Wilcox."

Billy said the only Jason registered at the convention was fifty-six years old and lives in Cincinnati. He couldn't mail a packet from Illinois. And this Jason was happily married.

"What about Ralph?" Scott asked. "Maybe he wanted Dana to drop out of the band and work with him. A guy who's smart enough to set up a meth lab can figure out how to run a tape machine."

Alex removed the tape from the machine. "I think we should turn this over to the police."

I grabbed the reel and said I'd take care of it, although I had no intention of letting Braxton get his paws on it. Since nobody could decipher the clue of the mysterious tape, the band members left to set up for rehearsal. Alex carried the tape machine to his car, and Red and Billy stepped into the outer room to inspect the food supplies.

That left Bunny and me alone in the inner room. I pulled up a chair to the desk and pushed aside a stack of papers. Bunny sort out her photos in neat stacks of the different convention events she had photographed. When she came to the crime scene pix, she gasped.

"Don't look if it upsets you," I said.

"No, I can take it." She sat down in a chair beside me.

Billy came in and look over my shoulder. "What's that?"

"None of your business." I turned my back to him to block his view.

From the other room Red called, "Billy, I told you get more ice."

"I want to see the pictures!" The kid knelt down beside me and rested his arms on the table.

"You better go take care of the ice," I said.

Billy stuck his hands in his pants pockets. "I don't have my room key. I forgot it. I'm locked out of my room."

Red entered the room. "What does that have to do with getting ice?"

"Nothing. I'm just saying."

"So go to the front desk and ask for another key. Honestly, Billy, do I have to tell you how to do everything?" Red peeked around Bunny. "Is that a picture of a dead man?"

I sighed. Trying to keep secrets from this group was harder than crashing an Oscar Night party in Hollywood.

"You can't breathe a word of this to anyone," I said to the guys. "What we talk about stays right here in this room."

"The pictures, they aren't too good," said Bunny.

She was far too modest. In spite of the low lighting and shooting from a distance, the pictures turned out remarkably sharp. I picked up a photo and studied Dana's body lying face up on the floor. For a moment the grisly scene brought back bad memories of that fateful evening.

"What are you looking for, Sandy?" Bunny asked.

"I'm not sure. Anything out of place. There's something on the floor by the body." I pointed. "See those shiny specks on the carpet?"

She pushed her glasses up on her nose and squinted through the lenses. "Yeah, but what is it?"

"When I walked into the room I stepped on something that made a crunching sound. I wished we could enlarge the photo so I could see."

"Would a magnifying glass help?"

"Yes, except I don't have one."

"I do."

Resourceful Bunny apparently carried a complete crime lab in her Yellow Submarine tote bag. She reached in the bag, took out a gold compact and opened it. One side of the compact had a regular mirror and the other side held a magnifying lens. Bunny handed the compact to me and I positioned the enlarging lens over the photo. In the glass the image appeared reversed, but larger.

"Looks like bits of broken glass," I said.

Red leaned over for a closer look. "Broken glass? Like from a broken bottle?"

"I don't think so. A broken beer bottle would leave bigger pieces and the glass would be brown, not clear like this. Besides, dropping a beer bottle on a carpet wouldn't break it." I knew all about broken glass, especially after my arrest last year during a bar fight in Hollywood when my face intercepted with the business end of a broken bottle.

"Maybe the killer busted out the window to get in the room?" Billy offered.

"Don't be silly," Bunny said. "Nobody's gonna climb three stories up the side of the hotel."

"I heard three gunshots that night," I pondered. "One bullet hit Dana. Maybe the second shot hit something made of glass and broke it. But that still leaves the third shot unaccounted for."

Red said, "Maybe the bullet hit a wall or the furniture."

"Or the killer," I said. "Maybe Dana fired first and wounded the killer. I bet the cops didn't bother to test Dana's hand for gunshot residue."

"I got an idea! Maybe the injured guy, he went to a hospital for first aid."

"Good thinking, Bunny. How many hospitals are in town?"

"Three. Deaconess, Welborn and St. Marys. He wouldn't go to an urgent care 'cause they're closed late at night."

"Can you call the hospitals and see if anyone came in Friday night with a gunshot wound?"

Bunny agreed as I picked up another photo, a close up of Dana's face. My stomach churned, but I forced myself to hold the magnifying lens over the print.

"He has a big bruise on his face," I said.

"Maybe he hit his face when he fell down," Red said.

"No, can't be. I've fallen on my face plenty of times when I was drunk and never had a bruise like this. Look, one of the hotel ashtrays is on the floor. I remember kicking it out of the way when I came in the room."

"Dana smoked," said Bunny. "Maybe he was smoking when I died."

"The cigarette butts are scattered all over the floor. If Dana had the ashtray in his hand and dropped it, the butts would have fallen in a pile beside him. Besides, Dana didn't strike me as a clean freak. I doubt that he'd carry around an ashtray when he lit up. I never did when I used to smoke."

"So what does that provide?" Billy asked.

"I don't know." Exasperated, I tossed the photo onto the table. "Maybe nothing."

Before I could deduct some more, a group of female fans barged into the suite. They greeted Bunny and one of them exclaimed, "Whatcha got there, Bunny? Are those pictures of the convention? Let's see them!"

My partner in crime-solving and I exchanged worried looks. She grabbed one of the other stacks of pictures and shoved them in the girls' faces. "Look, here's the Friday night dance!"

With the intruders distracted, I palmed the crime scene photos, stuffed them into my pants pockets and beat a hasty retreat.

❖ ❖ ❖ ❖ ❖

Some detective I was. I had enough suspects to stock a police line up and so many clues I could write an episode of *Diagnosis Murder*. Buddy Brave would crack this case in sixty minutes (minus commercials) but after two days Ernest Farmington was still baffled.

When I arrived at the Lancelot Room for band rehearsal, I climbed up a backstage ladder and inspected the catwalk to see if the Apple Bonker had planned another attack. The area was clear, so I came back down and strapped on the Rickenbacker. But I couldn't get the mystery tape out of my mind and the mystery had me so flustered I couldn't keep focused on the music. The way I muddled through the songs must have sent Lennon, may he rest in peace, spinning in his grave. (Yes, Beatle fans, I know Lennon was cremated, not buried. It's a figure of speech). My injured hand hurt and so did my brain. The songs blended together in my head until I couldn't tell "The Inner Light" apart from "Ob-la-di, Ob-la-da."

And to make matters worse, Detective Braxton came into the room to spread his good cheer. "Mr. Farmington, I need to see you."

I lowered my guitar and my blood pressure shot sky high. "What do you want now, detective?"

My worst nightmare approached the front of the stage. Two burly uniformed officers flanked him. They looked as if no one had fed them for two days and they were hungry for raw meat.

"This morning I called some of your connections in Los Angeles. I talked with your girlfriend, a Miss Helen Wheeler."

Whatever Braxton had to say to me about the psychotic woman, I didn't want the band to hear. I excused myself, set the Rickenbacker in the guitar stand and followed Braxton and his hounds into the hallway.

"Helen isn't my girlfriend. We broke up recently." Actually, I was the only one who ended the relationship. Helen still harbored some warped idea that she's still my one and only. "I wouldn't take anything she says as the truth."

"Miss Wheeler said you could easily become angry enough to kill someone."

"Detective, are you here to investigate Dana's death or to give me advice on dating? My personal life has nothing to do with the murder, unless Helen was sleeping with Dana. Which wouldn't surprise me. She probably ran out of men in L.A. to bed with. Did you drag me out of rehearsal to tell me Helen was spreading lies about me? Because I already knew that."

"Actually, Mr. Farmington, I came to search your room."

My heart flipped a quadruple somersault, but I kept a straight face. "Why?"

"To find evidence relating to the murder of Dana Mumford."

"You need a search warrant."

"Or your permission. You can voluntarily let me search your room or not. Of course if you refuse, I'll assume you have something to hide."

I despise people who shove me into a corner. Out of spite I could force the dick to cough up a warrant, but prolonging the inevitable would only increase my anxiety. I may as well get this over with so Braxton would leave me alone.

"I have nothing to hide. I'll let you in my room but before I do, can I get a witness?" For all I knew he might plant some evidence in my room so he could wrap up the case and relax for the rest of the holiday weekend.

At that moment Bunny came down the corridor with some of her friends. I called out and motioned for her to come over, as if my biggest fan needed any coaxing to get close to me.

"Hi, Sandy!" She glanced at the police. "What's going on?"

I spoke to her softly. "The cops want to search my room. I need you to come along and make sure they don't do anything sneaky."

Her happy face turned into a frown. "Okay."

She and I marched to the elevators with the Three Stooges on our heels. I felt like a condemned man walking the final mile to his place of execution. Our parade attracted attention from the convention people standing in the lobby. I hurried along before they could talk to me. The five of us crowded into a cab for the longest elevator ride of my life. Bunny started to speak, but I placed my finger on her lips to shut her up. In all innocence she might blurt out something incriminating. The cab stopped at the fourth floor and we made our way down the corridor.

As we approached my room, I said to Braxton, "The room's a mess. I didn't have time to clean up this morning."

He only offered a grunt in response. I unlocked the door and stepped back to let the cops in. The gorilla brothers pulled the mattresses off the beds, rummaged through the closet and dumped out the contents of my suitcase. I retrieved the ice bag from the bathroom with the intention of soothing my aching hand but the ice inside had melted. I left the bag in the sink and sat on the straight back desk chair. Bunny stood beside me. I kept my eyes locked on Braxton, noting his every move. As I silently fumed I punched my fist into my palm.

The flatfoot picked up the instrument case. "What's in here?"

"That's a guitar case," I said. "There's a guitar inside."

Honestly, how stupid is this guy? His musical appreciation probably ended with Muzak and *Hee Haw*. Braxton handed the case to a member of the wrecking crew, who placed it on bed, opened it and pulled out the guitar.

"Easy with that or you'll damage it." I stood up. "That's a delicate instrument."

The uniformed cop eyed me and poked his fingers into the sound hole.

"I'm not smuggling drugs, if that's what you're looking for."

Braxton scowled at me. "Mr. Farmington, we don't need your comments."

The cop inspected the guitar and the case. I worried he might tear the instrument apart in his eagerness to find contraband. I didn't breathe or sit down until after he replaced the guitar, undamaged, back in the case.

As the cops continued their probe, Bunny tugged on my sleeve. I brushed her off. She pulled again.

"Bunny, stop it."

Braxton glanced at me and resumed poking around in the desk drawer.

"Sandy!"

"Not now, Bunny."

"Sandy!" She sounded agitated, like a kid with an urgent need to use the bathroom.

"What is it?"

She looked terrified. "A thingy!" She pointed at the chair against the wall, her arm shaking. "A fiendish thingy!"

From beneath the chair a thin stream of black smoke poured from an oval-shaped container.

I jumped to my feet. "Everyone out of the room! It's a bomb!"

❖ CHAPTER EIGHTEEN

Nowhere Man

ONE OF THE officers intercepted me. "You can't leave until we're finished."

I nodded towards the plume of smoke rising from under the chair. "If we don't leave now, we're *all* finished!"

Braxton finally noticed the smoldering device and ordered us out. Bunny and I dashed from the room first, with the cops close behind. Braxton slammed the door behind him and yelled for us to get down. I flung one arm around Bunny's shoulders and threw her onto the carpet beside me —a move that Buddy Brave frequently used to save his pretty guest stars from close calls. I hid my face under my arm as a loud *boom*! echoed through the corridor. Streams of foul-smelling black smoke seeped out from beneath the door. The fumes almost choked me.

"Bunny, are you all right?"

She raised her head, coughed and nodded as I helped her to her feet. Some of the hotel guests stopped and watched. Braxton ordered them off the floor. He stood by the door for a moment in case of a second explosion, but nothing happened. He asked for my keycard, got it, and opened the door. Foul smelling smoke spewed out and Braxton waved it aside as best he could. He told me to stay in the hall, so naturally I followed him inside the room. I gagged on the putrid smoke and my eyes watered. I covered my mouth and nose with my handkerchief so I could breathe. The cops tried to open the windows to let out the smoke, but the panes were stuck and wouldn't budge. The smoked began to dissipate through the door and out into the hallway.

The furniture and my belongings appeared intact—the bomb only spewed smoke, not destruction. Braxton found the phone and called for the bomb squad. After he hung up, he got down on his hands and knees and peered under the chair at the remains of the explosive device. Bunny eased into the room and stood by me.

Braxton stood up and eyed me. "What's the meaning of your little stunt?"

I lowered my handkerchief. "You think *I* set off that stink bomb? You're crazy!"

"Then who did?"

"The same guy who dumped apples on me yesterday."

Braxton squinted an eye at me. "Mr. Farmington, I don't know whether to put you in jail or the nut house. What are you talking about?"

I summarized Saturday's ferocious fruit attack and Bunny corroborated my story.

"So you dodged a few apples," Braxton said, unsympathetic to my plight. "Someone pulled a prank, that's all. One of those nutty people at your convention."

"Detective, you don't understand," I said. "Someone's trying to kill me!"

He crossed his arms and surveyed the smoke hovering in the room. "Apples and a stink bomb. Not very effective murder weapons, are they? Mr. Farmington, you'll have to do better than that."

"All right then, Braxton, how did I set off the bomb? I was sitting on the other side of the room."

"Either you rigged a trip wire for it to go off when we entered the room, or you have a remote control device hidden on your person."

"How did I know you'd be in my room today?"

"You set it up this morning as a precautionary matter to protect whatever you're hiding."

I clenched and released my fists. "I'm a musician. I don't know how to set off bombs."

"Yes, you do, Sandy," Bunny said. "Remember the *Buddy Brave* episode, 'The Gruesome Gang Caper?' You buried a bunch of dynamite around the villain's hideout and set it off as a diversionary tactic."

"Bunny, that was a TV show! I was following a script! And those were fake bombs that I used! The special effects guys set off the real explosives, not me!"

Just when my life couldn't get any worse—it did. The hotel manager stomped into the room. "Who made this mess!" He coughed. "My asthma!" He jabbed his finger at me. "You! The kook from L.A.! Did you do this?"

"No!"

"This is your room, isn't it?"

"Yes, but I didn't—"

Braxton interrupted. "Mr. Bluefield, I have the situation under control."

The Blue Meanie ignored him and continued his tirade at me. "I'm charging you for the cleanup expenses."

"That isn't fair," I said. "Find out who set the bomb and make *him* pay."

Bluefield put his fists on his hips and stared me down. "I want you out of my hotel!"

"Believe me, there's nothing I'd rather do than get on the next flight back to L.A., you Blue Meanie."

The manager furrowed his brow. "What did you call me?"

Braxton jumped into the fray. "Mr. Farmington is staying right here until I finish my investigation."

Bluefield turned to the detective. "This man's a menace to my business. He's been nothing but trouble all weekend."

"I agree with you on that, Mr. Bluefield, but for now he stays."

"He has to go!"

I held up my hands in resignation. "While the two of you fight this out, may I please go and rehearse for the show tonight? I really need to practice."

The sourpuss shamus glared at me. "All right, but don't leave the hotel."

Before Braxton changed his mind I grabbed the guitar case and hotfooted out of room, with Bunny right behind me. We rode the elevator down to the lobby. Something in the cab smelled rotten—I did. The smoke had penetrated my duds. I needed a change of clothes in the worst way, but I didn't dare return to my room until the mean cop and Blue Meanie had both cleared out.

"If you're looking for a place to play," Bunny said, "you can use my room. It's empty 'cause Trish and I, we're both going on the trip to Angel Mounds."

"Thanks, but I'm dying to go outside. I've been cooped up inside this building since Friday and I think I'm going out of my mind."

"Just like The Beatles in 'A Hard Day's Night.' They got tired of sitting in hotels and dressing rooms so they ran outside to play in a field as the soundtrack played 'Can't Buy Me Love.'" Except that my life didn't come with a musical backdrop and might not conclude with a happy ending. "But the detective told you not to leave the hotel."

I made a nasty comment about what Braxton could do with his order.

The cab door opened on the ground floor. The bomb squad, decked out in padded protective suits and carrying cases of gear, was waiting to get on.

"Gentlemen, you want the fourth floor," I said as Bunny and I disembarked.

We passed through the lobby and down a hallway that led to the back of the hotel. Up ahead hung an exit sign, the most welcoming sight I'd seen all day.

Bunny continued our conversation. "I don't mind staying indoors most of the time."

"How can you stand it?"

"I'm used to it. It's the weather, I guess. Winter is too cold and icy to go outside. Spring rains all the time and summer's too hot and humid. I bet it's nice in L.A. all the time, isn't it, except for the earthquakes."

Yes, the common stereotype. People think the West Coast is constantly vibrating from the daily earth tremors.

"I almost forgot," she continued. "Red gave me a message to give to you in case I saw you first. He checked on the phone calls to Dana's room on Friday night. He got a couple of calls from Indy and one from the hotel lobby. What's that all about?"

"I think Dana's killer called him Friday before he came to the room."

"So the murderer called from the lobby. He wouldn't have time to drive down if he phoned from Indy."

"Yes, but that doesn't help us. With the convention going on, dozens of people must have used the lobby phones. Someone might have walk in off the street to call. Someone who was already checked in might have phoned from the lobby so the call couldn't be traced to his room." *And what about Scott? He had a keycard to Dana's room, so he wouldn't need to call at all.* "So much for that lead. Bunny, do you have any idea who broke into my room and planted that bomb?"

"I don't know, Sandy. I didn't tell anyone which room you were in."

"But we switched rooms, remember? Who knew about that?"

"I never told anyone I changed rooms with *you*. I said the hotel mixed up my reservation, that's all. But nobody wants to hurt you, Sandy. Everybody likes you."

Obviously one person hates my guts.

We stepped outside into the blistering heat and glaring sunlight. I silently cursed myself for not picking up my sunglasses on my way out of the room. In the parking lot a charter bus idled nosily, spewing exhaust fumes from the tailpipe. The people inside the bus, all wearing convention nametags, waved and shouted at Bunny.

"Be right with you!" she called. To me she said, "I'm the tour guide for the trip. Before I forget to tell you, I called the hospitals and asked about gunshot patients for Friday night."

"And?"

"Nothing."

Damn! That ruined my best theory. "That can't be right. I'm positive one of the bullets hit the killer."

The bus driver honked the horn. Bunny motioned for him to wait. "I got to go now, Sandy. Sure you don't want to come along with us? We'd sure love your company."

"Sorry, but this guitar needs me even more. One more thing, Bunny. What's a 'fiendish thingy?'"

She grinned. "It's from the movie 'Help!' The mad scientist put a bomb in a curling stone while the boys were playing on the ice. George sees the bomb smoking and he called it a 'fiendish thingy.' Don't you remember?"

"Afraid not. I haven't watched the movie in a long time." What rotten luck—a Beatles film buff with a deranged sense of humor was stalking me.

She touched my hand and looked at me with genuine alarm in her eyes. "Be careful, Sandy."

I smiled as I patted her hand. "Don't worry about me. I'll be safe. You go on and have a good time."

Bunny climbed on the bus and I, with guitar in hand, hurried across the street towards the river. The humidity hung in the air like a wet blanket. Since I hadn't put on any sunscreen, the sun was baking my bare arms like pieces of toast. But at least I was outdoors, breathing fresh air, looking at a clear, blue sky and away from demanding fans and nosey cops.

I raised a hand to shield my baby blues from the sun and searched for a place to practice. The riverfront was practically deserted, save for an elderly couple out for a stroll, a dog walker and some smokers with convention nametags. Across the street in Dress Plaza stood an interesting structure. Atop a small mound terraced with grassy steps stood four huge stone pillars that punched the sky. A plaque identified the structure as the Four Freedoms Monument, dedicated to free speech and religion as well as freedom from want and fear. Fifty waist-high pedestals, one for each state, encircled the pillars. On the side of the hillock facing the river I sat down on one of the steps. Back home I liked to hang out at the beach, watching the crowds, the sailboats, the seagulls and the Pacific Ocean that stretching endlessly into the horizon. The riverfront in Evansville offered crows overhead, tugboats pushing a barge downstream and the Kentucky shore a few miles away. But no mobs and little noise, a quite place to sit and reflect. This nutty little town was starting to grow on me.

Sitting in the open left me an easy target for the killer. A sniper could easily hide in the nearby apartment buildings or crouch behind one of the monument columns. A plane flew overhead and I raised my arm to protect myself against falling apples. The paranoia was killing me. I shook my head to clear out the craziness and unpacked the guitar. Fortunately the stink bomb didn't hurt the instrument. I tuned up and ran through the songs for the show. Then my fingers idly plucked a riff while I thought about Dana's death. Which one of my suspects did it?

Scott admitted he didn't like Dana. He had no alibi for Friday night but he had been on stage during the apple attack and Scott probably knew nothing about setting bombs.

Valleri was in Dana's room the night he died. Although some phone calls came through to Dana's room, Valleri might be lying about what Dana said on the phone. She was beefy enough to carry all those apples and mean enough to bully a passkey from a maid to get into my room to set up the bomb.

Maybe Hank intended to pick off the band members one by one but was foiled after he bumped off Dana. But why the bomb in my room? Possibly my playing with the guys made me a target. Or maybe he hated bubblegum music. I've met hard rock fans that would rather pierce their eardrums than listen to my pop ditties.

What about the phantom Jason? I wished I'd asked Elizabeth for a description of the guy. I might have seen him this weekend and never known it. Checking the hotel registrations wouldn't help. Someone smart enough to construct a bomb with a trigger mechanism wouldn't be dumb enough to sign in under his real name.

Ralph? He seemed like a long shot, but a guy sick enough to deal in drugs wouldn't have any moral scruples regarding murder. A guy who cooked up meth could easily make a bomb.

I refused to consider Bunny, but in the movies the killer was usually the character nobody suspected. She was in my room before the bomb went off, but she warned me in plenty of time that she could escape. Maybe she was cozying up to me all weekend as ploy to win my trust.

And what about Winston?

He was walking along the riverfront, his sneakers slapping the water as it kissed the shoreline. He stared down at his feet and swung his arms defiantly. The earphones on his head were wired to a portable tape player clipped to his belt. He was dressed in blue jeans and a T-shirt printed with "Working Class Hero." His convention badge hung around his neck but was tucked under his shirt.

I waved at him and called for him to join me. He stopped and pushed the headphones down around his neck.

"Sit down. I'd like to talk to you."

He hesitated for a moment. "Sure, I'll give it a bash." At least he sounded more cooperative than Valleri.

"Nice day for a walk, isn't it?"

"Yeah." He sat on the grassy step by me and gazed off at the river, avoiding eye contact.

"Are you coming to the concert tonight?"

"It's not my bag, man. I don't do that scene."

"I think you'll enjoy it."

"Why do I need fake music when I can listen to the real thing?" He patted his tape player. Through the earphones came the faint sounds of Lennon's "Jealous Guy."

My investigation was going nowhere fast. Recording a Grammy-winning album at my age might prove easier than prying a conversation out of Winston. "I see you're playing hooky from the convention. I thought you'd be at the trivia contest. You'd probably win. You seem to know a lot about John Lennon."

"Sometimes I like to think. You know, be by myself and think." He turned off the tape machine and watched a motorboat zip down the river. I wished he'd do less thinking and more talking.

"What did you do this morning?" As soon as I said it, I realized how stupid I sounded. If Winston had set the bomb, he wouldn't admit to it outright.

"Keeping busy, you know, talking to the people about peace and love. How we'll never have peace as long as we all buy into the military industrial complex that runs the country. The people have the power, not the government and not the politicians." For several minutes he rambled on incoherently as I nodded and muttered "uh huh" occasionally. His eyes kept sliding off of me.

"If all the people rose up and made their voices heard, we'd have peace. That's what John and Yoko were trying to say at the bed-in at Toronto, but nobody listened. The press was too caught up in the happening to listen and that's the trouble with fame. Some people can't get past John the famous singer to hear John the activist. That's what killed him—the evil man who thought he could grab a piece of John's fame for himself."

I couldn't get any answers about Dana's death as long as Winston kept channeling the lost Beatle. Somehow I had to smash through his façade.

"I heard you sing at the Friday night dance, Winston. You're good." I held out the guitar. "Would you like to play something?" He looked at me, puzzled. "Go on, play anything you want."

"Why?"

"Because that's what Lennon would do. He never passed up an opportunity to make music."

I knew he couldn't resist a challenge like that. The kid took the instrument, strummed with his right hand and made a terrible sound.

"Excuse me, I forgot the instrument's set up for a lefty." I retrieved the guitar. "Tell you what, I'll play and you sing. What would you like to sing?"

His eyes sparkled. "'The Ballad of John and Yoko.'"

What else would I expect from a Beatle wannabe except Lennon's lament over his struggle to marry Yoko and the media circus that tagged along. Winston told me the chords and I strummed, singing along on the second verse. By verse three Winston loosened up and we had a good time with the rest of the song. Next we tore through "Mind Games" and "Watching the Wheels." After the third song I packed up the guitar. As much as I loved singing, I needed to squeeze some information from my suspect. The boy sleuth was hot on the trail.

"Let's take a walk," I said.

I picked up the guitar case and we moseyed along the shore as the tugboats tooted their whistles. "How long have you been a Beatles fan?"

"All my life. Ever since I can remember. Me mum had all the old records and she played them for me. In fifth grade we had to write a report on the person we admire the most. I wrote about John and got an A. In high school I wrote a short story about John and Yoko starting their own art gallery. Got an A on that too. Only times I ever got an A in English class."

"Did your father like The Beatles?"

"Don't know. He left home when I was three."

Lennon was three years old when his own father left the family and the Liverpool lad didn't see his dad again for twenty years. Was Winston's fixation with Lennon an attempt to find a father figure?

"It's tough to lose someone you love, isn't it?" I asked.

"Never knew me dad. Can't say that I loved him."

"I didn't know Dana Mumford either, but I liked him. It's a shame the way he died. Shot down in cold blood, just like John."

Winston stopped walking and scowled at me. "No! Not like John! Dana wasn't murdered by a man who said he was a fan."

"Now how would you know that?"

The kid stared at me in shock and then turned his head away. I held my breath. Had I pushed him too far? Someone as emotionally fragile as Winston could easily snap.

He said, "Everyone was at the movie when Dana died, right? And those were his fans."

"You didn't watch the film. Where did you go after you left the dance?"

He bit his lip and scrunched up his eyes as if searching for an alibi. "I went on a walk. That's what I did. That's what John did when he lived in New York City. He walked around the city a lot and nobody bothered him."

I didn't believe a word he said. "You took a walk through downtown, alone, late at night? That's not safe. You're lucky nobody mugged you."

Winston set the headphones back on his ears and switched on his tape player. I pulled the 'phones off his head. "Did you kill Dana?"

He shrugged and smiled. "I couldn't do that. John would never do that. Love and peace, he always said. He wouldn't hurt—"

I set down the guitar and grabbed the kid by both arms. "I am not talking about Lennon, I'm talking to *you*. Whoever you are, whatever your real name is, I want *you* to answer me. John Lennon isn't here, *you* are. I want to know what *you* did. Now talk to me!"

Winston's lower lip trembled and his eyes moistened. I lowered my hands and he turned his head away. He removed his glasses and wiped his eyes and runny nose with the back of his hand before putting the spectacles back on.

I said gently, "What's your name, son?"

"Charlie," he muttered. "Charlie Merkle."

"Charlie, did you kill Dana?"

"No, no, no. Please, Mr. Fairfax, I didn't do it. It wasn't me. I'd never ever kill nobody."

"You didn't go on a walk Friday night, did you?"

"No." His voice was barely audible.

"What did you do?"

He sank down on his heels and I squatted beside him on the shore. He drew lines in the damp earth with his finger as he talked. "I left the mixer and hung out in the lobby. I asked some girls if they wanted to go to the dance with me but they said no. Some people were going out to a nightclub and I asked if I could go with them but they said no. I went to my room and called some people I knew and asked if we could do something, but all of them had other plans."

He scooped up a handful of wet sand in his hand, squeezed it and let the grains trickle through his fingers. "So I went to the video room down in the basement and watched the films. I was the only person in the room, 'cause the projectionist had set up an extended-play video and left for the night. I fell asleep and didn't leave the video room 'till morning. Guess that's not a good alibi, but that's what I was doing when Dana died. I was the only person in town who didn't have a friend on Friday night."

For a few minutes we sat in silence, watching the sun glint off the water as the crows cawed overhead.

I stood and picked up the guitar. "C'mon, it's getting late. Let's get back to the action." He rose, wiped his dirty hands on the seat of his pants and walked beside me as we headed for the hotel. "Why are you so obsessed with John Lennon's death?"

"Everything in the world died that night."

"You're still alive."

"Yeah, so what?"

"You don't see the three surviving Beatles giving up, do you?"

"John Lennon was somebody great. I'm nothing."

"I don't believe that. Everybody's worth something."

"I'm not as talented as John."

"Who is? He was one of a kind. *You're* one of a kind. You can't do what he did, but you can do plenty. Charlie, you've got to stop hiding behind another man's name."

He looked at me. "You don't use your real name."

"Don't change the subject. All I am saying is give people a chance to know Charlie. They'll like you. I know they will."

We reached the back doors of the hotel. I thought Charlie might be angry—I'd pushed him hard—but when he spoke, he sounded curious and childlike. "How do I act like myself?"

"I don't know, but I'll tell you this—John Lennon was always honest. He valued honesty above all else. So be true to yourself. That's the highest tribute you can pay to the man."

I pushed the door open to let Charlie through first. A group of convention fans stood inside. "Oh, hi, Winston," one of them teased. "How's John Lennon doing today?"

He shot me a look of distress. I nodded and smiled. His voice sounded pained as he spoke to the fans. "Uh . . . you don't know this, but . . . my name's Charlie."

I walked away, confident in his ability cope. But my euphoria soon faded. Red ran up to me, distraught and out of breath.

"Sandy! There you are! Where have you been! I've been looking everywhere for you! Have you heard the bad news?"

As if I needed more difficulties this weekend. "What's the matter now? Did the Apple Bonker strike again?"

"Worse than that. The Blue Meanie shut down the convention and cancelled the concert."

❖ CHAPTER NINETEEN

With A Little Luck

OF ALL THE possible dire events, I never saw that one coming. I thought I had a few more hours of sleuthing available. Once the convention ended, the suspects would scatter, I'd never find the killer and Braxton would lock me up in chains.

"What do you mean, cancelled?" I asked.

"Mr. Bluefield said everyone associated with the convention had to leave the hotel immediately. Said Dana's murder is causing too much commotion."

I frowned. "He can't blame that on *us*!"

The foot traffic around us picked up. Red glanced at the gathering crowd and ducked through a doorway marked "Employees Only." I followed him into an empty hallway lined with storage rooms. A flickering florescent tube in the ceiling cast intermittent lighting. Red, being a few inches shorter than myself, craned his neck look up at me.

"The manager said if we don't leave right away, he'd call the police. I can't let the fans get in trouble with the cops. That's a rotten way to end a convention."

I set down the guitar. "Look, Red, in my career I've never, ever missed a show, not when I had a hundred-and-one-degree fever and was throwing up backstage and not when I sprained my wrist and sang with my arm in a sling. The boys and I have put too much effort into this concert. I have too much at stake for some stinking murderer to shoot down my show."

"But where would we go? We can't book another venue at the last minute."

I stared at the wall and tried to clear my head so I could get a handle on this bizarre merry-go-round of a weekend. I chewed my thumbnail. I craved a drink so badly I nearly gnawed my hand off.

"The Blue Meanie said we have to leave the hotel. What if we go *outside* the building? What about the courtyard in the back?"

"He doesn't want to see or hear us at all. I'm sorry, Sandy, but I don't know what we can do. I think we better forget it and get back home where we belong."

The last part of that sentence triggered something in my befuddled brain. I remembered another band, all those years ago, playing "Get Back" atop a building.

"Can we get up on the roof?" I asked.

"The roof? What roof?"

I jerked my thumb toward the ceiling. "Up there. That roof."

"Why would we want to—oh!" Red grinned as he figured it out. About time. "You mean the Mersey Marvels play on the roof like The Beatles did at the end of their movie *Let It Be* when they performed their last live concert from the rooftop of the Abbey Road studio."

"Yes, just like The Beatles."

"I don't know, Sandy. I don't think Mr. Bluefield will like it."

"So don't tell him. Pretend you're packing up the band equipment to leave and sneak it upstairs. We can probably play for at least an hour before the Blue Meanie finds out."

I could see the *Courier* headlines now: OVER-THE-HILL TEEN IDOL IN SLAMMER FOR CRIMINAL CONCERT—*Forgotten star goes through the roof playing his swan song.*

Red asked, "What if the roof doesn't have any electrical outlets for the instruments?"

"Then we'll play unplugged. Come on, Red, we're wasting time. Go tell the band so they can get ready. And if Bluefield complains, tell me and I'll knock some sense into his pea brain."

"I'll do that. Thanks, Sandy."

Red started towards the hallway door and I checked my watch: three o'clock. I wasn't prepared for this concert. I desperately needed another group rehearsal.

As I picked up the guitar case, I heard the click of a door latch. One of the doors opened a crack. The top half of the door was frosted glass, with a silhouette of a person faintly visible through it. A thin hose poked through the opening. A stream of red paint shot through the pipe and doused me, head to toe. I dropped the case, ducked my head and raised my hands to cover my face.

"What the—!" I wiped the goo from my eyes and shook the sticky glop from my bare arms. The paint dripped off my hair and ran down my face.

Red stared at me. I expected him to laugh—I'm sure I looked ridiculous—but he didn't. "Sandy!" I never heard a man's voice screech so high. "Get down! Get down!"

"What?"

He ran down the hall and tackled me (did this guy play football?). He knocked me down on my back and pressed my shoulders to the cold tile floor.

"Red! Get off! I mean it!" He had me pinned in one heck of a compromising position.

"Sandy! Stay down!"

I tried to wriggle my arms free, but this guy was strong. "Red, if you don't get off me in two seconds, I'll—"

Something flew through the air over our heads with a loud whoosh! and slammed into the wall. Red got off me and stood up, grabbed my hand, and helped me to my feet. A long, curved East Indian scimitar was embedded in the wall right where I had stood a moment ago. The sword wobbled in the woodwork.

"Are you hurt?" he asked.

Covered in red paint, I looked like an actor in a slasher movie, but at least I wasn't sliced and diced. "No, I'm in one piece. You saved my life, Red. Thank you. And you're looking colorful too."

When Red landed on me, some of the red paint had rubbed off on him. He inspected his clothes. "My wife gave me this shirt for my birthday! She'll kill me!"

I jerked my head towards the weapon in the wall. "Speaking of killing, how did you know about this?"

"It's a scene right out of the movie *Help!* An Eastern cult that worships the goddess Kaili chases Ringo because he's wearing the sacrificial ring. But before they can kill him, they first color him red. When I saw the paint, I knew what was coming next."

Apple Bonkers, fiendish thingys and now the knives of Kaili. The writers on my TV show never dreamed up such zany plots.

"What's this?" I untied a piece of string holding a slip of paper to the knife handle. I unfolded the paper and read the message, typed in all caps: DANA IS DEAD. LET IT BE. STOP INVESTIGATING. I showed the paper to Red.

"This guy can't send me a letter in the mail?"

Red's eyes grew wide as he read the threat. "Should we call the police?"

"Are you kidding? You tell Braxton about Kaili and sacrificial rings and he'll fit us both with straightjackets."

"Too bad the knife thrower typed the message," Red observed. "If the handwriting matched the words on that envelope with the mystery tape, we'd have the killer."

The killer would easily fit a small printer or portable typewriter inside a suitcase or the trunk of a car. The police wouldn't search every vehicle or piece of luggage in the hotel. I had enough dead ends in this mystery to open my own subdivision. I stuck the paper in my pants pocket and studied the door, now closed, from where the attacker had sprayed me. Tiny globs of red paint glistened on the floor. I opened the door.

The room inside was lined with shelves of folded white sheets and towels. The wannabe Picasso had escaped through a door on the other side of the room. As much as I wanted to chase the cretin, I needed to clean up first. The stink bomb left me as fragrant as a compost heap and the paint made me look like a Jackson Pollock art piece. I returned to the scene of the crime and studied the blade stuck in the wall.

"That's an unusual weapon," I said.

"Looks exactly like the knives used in the movie. Excellent replica." Red sounded more like an enthusiastic collector than a convention host who nearly lost a guest star through decapitation.

"Did the attacker purchase the knife from the dealers' room? If so, the vendor could tell us who bought it."

"Nope. This afternoon I checked every table for fake merchandise and nobody had a knife like this. I'd remember it. The killer must of brought it with him."

Isn't it a pity. Why do people always poke holes into my brilliant theories? "Let's get out of here. I need a hot shower before fungus starts growing on my skin."

"You'll need this." Red gave me a keycard. "We moved you into another room. The one with the stink bomb won't air out for a couple of days." My third room in three days. Maybe I should camp out on the lawn in a pup tent. "Billy and Bunny and I moved your things into a room on the second floor. If anything's missing, please let me know."

"Bunny? I thought she went on the road trip."

"She changed her mind at the last minute and got off the bus before it left. She told me she wanted to stick around in case we had more problems. I'm glad she did."

Bunny? That meant she was in the hotel and could have attacked me. Acting out a scene from a Beatles movie would be right up her alley.

Red pulled the scimitar out of the wall and tucked it under his arm as we started for the lobby. "I'm adding this to my Beatles collection. If it's an authentic prop from the movie, it might be worth quite a bit." His face glowed with the special pride of a collector discovering a rare piece. "Unless you want it."

I held up a hand and drew back. "No, no, you keep it."

"Sandy, I talked with your manager. He said you can't perform the show unless we agree on your fee."

Red peeled a sticky note off his clipboard and handed it to me. The small yellow square had a figure written on it. When I saw the price, I blanched. Bunny and Red couldn't possibly afford to pay me this much. Normally I stay away from money matters and let Marshall do the haggling, but going through with this concert seemed more important than a paycheck.

"Don't worry about it," I said.

"But Mr. Ellis said—"

I crumbled the note and shoved it into my pocket. "We'll talk about it later. Right now I've got a show to do."

❖ ❖ ❖ ❖ ❖

As soon as I entered the lobby, I knew I should have taken a back route to my room. People tend to stare at me anyway, but today everyone stopped to gawk at my paint job. As tall as I am, I can't easily hide and today the lobby seemed more crowded than usual.

A few bold fans approached me. "Excuse me, Sandy, but why are you covered in paint?"

"No reason," I replied through clenched teeth.

Red and I separated, he to find the band members and me to run up the stairs to the second floor—waiting for the elevator would take too long. I quickly found my new room—by now I knew the hotel layout like a pro.

I slid the keycard halfway into the door slot and froze. Had the killer booby-trapped this room as well? Would I open the door and set off a rifle? Was the ceiling rigged to collapse on me? I pressed my good ear against the door and listened—no one was moving around inside. I pushed in the keycard and withdrew it rapidly. Nothing happened. I slowly pushed down on the door latch. Okay so far. I shoved the door open and jumped back to avoid any flying objects. A couple walking by eyed me curiously and moved on. I peered around the doorframe before I entered. I tiptoed around the room in slow motion, lifting my feet high and checking the floor for trip wires. I searched under the furniture and in the drawers for bombs. In the bathroom I turned on the tap to see if the water looked discolored, possibly poisoned. I'd reached new heights in paranoia.

My travel bag stood at the foot of the king-sized bed—at last, a decent sized bed. The kids had hung my clothes on the closet rod and placed my toiletries in the bathroom, disorganized but all accounted for. As I stripped down for a shower, I peeled off the paint-drenched Ace bandage from my left hand. The bruises had faded and my hand didn't hurt as much as the day before. I wasn't certain I could last through the show without a bandage, but this one was unusable and I didn't have time to find a fresh wrapping. I'd have to deal with any discomfort as best I could.

In the bathroom I opened a couple of packets of hotel soap, grabbed a complimentary washcloth and bottle of shampoo and settled down to business in the shower. To my relief, the paint rinsed right off under the hot water and suds. I panicked—had the killer rigged the shower water to heat up and scald me? Would the murderer rip off the shower curtain and slash me with a knife like in the movies? If I didn't find Dana's assassin soon, I'd worry myself into a nervous breakdown.

I tried to relax and focus my thoughts on the concert. As I bathed I ran through some vocal warm-ups to prep my voice. After the shower I felt revitalized and ready for the show. I put on my bathrobe, brushed my teeth, and combed and blow-dried my hair. As I tied the mane in a ponytail, I hummed a happy tune. I pulled the brown suit from the closet and my singing turned into a groan.

The suit was ruined.

Debris from the stink bomb had fallen on the suit and burned holes in the fabric. Ashes covered the clothing and the outfit smelled like an angry skunk. Not even a jiffy cleaning and repair service could salvage this mess in time. I had no other clothes suitable for the stage and no time to buy new ones. I considered opening a window, jumping to the ground and running away.

Before I could carry out the plan, someone knocked on the door.

"Go away!" I yelled.

"Sandy, it's me, Bunny," came a muffled reply from the other side of the door.

"I don't have time to talk with you now."

"I brought your clothes for the concert."

"My what?"

"What you're wearing for the show."

I opened the door and stood in the doorway without stopping to consider that I was wearing nothing more than my slippers, bathrobe and Jockies. That's me, always dressed for the occasion.

Bunny held a hanger and the costume on it made my eyes bug out—the most incredible recreation of John Lennon's uniform from the *Sgt. Pepper's* album cover. A fluorescent lime green satin long-sleeved band tunic decorated with red cording around the high collar and the front, cuffs and epaulets trimmed in red fringe, red cording hanging across the chest and red fringe around the tunic hem, along with a black T-shirt and matching line green pants.

"Where on earth did you get that?"

"From one of the vendors downstairs. When I moved your things from the other room, I saw that your suit was messed up. So I got this for you. How do you like it?"

"Bunny! I don't want you buying things for me! I can look out for myself!"

To my surprise, the meek and mild fan lost her temper. "Sandy, I *like* doing nice things for you. I wanted so much for you to have a good time this weekend but everything's gone wrong and I'm trying to make things better but you don't appreciate it. You must think we're all a bunch of dumb hicks out here. I went to all this trouble for you and you don't want it. Never mind, I'll take it back to the vendor and tell him it isn't good enough for you." She turned on her heel and started down the hall.

"Bunny! Come back here!"

She stopped and looked over her shoulder at me. I crocked my finger at her for her to come closer. She did. I lifted her chin with my finger and smiled.

"Don't be angry with me, Bunny. You can't help what's been going on around here. I've been under a lot of stress this weekend and I don't mean to take it out on you. I haven't been the kind of guest you were expecting. I'm sorry."

She blinked back the tears. "Sandy, I've looked forward to meeting you for so long and dreamed that when I did we'd have fun together and everything would turn out great. Just like in your movies."

Her sincerity touched me. "Let me see the clothes." She handed me the costume. "What if it doesn't fit?"

"Sandy! I have all the teen magazines about you and they list your measurements and clothing sizes. I told Trish your size and she altered the clothes."

I burst out laughing at the lunacy of it all—a fan remembering my vital statistics and those goofy teen mags from long ago saving my hide. Bunny giggled too, although not for the same reason. My bathrobe had gaped open a little in the wrong place. Blushing, I pulled the robe shut and tightened my terry cloth belt.

"Isn't this outfit too showy for the concert?" I asked.

"The band brought along their Sgt. Pepper's outfits too. They usually wear them in the second half of the show."

I draped the costume over one arm. "Thanks, Bunny. This is very kind of you. I'll get dressed and see you on the roof in a few minutes."

"Do you want something to eat? I know you usually like a light snack before shows. Can I get you anything?"

Now that she had mentioned it, I was famished. I'd only had some snack food since breakfast. She was right about the light snack—a heavy meal before a show makes me sluggish. I wait until after a concert before chowing down with a hearty dinner.

"The ground floor has some vending machines. Do they carry PowerPunch?"

"I'm not sure. I can check."

"Would you?" I placed the costume on the bed, fished a couple of bills from my wallet and handed her the money. "Get me a PowerPunch or any energy drink. Whatever you can find. At this point I'm not fussy."

"Do you want anything else?"

I lusted mightily for a stiff drink to get me through a show I felt totally unprepared for. I was tempted to ask Bunny to pick up a drink from the lounge, but she gazed at me with that you-can-do-no-wrong adoration and my resolve stiffened.

"No, thank you."

"I'll bring back the change."

"Keep it. Get something for yourself, you deserve it. Run along now."

After she left, I closed the door and tried on the costume. Son of a gun, the outfit fit perfectly. God bless Trish and Bunny and all the wonderful fans. I'll pay her for the clothes no matter how much she protests. And now, shoes. I could either wear my sandals, go barefoot, or put on the brown dress shoes that matched the ruined suit. The shoes looked odd with the lime green fabric, but at this point I didn't care. The pants were long enough to hide the shoes. I stuffed the crime scene photos and the tape reel into my pockets. I must be insane, heading out for a show with police evidence in my possession. When I left the room I made certain the door was locked behind me.

In the hallway I realized I had no idea how to get to the roof. I could look for Bunny and ask her, but I didn't want to march around the hotel looking like a neon Christmas tree. The most logical place for rooftop access was the top floor, so I headed for the elevator and pressed the "up" button. The elevator door opened and the cab was crammed full of fans wearing convention nametags, each one holding either a folding chair or a piece of band equipment. The cab exceeded the legal limit of permitted passengers, but nobody cared. I squeezed in between Prudence and a cute young fan who liked having me squashed against her. The door strained to shut behind me.

The fans spotted my band uniform and cheered. Some of them wolf whistled and the rest burst into a chorus of "We're Sgt. Pepper's Lonely Hearts Club Band." A wise guy in the back shouted, "Lookin' good, Sandy!"

Prudence pushed the top floor button. She held a clear plastic suit bag containing an orange satin band uniform with white trim for Grant. She wore a brightly colored '60s-style jumpsuit, love beads and silver peace-symbol earrings, right in style for a Beatles festival.

"You look handsome, Sandy," she said.

I smiled. "This old thing?" I glanced at the crowd around us. "Looks like everyone knows about the change in plans."

"When the fans heard the show was still on, they offered to pitch in and help set up."

"That's great. With everyone helping out, the concert should go on without a hitch."

She sighed. "I hope so."

"What's wrong?"

"It's Scott. He's been acting strangely today. He disappeared for a couple of hours this afternoon and he won't say where he went. And something else."

"What's that?"

"Ralph's here."

❖ CHAPTER TWENTY

Band On The Run

PRUDENCE STARTED TO say more, but I whispered, "Not here. We'll talk later." The eavesdroppers crowding in around us made me uncomfortable.

When the doors opened on the top floor, the mass of humanity poured out into the hallway. Prudence and I hung back so we could talk.

"Ralph," I said, "He's the guy in Dana's high school gang, right?"

She nodded. "I saw him in the lobby about an hour ago. He got on the elevator before I had a chance to stop and talk to him."

"Was Scott with him?"

"No, not when I saw him. I don't know how long Ralph's been in town. Maybe he's been here all weekend, but I only saw him today."

Ralph might be Scott's accomplice and alibi, the muscle behind the attacks on me and the triggerman for the murder.

"Does Scott usually disappear before a show?" I asked.

"No, the guys stick together during gigs so nobody gets lost or shows up late."

Prudence couldn't account for Scott's whereabouts at the time I was nearly nicked by a knife, which didn't prove anything, of course. Maybe Scott dashed over to the casino for a quick game of blackjack. Maybe he shacked up in his room with a female fan for some afternoon delight. Perhaps he took a nap. Or possibly the musician hid in a linen closet with a spray gun full of red paint.

I told Prudence about the knife attack. To my amazement, she said, "That sounds like something Hank would do."

"It does?"

"During the shows, whenever the band played 'Help!', Hank would jump up and yell, 'Kaili!' like the characters do in the movie when they're chasing Ringo. One time he actually threw a knife at Art."

"He did?"

"A plastic knife, but still, it's the principle. That's when the guys banned him from the shows. Grant was afraid that next time, Hank might use a real knife."

A door marked "Roof Access. Staff Only—No Admittance" opened to a short flight of steps leading to a heavy metal door. We stepped through the door and onto a roof covered in dust, dried bird droppings and litter left by other trespassers. The sun beat down cruelly. Inside the heavy satin costume I baked like a ham hock inside an oven. Large metal heating and cooling units dotted the rooftop. The fan blades inside the air conditioners roared. Between that and the traffic noise from the street below, the band would have to play at full tilt for anyone to hear us. So much for preserving the hearing in my good ear.

The roof was as flat as the Indiana countryside. Since nobody had put up a platform for the stage, the instruments were set up in an area marked off with duct tape. If the killer wanted to pick us off during the show, we made easy targets. The fans dropped off their cargo and returned downstairs for another load while other convention people arranged the chairs in rows facing the stage. Art adjusted his drum kit. Scott, squatting beside a monitor, plugged in cables. Some fans helped Grant put a large speaker in place. Prudence and I approached the guys—along with an unwelcomed guest.

"Hey, Beatles! You say hello, I say goodbye! How ya'll doin'!" Hank yelled loud enough for the folks in Kentucky to hear. He wore a white wife beater shirt and shorts that exposed a pair of ugly hairy legs. "Hey, this is crazy, a rooftop concert! So ya gonna play 'Get Back,' right? If you're on a roof, you gotta play 'Get Back.'"

Scott started to speak, but I stepped in to stop a potential blood bath. "We're busy setting up, Hank. Why don't you take a seat and stay out of our way?"

Hank noticed my costume and grinned. "Hey, look at you. Great threads! Buddy Brave joins the Sgt. Pepper's band! Are ya gonna sing? Huh? Huh?"

I wished I could prove that Hank was the killer so I'd have a good excuse to knock his block off. "Please, Hank, we're all very busy. Sit down and be quiet."

"Yeah, okay."

The early birds had claimed the front row of chairs, marking their spots by leaving a convention program or some other personal item on the seat. Hank plopped his keester on one such saved chair. Immediately a middle-aged woman came over to him.

"That's my seat," she said.

"I think it's mine." He leaned forward and rubbed his caboose. "See? It's on pretty tight."

"You're in my chair."

"Ain't got your name on it."

"You're sitting on my program and that has my name written on it."

Hank blew a raspberry at her.

Scott shouted, "Hank, give the lady back her chair."

"Awww, come on!" Hank protested.

"She helped us set up before you showed up. Now move your fat butt before I toss it off the roof."

Hank jumped to his feet and stood over Scott, his fists balled. "I dare ya!"

Scott stood up and faced Hank with that same mean look in his eyes that I saw when I challenged him on Saturday.

"Scott, please!" Prudence begged.

"I'm gonna get you!" Hank said. "You and every one of the Marvels!"

I grabbed Hank's arm, squeezed hard and steered him to the back row. I pushed him down into a chair and returned to the "stage." Was he planning to knock off the musicians during the show? Would the band play its last gig in rock 'n' roll heaven? Was I destined to become number one with a fatal bullet? I didn't see a gun bulge under Hank's T-shirt, but with his large hands he could easily strangle or beat a person to death.

The guys ran a quick sound check and Prudence set out stacks of folded white towels and bottles of water around the instruments. She pointed out Ralph to me. He was a thin man with dirty hair as well as the gaunt face and listless eyes of an addict. The man stood off to one side and didn't take part in setting up. He eyes twitched and he scratched his arm.

"Why is he scratching like that?" I asked.

"He lives out in the woods, so maybe he picked up some poison ivy," she replied.

Ralph looked weak, but a guy hopped up on drugs can turn strong and deadly. He sat down in one of the aisle seats, where he could easily make a getaway.

I put the man out of my mind and surveyed the stage setup, only a few feet from a sharp drop-off. "We're too close to the edge of the roof."

Scott said, "We're stuck here. If we move over there," he gestured towards the center of the roof, "those noisy air conditioners'll drown us out."

"I don't want anyone falling off the roof, that's all." *Especially me.*

"Nobody's gonna fall off the roof."

"Are you sure?"

Scott scowled at me for a long minute. "Yeah. I'm sure." He muttered something under his breath and stomped off.

Someone tapped my shoulder from behind and I nearly leaped out of my costume. I spun around. "Billy, don't ever sneak up on me like that again."

"Sorry. Bunny told me to give this to you." He handed me a lukewarm can of PowerPunch. In his other hand he carried his backpack.

"Where is she?" I popped the top and took a big swallow. The caffeine buzz hit my brain cells and I felt better.

"She's calling people to tell them concert's been moved up. Be tough if they showed up at eight tonight and no show."

"Yeah, real tough. What's in the backpack?"

"My stuff. I already checked out. I'm heading home right after the show."

"You're not helping Red and Bunny close out the convention?"

"Naw. They don't need me. There isn't much left to do."

I'm sure the organizers had plenty of cleanup duties left, but Billy wanted to scoot out and avoid any more work. He rambled on about how busy he'd been this weekend but I only half-listened to the kid. I was more interested in figuring out possible escape routes off the roof in case the murderer struck.

"Have you caught the killer yet?" he asked.

"What? No, not yet. A couple of my suspects washed out."

"Which ones?"

Billy didn't strike me as someone who could keep a secret. "It doesn't matter. Excuse me."

I hid behind one of the heating units to get psyched up for the concert. I never liked to interact with the audience before a show. Staying hidden made my entrances more spectacular and helped to build excitement among the fans. But I also needed privacy to deal with my nerves. I've performed before crowds of ten thousand and more but I'd never suffered stage fright as badly as I did now. I'd forgotten every note and lyric. Why was I so jittery? If I didn't finish this show, I'd never have the confidence to perform in public again. I reached in my pocket and fingered the piece of pottery. I couldn't let my kids see me as a failure.

I peeked around the corner of the metal box. The crowd looked about two hundred fifty, larger than the group at my Saturday appearance. The fans filled up seats and chattered anxiously among themselves. I can read an audience pretty well and this mob was wound tighter than the top E string on a guitar. I felt some weird vibes and took a deep breath to steady myself. Somehow I knew the murderer was here on the rooftop. And right now I'd kill someone for a drink.

I heard footsteps coming up behind me. The killer? I whirled around, holding out the empty PowerPunch can as a weapon. Then I regressed through a time warp as St. Pepper's Lonely Hearts Club Band stood before me. The guys sported fake wigs, sideburns and mustaches, identical to their counterparts on the album cover. All wore band costumes as elaborate as mine—Grant/"George" in an orange satin tunic and pants, Scott/"Paul" in blue and Art/"Ringo" in pink. I felt lost in a number nine dream. I expected Lucy in the Sky with Diamonds to waltz by with a plate of Scotch and cokes, jam butties and jelly babies.

"Didn't mean to startle you," Grant said in a Liverpudlian accent, which made his uncanny resemblance to George Harrison even more unsettling.

I waited a moment for him to break into a Hare Krishna chant, but he didn't. "You guys look like the real thing."

"Let's hope we sound like the real thing," Art drawled in his "Ringo" voice.

"Didn't mean to get on your wick earlier, Sandy," said Scott in a "Paul"-perfect voice. "We're all feeling a bit stroppy today."

"Sure, I understand."

Grant laid a hand on my shoulder and resumed his normal voice. "I know we're asking a lot out of you, Sandy, stepping in like this at the last minute. You don't have to go through with this show. If you don't want to play, you can leave and no hard feelings."

I set down the can and glanced at the exit door. I could go downstairs, get a bottle of wine, kick up my feet, relax and let the cops take care of the murderer. Who was I trying to fool? These guys could play better without me. But the time had come for this ex-lush to face the music.

"I'm ready. Let's do it."

A whine of feedback blasted from the speakers as Alex addressed the audience over a microphone. "Good afternoon, fellow Beatles fans. I want to thank all of you for your patience and your help in making the concert happen. We might experience some technical difficulties due to the circumstances, but please bear with us."

Bunny's voice came over the speakers. "We'd like to dedicate this concert to the memory of Dana Mumford. After the show I'll be collecting donations for his family. I hope all of you will be generous and give from the heart."

The bandmates huddled in a tight circle, facing inward with their arms on each other's shoulders. Art said to me, "Before a show we always do a group hug. Wanna join us?"

"Sure, why not?"

I'm not a touchy-feely guy, but a gathering of only three Beatles didn't look right. Besides, I needed their support to pull me through. I squeezed in beside Scott and Grant and placed my hands on their shoulders. The guys did a pep chant, bounced up and down and raised their arms in a rebel yell. By now my adrenaline—and anxiety—was so pumped up I could barely keep my feet on the ground.

Alex announced, "And now, fans, as we wind up our first ever Swingin' Sixties weekend, will you please give a terrific welcome to the best of the Beatles beat meisters, the most fabulous fab foursome, our favorite Hoosier tribute band . . . the Mersey Marvels!"

The guys ran to their instruments and I followed. The fans greeted us with tepid applause. I expected more noise from die-hard fans. Possibly they were tired from lugging band gear up the stairs, or ready to drop from the sun beating down on their heads, or waiting to see if we could actually pull this off. I stood behind my microphone stand and strapped on the Rickenbacker. The ringside girls sat on the hard, dirty roof inches from the duct tape border, their tushes resting on sweaters or hotel pillows. Bunny, of course, was camped right at my feet. Alex stood halfway down the center aisle and operated a video camera set on a tripod, all the better to record my blunders. Prudence was in the back, working the soundboard.

Red, his wife and Billy sat front row center along with Hank, who had apparently worked his way forward from the back row. Valleri stood at the end of the row of ringside girls, her shopping bags at her feet, her arms crossed and her face contorted in a perturbed look. Ralph was still in his chair. To my surprise, Winston/Charlie sat in the front row. After all the negative things he'd said about tribute bands, why was he here? With all my suspects present, I might be dead before my comeback show even started. Elmer stood guard a few feet to my left, which didn't give me much hope. If anything went down, Elmer would be the first one out the exit door.

Grant and Scott put on their guitars and Art settled on the drummer's throne, his sticks raised. My hands felt sweaty and I griped the pick tightly as not to drop it. Grant raised his eyebrows as if to ask if I was ready. I nodded.

Showtime.

Scott counted off the beats, "One, two, three, FOUR!" and jumped into "I Saw Her Standing There." I hit a couple of sour notes and the guys glanced at me, but we kept going. We plowed straight through "All My Loving," also with Scott on lead vocals, followed by Art on "Boys." The band paused for a breather and the audience responded with decent applause.

Scott addressed the crowd in the "Paul" voice. "Welcome to the show. You might have noticed that John isn't with us today. He popped out for a spot of tea, but not to worry, he sent over a good buddy to fill in. Please say hello to Mr. Sandy Fairfax." The ringside girls screamed and I flashed them a smile.

Time for me to shine as I sang "She Loves You." I goofed a couple of words and I worked too hard on the mechanics to put in as much feeling as I wanted, but otherwise we sounded good. The crowd responded warmly, especially when the four of us wagged our heads in unison on the "ooooooos." On the next tune, Scott's "Things We Said Today," we hit the pocket with a flawless performance. Grant played right handed, so he and I "crossed" the necks of our guitars for a visual treat. The audience approved of our efforts and applauded. Then Grant treated everyone to a Harrison double header with "Everybody's Trying To Be My Baby" and "Here Comes the Sun."

According to the set list taped to the roof at my feet, up next was "Day Tripper." I started the intro, but Grant motioned for me to stop.

Scott shot me a pranker's grin. "We're gonna do something a little different right now, change the pace a bit. We'd like to do a special song in honor of our guest star."

To my horror, the trio started a riff I knew all too well, an infectious beat with a musical hook big enough to land a whale—the lead-in to my hit song, "Girl Of My Dreams." The fans, of course, instantly recognized the tune. The ringside girls clapped and shouted in delight. My jaw dropped and I stared at the guys, dumbfounded and annoyed. My shows were always meticulously choreographed, scripted and rehearsed; the unexpected always threw me off.

"Am I the only one who didn't know about this?" I said.

I shook my head, but the band kept playing and the crowd urged me on. I removed the guitar and set it on the stand. I took the mike in one hand and with the other hand flipped the chord out of my way.

"I haven't done this one in a while, but here goes."

I waited for the downbeat of the riff to come around and plunged into the first verse. The words came more easily than I expected. As I sang I prowled the front of the stage area, just inches from the outstretched hands of the ringside girls trying to grab my legs. I clutched the mike in both hands, leaned over the girls and sang my heart out to them. I'd move in close to tease, and then retreated. I wiggled my hips—the fans loved that. When I saw a camera aimed at me, I posed until the fan snapped the shot. And they took endless photos. Thanks to the sun, at least my eyes didn't suffer from camera flash. I played up to the video camera—old habits die hard.

She kissed my lips and held me tight/We danced together throughout the night
I ran my fingers through her hair/Then I woke up, to my despair
The girl I loved had disappeared/She left me, the one I had so near

Have you seen the girl of my dreams?/The only one for me
Tell me, quick, where can I find her?/Prettiest girl I've ever seen
Are you the one, the girl of my dreams?/The one I'm longing for
Will you make me happy and glad?/Love me forever more.

I zipped along until I noticed I was singing a half beat ahead of the guys. I actually *heard* the Marvels while I sang. Amazing. Back in the days before feedback monitors I couldn't hear the accompaniment over the audience screams, so I raced through the songs regardless of the band's tempo and hoped that at some point we caught up with each other. I slowed down until the band and I synced up.

On the second verse my mind blanked on the lyrics, completely clueless on what came next. I said to the ringside girls, "Little help, please." They shouted the words at me until I got back on track.

I pray I'll see that girl once more/Before I go to bed each night
I search for her in all my slumbers/But she keeps away, out of sight
I'm lost and sad without my friend/I'm lonely without my lover
I can't rest until I find her/As I sleep beneath the covers.

I'll roam the world to find my love/I'll search both day and night
When I find her, girl of my dreams/I'll hug and squeeze her tight
Can you be the girl of my dreams?/I see her each night in my sleep
I'll marry her now, the girl of my dreams/She's the one I'll always keep.

The love flowed from the crowd and in return I pumped up my energy for them, which in turn generated more fervor from the fans. I crave the symbiotic relationship between performer and audience. The pure pleasure of performing swept me away. I could keep going like this for the rest of the day. I enjoyed myself so much I felt guilty calling this "work." At last I finished the song (or rather, it finished me), drained but feeling like a million bucks. The crowd rewarded my hard work with a standing ovation. I wished my kids were here to see this.

Bunny handed me a rose in token of her appreciation (I found out later she was the one who put the band up to this). I acknowledged the crowd's affection with the stage bow my handlers had taught me: lean forward from the waist until my torso was parallel to the floor, arms down at my side, lower my head to let my hair hang, hold for a two-count, then straighten up and snap my head up to flip the hair back.

On my way back to the mike stand I placed the flower atop a speaker, picked up a towel and wiped the sweat off my face. I was perspiring so much it's a wonder the color dye in my costume didn't run. I picked up the Rickenbacker and we continued with Scott singing "Day Tripper," which got some of the fans out of their chairs and dancing. I knocked 'em dead and kept 'em dancing with "I'll Cry Instead."

Hank starting shouting requests. We ignored him at first but he grew more persistent. He kept insisting on "Rocky Raccoon." I couldn't understand his desire for that particular song—unless he was taunting us.

Grant stepped over to me and whispered in my good ear, "You okay with 'Rocky Raccoon?' We didn't rehearse it."

After watching Dana die, no, I didn't want to play the song, but provoking Hank might not be a good idea. I nodded my approval.

Scott told the crowd, "Due to popular demand, we're gonna do a song off our 'White Album' you might of heard before, 'Rocky Raccoon.'"

Hank got on his feet and pumped his fists. "All right! All right! You guys rock!"

Scott handled lead vocals on this one, so I listened and picked up on the music, mostly C chords and sevenths, nothing tricky. The audience sang along, with Hank braying in full voice. I concentrated on the music and didn't sing along.

Then it all clicked.

Near the end of the song, out of the blue, the puzzle pieces snapped together. I understood what Dana was trying to tell me. The realization shocked me so much I stopped playing. The song ended, the crowd cheered, but I stood motionless with a glazed, deer-in-the-headlights look on my face.

Grant stepped over to me. "Something wrong, Sandy?"

I forgot I was standing in front of an open mike. Everyone on the rooftop heard me say, "I know who shot Dana and why."

❖ CHAPTER TWENTY ONE

In Spite Of All The Danger

NOBODY MADE A sound. Art set down his drumsticks, the audience stopped cheering and everyone glued their eyes on me. I strummed my guitar to keep the music going, but Grant and Scott didn't join in. I glanced around, afraid my suspect might strike me down before I named the name.

"Tell us!" someone yelled from the back row. "Who killed Dana?"

The other fans repeated the question. I unplugged the Rickenbacker and set it down in the stand. All of a sudden the guitar felt heavy and clunky. I stepped up to the mike and took a deep breath. What if I was wrong and fingered the wrong person? Nevertheless, I plunged ahead with my deduction.

"Right before Dana died, he said to me 'Rocky Raccoon.' The clue isn't in the song title but in the words. The lyrics explain how Dana died. The song tells the story of Dan and his girl, who was also known as 'Lil' and 'Nancy.' Dan, of course, is Dana. Lil is short for Elizabeth, his fiancée. She works at a preschool. In England, someone who cares for children is called a nanny, which sounds like 'Nancy.'"

The fans that were dancing returned to their chairs and the audience listened with rapt attention. I waited, hoping I could flush out the killer with the threat of exposure, but nobody made a move to leave.

"In the song, Dana steals Rocky's girl and Rocky seeks revenge. He checks into a hotel and confronts Dan. Dan shoots first and wounds Rocky. That's what happened Friday night. Jason had dated Elizabeth and was jealous at her engagement. Jason mailed Dana a tape with a warning to break it off. When that threat didn't work, Jason came to the hotel Friday night. He called

Dana from the lobby to see if he was in. The two men met in Dana's room. They talked, they argued, and three shots were fired.

"Dana took out the gun tucked in his pants and shot Jason. Bullet number one. He's tipsy and couldn't aim straight, so he only wounded Jason in the arm. Jason threw the ashtray at Dana to stop him from shooting again. The ashes were scattered all over the floor. The ashtray conks Dana in the face and leaves a bruise. Dana drops his gun. Jason picks it up and shoots. Dana falls down, mortally wounded. Bullet number two. Jason's scared and shoots out the ceiling light to hide what he's done and to cover his escape. The broken light left bits of glass on the floor. Bullet number three. Jason ran out so fast he didn't close the door all the way shut. That's how I could get into the room. He went home, but returned the next day to establish his alibi."

I stared Billy Shears square in the eye. "And that's the way it happened, right, Jason?"

On my TV show, whenever Buddy confronted the villains at the end of the episode, they confessed, or cried, or expressed remorse, or held out their wrists for the handcuffs. Billy/Jason, however, reached into the backpack stored under his chair, whipped out Dana's gun, stood up and aimed the weapon at my face. And unlike the firearms on my show, this gun was loaded with bullets, not blanks. Why can't reality be more like the movies? I needed better scriptwriters in my life.

Jason gripped the gun with both hands, straightened his arms and locked his elbows. His eyes hardened like I'd never seen before. "Put your hands up!" I didn't like this dark side emerging from the twerp.

"Billy, er, Jason, put the gun down." I sounded far calmer that I felt. Had to keep talking to keep myself from panicking. "Come on, please, put it down."

"Shut up and put your hands up!"

I raised my hands level with my head. Jason's hands shook as much as mine. A cold-blooded killer can control his actions, but a terrified kid like Jason might let his trigger finger slip at any distraction. I took deep breaths. Keep breathing so I don't faint. Stay calm. Keep watching Jason. Don't take my eyes off him.

Grant and Scott stepped towards me. "No! Stop! Don't move!" I yelled, my eyes still on the kid. A lady in the audience screamed and some fans started to leave for the exit door. Jason spun around and pointed his gun at the crowd.

"Jason!" I shouted. "Leave the audience alone! Your fight's with me."

I wasn't as heroic as I sounded. I simply couldn't bear the thought of watching another person die this weekend. The gunman focused his crazed eyes back on me.

I spoke into the mic. "Everyone, please sit down and stay seated. Keep calm and stay quiet and nobody'll get hurt."

Can't let the fans get hysterical and trample each other in a stampede for the exit door. I glanced down at the ringside girls at my feet. They sat right between the gunman and me. A stray bullet might hit one of them.

"Bunny, get the girls out of the way. Hurry!"

I didn't need to tell her twice. Bunny sprang to her feet and hustled the ladies off to one side. They stood in a clump and whispered among themselves until Bunny hushed them.

I stepped away from the mike to speak to Jason one-on-one. He might feel less threatened if I diverted his attention from the crowd. My mouth was dry. I swallowed. I needed a sip from a water bottle, but I didn't dare lower my hands to fetch it. I spoke to Jason the way I talked to my kids when they were little.

"Jason, you don't want to shoot me in front of these witnesses. That's not a good idea."

"I'm not going to jail!" he shrieked, his weapon still pointed at my head. "Nobody's gonna put me in jail!"

Don't panic. Can't afford to lose my temper. Talk softly to this guy. "Jason, think about what you're doing. You can't get away with this."

"Yes, I can! I have you." He moved to my left side and jabbed the cold metal barrel against my temple. I caught my breath. I blinked to keep the sweat from dripping into my eyes. "Let's go."

"Where are we going, Jason?" Keep him talking. Keep stalling until help comes. Who's going to rescue us? Nobody knows we're up on this roof.

"To my car. We're getting' outta here. Nobody's gonna stop me as long as I have you."

I watched Jason from the corner of my eye. My arms ached from holding them up. I gulped down deep breaths. Can't let him take me away from here. Soon as he's safe and we're alone, he won't have a reason to keep me alive. Keep him occupied.

"What are you going to do to me?"

"Shut up!" His voice quavered and his hands shook.

"Are you going to shoot me after we leave here? Dump me in an empty cornfield?"

"Move!"

Jason rammed the barrel against my head. I shut my eyes and nearly suffered a heart attack from fright. *Dear God, I know I haven't been to church in years, but please, help me get out of here alive. I don't want to die like this.*

"All right, calm down, Jason. I'm moving." I opened my eyes and walked across the stage area as slowly as I could. I hoped Jason wouldn't notice my pokiness.

"Billy!" Bunny shouted. "Don't hurt Sandy!"

I stopped and turned my head. Bunny took a step towards Jason, her arms out to grab him. The silly girl would get herself killed.

"Bunny!" I yelled. "Stop! Don't do it!"

Jason took the gun off my head and pointed it at Bunny. That split-second relief gave me the time I needed. I glanced around for a weapon and seized the first object I saw.

The Rickenbacker.

I grabbed the neck of the guitar with both hands and swung it hard at Jason's hands. He fired. The blow knocked his aim off course and the bullet struck one of the cymbals on the drum kit with a sharp *zing*! Art ducked behind the bass drum for protection. My attack also forced Jason to drop the gun. The weapon skidded across the rooftop. The killer lunged at me. I swung the musical club again and smashed the instrument against the side of his head. A solid body guitar packs a wallop and Jason fell face down on the roof. I threw away the ax and fell on my knees. I straddled Jason's back, grabbed one of his wrists and jerked his arm behind his back. He yelped in pain.

"How dare you try to kill me, you scum sucker!"

"Sandy, no!" Bunny grabbed my arm. "Don't hurt him!"

I shook her off, but she was right. The punk wasn't worth a battery charge on my police record. I relaxed my grip on his arm but held on. I felt Jason's body sag in defeat. Bunny reached down to retrieve the gun.

"No, don't touch it!" I said. "Fingerprints!"

I looked up to see if the audience was safe. The fans sat riveted in their chairs, their faces frozen in shock, except for Alex, who fiddled with the controls of the video camera.

"Alex!" I called. "Did you record any of that?"

"I think so. The machine's still running."

"Take the tape to the TV station, Channel 14. Give it to Clyde Danvers. He'll want to run it on the evening news." That'll give Danvers one hell of a scoop.

Alex grinned as he removed the cassette from the recorder. "You got it!"

I shouted to nobody in particular, "Somebody get the police!"

The roof access door opened and out came Bluefield, some hotel clerks, Braxton and several uniformed officers. Talk about quick service. I assumed the cavalry had arrived to save the day, but as usual I was wrong.

"There he is!" The Blue Meanie pointed to me and from the look on his face he wasn't planning on giving me a medal. "He's the one! And all of these people are trespassing!"

Braxton grabbed my arm and yanked me to my feet. "Ernest Farmington, you're under arrest for the murder of Dana Mumford. You have the right to remain silent—"

"I will *not* remain silent," I shouted. "I'll make as much noise as I want. And wouldn't you rather have the *real* killer?"

Jason scrambled to his feet, but I stuck out my foot and tripped him. He fell down again. I planted one foot in the small of his back and applied just enough pressure to convince him not to try another escape.

"Detective Braxton, this is Jason Wilcox," I said. "He shot and killed Dana on Friday night and today he tried to kidnap me and murder Bunny. That's the murder weapon over there with his prints on it."

Braxton's face turned red with anger. "Are you trying to pin this on someone else?"

I dug my heel into the creep's back. "Talk to the man, Jason."

The kid squirmed. "Okay, okay, I did it."

Two officers lifted Jason to his feet and handcuffed his wrists behind his back. He dropped his head and started at his feet.

"But Billy wasn't here Friday night," Bunny said. "He was at his job."

"That's his alibi," I said. "What did you do, Jason, leave work early so you could drive here?"

"I didn't go to work." Jason spoke softly as the bravado drained from his soul. "I called in sick."

"When I checked in on Friday, I studied the state map that's in the lobby," I said. "Princeton is only thirty miles due north of Evansville, a straight shot on the highway. Jason could easily drive from Princeton, meet Dana, return home the same night and come back Saturday morning."

"But Jason wasn't shot," Bunny said. "He didn't go to any of the hospitals."

"Not the ones in Evansville. I'm guessing the bullet only grazed Jason's arm and he could wait a while before getting medical help. I'm sure Princeton has its own hospital, right, Jason?"

The kid nodded. "Gibson General Hospital."

"Jason wore long sleeves all weekend to hide the wound. He wasn't cold from the air conditioning like he said. And the clothes also explain the clue Dana wrote out before he died, '28IF GEORGE.' The number referred to the *Abbey Road* album cover which shows George Harrison dressed in a long-sleeved denim shirt and pants—just like the outfit Jason was wearing when I saw him Saturday morning. I'm guessing Jason had on the same clothes Friday night as well. That's why the clothes were wrinkled."

The kid confessed to causing the attacks on me with the apples, the bomb and the knife. He started blubbering. "I only wanted to you to stop nosing around. I didn't mean to hurt you, Sandy. I'm sorry. I never wanted to kill Dana. It was an accident. All I wanted to do was scare him. I wanted him to give me Elizabeth back. I loved Elizabeth. I really did. Why didn't she want me? Nobody likes me."

Jason sniffed back the tears and dragged his feet as the officers led him away. I felt sorry for the kid. Here he was in the perfect environment for a loner like himself, surrounded by like-minded fanatics willing to share with him their enthusiasm for all things Beatle. Instead of making friends with the people he could relate to, he kept lusting for a woman completely out of his class.

I smiled at Braxton as I turned over the crime scene photos and tape reel to him. “Looks like I found your killer for you.”

The flatfoot narrowed his eyes and set his thin lips in a straight line. “Are you expecting a reward or something?” Braxton scrutinized my Sgt. Pepper's costume. “What kind of getup is that?”

“It's the latest leisure wear in La-La land.”

He snorted. “You Beatles freaks—you're all crazy!”

I started to walk away when he said, “Stop right there! I'm not finished with you yet, Mr. Farmington.”

I cringed. What now? Was he going to haul me in on another charge? Arrest me for impersonating a Beatle? Take me to the station and force me to watch slides of his family vacation?

Braxton had a paper bag under one arm. He opened the bag, took out an old record cover, and thrust it at me. “My wife wants your autograph.”

As far as everyone on the rooftop was concerned, the concert was over. The band was in no mood to keep playing and neither was I. The audience was too jazzed to sit still any longer. The fans wandered about, talking about what they'd just witnessed and gawking at the cops. Braxton grabbed a microphone and ordered the fans to sit down and be quiet so the police could take statements, but everyone ignored him.

After I finished telling my tale to one of the uniformed cops, the fans surrounded me and thanked me not only for unmasking the murderer but also for the fantastic concert. They loved the show, especially my impromptu solo. Their affirmations made the difficulties of the weekend fade away. The convention goers took endless photos with me, enough though I looked like death, tired and disheveled, my clothes a mess and soaked with sweat and grime. But I put on my best smile for them, grateful that they were the ones snapping my mug shot instead of the deputies down at the jail.

Hank's belly jiggled as he sprinted towards me. Why didn't the police bust him for indecent exposure? “Hey, kid detective, terrific concert. You're the greatest! I liked when you and that guy staged the thing with the gun. Great stunt! Just like your TV show!”

“Hank, that wasn't a stunt,” I said. “He had a real gun and he tried to kill me.”

His eyes bulged as big as his stomach. “You mean . . . for real?”

"Yes. He's the one who murdered Dana Mumford."

"Wow." He stretched out the word into several syllables. "Hey, you guys are too dangerous. I'm splittin' out of here." And he did, to everyone's relief.

Charlie was next in line. A young lady held his arm. "Hi, Sandy. I liked the show."

"Thanks, Charlie. That means a lot to me. I'm glad you came."

The lady said, "Charlie, introduce me."

He patted her arm. "Sandy, I want you to meet a friend of mine. This is Pam. I met her this afternoon in the dealers' room. John's her favorite Beatle too."

The young Asian-American woman was slender and short, with thick black hair that hung to her waist. She wore a miniskirt, blouse, knee boots and a wide-brim hat—all in black. "Hello, Sandy. Nice to meet you." She spoke in a childlike, high-pitched soft voice with a touch of an accent. "May I have your autograph?"

She giggled as she handed me a convention program and pen. Maybe on my flight home I'll finally open my registration packet and read the program. I signed my name and returned the booklet to her.

"Thank you." She held up two fingers in a V. "Peace and love, Sandy."

The gesture surprised me. "Yes, peace and love to you too, Pam."

They left hand-in-hand, smiling into each other's eyes. I couldn't believe it—Charlie had found his perfect match.

Valleri glared at me on her way to the exit door. "I told you I didn't do it."

As much as I wanted to say something sarcastic, I bit my tongue and replied with kindness. "Enjoy your records."

"They're scratched!"

Ralph meandered towards the band members. I joined them in case he wanted to pick a fight.

Grant signed an autograph for a fan and eyed the stranger warily. "Hi, Ralph. I didn't expect to see you here."

"Yeah, uh, I heard about Dana." Ralph rubbed his nose and sniffled. He twitched as he talked. "Real sorry he died. He was an all-right guy. Came over to pay my respects."

"That's nice of you."

"What are you doing in Evansville?" Scott asked.

"Uh, meeting some guy on business." Ralph glanced nervously at the cops. "Gotta go. Catch ya later." He ran for the roof access door.

"'Meeting some guy on business,'" I repeated. "Is Ralph expanding his meth empire into Southern Indiana?"

Scott shrugged. "With that guy, who knows."

The police wrapped up their investigation, the fans trickled away and the band ducked behind a cooling unit to change into their work clothes so they could pack up the gear. In an effort to cool down I unbuttoned my tunic and let it hang open (I wore the black T-shirt underneath). I picked up the Rickenbacker, inspected the damage and returned it to Grant.

"I'm sorry I broke your guitar. It's a terrific instrument. Send me the receipt for the repairs and I'll cover it."

"Sandy, you found Dana's killer. That's payment enough." He pumped my hand and slapped me on the back. "Thanks a million for helping us out. It's been a pleasure working with you. You don't know how much this means for us to play with someone of your caliber."

"I have to admit," I said, "I only sounded good because you guys backed me up. You've got a great band here. Don't break it up."

Art asked, "Sandy, if you don't mind, can you do us a favor?"

"What's that?"

"When you go on tour, let us open for you."

I laughed. "That's not a bad idea. I'll think about it." I did a double take. "What do you mean, *when* I go on tour? I'm not thinking of touring again."

"Come on, man, we all heard you today," Scott said. "You still got it. I'll bet even money that before the year's out, you'll be a hot ticket again."

Art jabbed his elbow into his band mate's ribs. "You'll bet on anything!"

Prudence came through the roof access door and ran up to us with a big smile on her face. "I called Elizabeth just now and told her about Jason's arrest. Sandy, she has a message she wants me to give to you." She stood on her toes, grabbed my head with both hands and planted a long, wet kiss on my mouth. She released me and I stared at her, dazed. These Hoosier girls sure know how to talk to a guy. "Elizabeth says thank you from the bottom of her heart for everything you've done for Dana."

"Tell her she's welcome." I waited expectantly in case Elizabeth had another message to give me.

The Mersey Marvels said their goodbyes and set about striking down the setup. I grabbed Scott's arm before he left.

"Wait a minute, Scott. Something I don't understand. Prudence said you left for a few hours this afternoon. Where did you go?"

"It's nothing. I left the hotel to talk to a counselor that Bunny knows. I felt guilty about Dana's death."

"Why would you feel guilty if you didn't shoot him?"

"You heard the way I yelled at him on Friday. We never had a chance to patch things up. I'm thinking if I'd kept an eye on him Friday, maybe he'd still be alive."

"It's not your fault, Scott. Jason was out to get Dana, if not here then someplace else. You couldn't have stopped him."

"Thanks, Sandy."

As Scott carried off the last of the band gear, Red shook my hand and thanked me profusely for being such a good sport and putting up with the lunacy this weekend—as if I had any other choice except to go with the flow.

"I'll call Mr. Ellis tomorrow and tell him what a bang-up job you did at the concert."

"You do that. Tell him I knocked 'em dead. No, don't say that. Bad joke. Look, Red, tomorrow's Labor Day. Go home and get some rest. You deserve it. Call Marshall on Tuesday. No, better make that Friday. Let him stew for a while. By then I'll convince him to waive my performance fee."

"We want to pay what you're worth, Sandy. You helped make this convention a success."

"No, Red. I owe you kids plenty for giving me the opportunity to perform again."

The Blue Meanie himself came up and shook my hand. "Mr. Fairfax, I owe you an apology. Looks like someone else was responsible for all the mayhem this weekend."

Looks like you were an idiot not to figure that out sooner. But I grinned and accepted his apology.

Bluefield looked hot and uncomfortable in his jacket. He loosened his tie and undid his top shirt button. "I heard some of that Beatle-ly music. Awfully loud, wasn't it?"

"Beatles songs sound best when they're loud," Red said.

"But it's not bad. Kinda swings, don't it? I was thinking, Mr. Hardiman, if you want to book your convention here for next year, I'll give you a special discount rate. Our way of saying thanks to you and Mr. Fairfax for helping out the police."

"That's great," Red said. "Thank you, Mr. Bluefield. Sandy, would you be interested in coming back again next year as our special guest?"

No! No! I never want to see this insane place again! "Absolutely." I couldn't believe I said that. The sun must be making me dizzy.

Bluefield cleared his throat. "But the discount price is good only if none of the guests end up dead."

❖ CHAPTER TWENTY TWO

End Of The Line

AFTER THE POLICE and fans left the rooftop, the hotel employees brought up wheeled carts to haul off the folding chairs. The clerks moved down the rows, slapping up the seats on the chairs with a bang and piling the furniture onto the carts. The band and their equipment were gone, leaving only the duct tape stuck to the rooftop. I plopped onto a chair, too tired to walk downstairs. The rhythmic banging of the chairs folding up almost lulled me to sleep. Usually after a high-rolling concert I stayed on an emotional high and took hours to wind down, but not today. A delayed reaction to my heart-stopping encounter with a loaded gun, along with fatigue, set in. I realized how close I came to joining the late John Lennon himself in the great beyond. Acting scared on my TV show was nothing like the real thing.

Bunny sat down in the chair beside me. "You left this on the speaker." She handed me the rose.

"Thanks. I don't want forget it." I sniffed the flower as Bunny giggled. "What's so funny?"

"I was thinking about the way you hit Jason with the guitar. You whacked him the same way you hit the villain on your TV show, remember, the episode we watched on Friday in the hospitality suite."

I was speechless. Now I was acting out scenes from my show in real life. I never did that when I was drunk.

I rested my arms on my knees. "Bunny, you shouldn't have rushed Jason like that. You almost got both of us killed."

"Sandy, I'm not going to stand by and watch somebody hurt you."

"Next time, be more careful."

"Next time? There won't be a next time. We'll never run into any more bad guys."

"I hope not. You sound hoarse."

She coughed and spoke in a raspy whine. "I am, from all the screaming during the show. I can't enjoy a concert unless I lose my voice screaming."

She pulled two Granny Smith apples from her tote bag and offered one to me, the last of the fruit from the hospitality suite. I took one and started eating. Performing and crime fighting certainly work up an appetite. I asked Bunny about the cardboard bucket in her lap.

"Donations for Dana's family." The container was nearly overflowing with dollar bills and checks. "Must be a couple of hundred dollars in here. Would you like to give something?"

I pulled out my wallet, grabbed all the loose bills and dropped the dough into the bucket. Since I was going home soon, I may as well get rid of my travel money.

She eyed my gift. "Thanks, Sandy! That's so generous of you!"

I peered into the bucket. "How much did I put in?"

"Do you want to take it back?"

"Keep it."

We ate our apples and watched the clerks haul off the chairs, leaving the roof in its original bare blandness, without a trace of the excitement or the jeopardy of a few minutes ago. I love the quiet that follows a concert, the lull after the storm. Bunny and I were the sole occupants on the roof. A breeze blew off the river and the temperature dropped a few degrees, providing some relief.

"Looks like Buddy Brave solved another case," Bunny said. That wretched character would follow me to my grave. "I'd never guess Billy, I mean, Jason, was a killer."

"How long have you known him?"

"Not long. I e-mailed him for a few months over the Internet. When Red and I asked for volunteers to help with the convention, he jumped in."

"Smart move on his part. Jason got in the loop so he could follow Dana. He had access to the room assignments. He knew where I was, too, so he could plant the bomb."

"How did he get into your room?"

"Easy. Remember this morning when he said he had locked himself out of his room? He lied. When Jason went to the front desk to get another keycard, he told the desk clerk *my* room number, not his, so he could get my keycard. The clerk didn't take time to check the number."

"What about the mystery tape?"

"At my appearance yesterday, Jason worked the sound board. He knows how to run audio equipment and make tapes."

"But the envelope had an Illinois postmark."

"According to the map in the lobby, Princeton's only a few miles east of the Illinois border. Maybe Jason had to go across the state line for an errand or to see a friend. He saw a post office or a mailbox, and dropped off the packet."

She finished her apple and placed the core in a plastic baggie. Such a tidy person. I, on the other hand, tossed my core onto a pile of debris left by the audience. Unless someone came up here to clean, the trash would stay here longer than the building.

"I don't understand how he could do it," Bunny said. "Jason seemed like a nice guy."

"Love and jealousy can make a heartbroken guy do crazy things."

A plane flew overhead, heading west. Tomorrow morning I'd be on one of those flyers.

"Sandy, I want to ask your permission for something. Can I set up a website about you? The official Sandy Fairfax homepage. So the fans can keep in touch with what you're doing."

"I'll say yes only if you do something for me. I saw your drawings in the art show. They're excellent. Why aren't you doing more with your art besides drawing pictures of me?"

She pretended to search for something inside her tote bag to avoid looking at me. "It's a hobby, something for fun, nothing much. I couldn't make a living with it."

"Doesn't matter how much it pays. You need to work on your talent. Promise me you'll take an art class as soon as you can."

"I'm not that good. My parents told me so."

"Yes, you are. I believe in you."

She looked up and smiled. "Sure, Sandy. If you want me to, I'll do it."

"Then you have my permission for the website."

"It's a deal!" We shook hands on it. "If you're not doing anything tomorrow, I can show you around town. Evansville isn't as glamorous as Los Angeles, but it's home."

"Sorry, but I'll be flying out as soon as Marshall can book a flight. I'm anxious to go home." And ask Becka to let me see my kids. What an incredible story I had to tell them about my weekend. "I suppose you'll be going home soon too."

"Oh, no, I haven't even started packing. Are you hungry? I'm starved. We can go out where ever you want to go."

"Normally I'd say yes, Bunny, but I'm exhausted. I'm going down to my room, order room service, soak in a hot bath and call it a day."

She leaned towards me and her eyes twinkled. "What are you going to do next, Sandy? Make an album? Star in a movie? Solve another mystery?"

"I don't know yet, Bunny. But don't worry." I gave her a wink. "I'll think of something."

THE END

Teen Idol Quiz

A TRUE FAN knows *everything* about her idol! See how well you know teen idol Sandy Fairfax, the star of the smash '70s TV show, *Buddy Brave, Boy Sleuth.* All of the answers can be found in *The Baffled Beatlemaniac Caper.*

1. What is Sandy's full given name?
2. What is his favorite soft drink?
3. How old was Sandy when he went on his first concert tour?
4. What type of music does he listen to at home to relax?
5. What are names of his children?
6. How many musical instruments can Sandy play? Name them.
7. In which part of Los Angeles does Sandy live?
8. What was the name of his first album?
9. How many *Buddy Brave* movies were made? Name them.
10. Which is Sandy's favorite *Buddy Brave* episode and why?

Count up your correct answers. How well did you score?

0 to 2—Apple Bonker

3 to 5—Nowhere Man

6 to 8—Sandy's Buddy

9 to 10—Girl of My Dreams

Answers:

1. Stanford Ernest Farmington Jr.
2. Mountain Dew
3. Nineteen
4. Classical
5. Robin Joy Farmington and Stanford Ernest "Chip" Farmington III
6. Three: Guitar, piano and violin
7. Hollywood Hills
8. *Sincerely Yours, Sandy*
9. Two: *Buddy Brave and the Suspicious Spy; Buddy Brave and the Dangerous Demon*
10. "The Sultan's Silver Caper." While filming this episode Sandy met an actress who became his wife.

About the Author

SALLY CARPENTER IS native Hoosier now living in sunny Southern California.

She has a master's degree in theater from Indiana State University. While in school two of her plays, "Star Collector" and "Common Ground," were finalists in the American College Theater Festival One-Act Playwrighting Competition. "Common Ground" also earned a college creative writing award. The plays received staged readings and productions in New York City.

Carpenter also has a master's degee in theology and a black belt in tae kwon do. She's worked a variety of jobs including actress, freelance writer, college writing instructor, theater critic, jail chaplain, and tour guide/page for a major movie studio as well as for a community newspaper.

She's a member of Sisters in Crime/Los Angeles Chapter. Contact her at scwriter@earthlink.net.

9091040R0

Made in the USA
Charleston, SC
09 August 2011